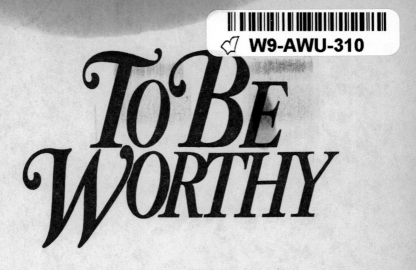

TO BE WORTHY

DONNA FLETCHER CROW

VICTOR BOOKS™

A DIVISION OF SCRIPTURE PRESS PUBLICATIONS INC.
USA CANADA ENGLAND

Cover art by Ken Call, showing Georgiana and Granville joining the Beaufort Hunt in front of Badminton House.

Library of Congress Catalog Card Number: 86-60876
ISBN: 0-89693-512-4

VICTOR BOOKS
A division of SP Publications, Inc.
Wheaton, Illinois 60187

To Be Worthy

The Cambridge Collection

There are so few people now who want to have any intimate spiritual association with the eighteenth and nineteenth centuries. . . .

Who bothers at all now about the work and achievement of our grandfathers, and how much of what they knew have we already forgotten?

Dietrich Bonhoeffer, *Letters and Papers from Prison*

DONNA FLETCHER CROW brings a lifetime love of English literature and history as well as intensive research to The Cambridge Collection—her historical series on the work of the Evangelical Anglicans. A former English teacher, she is now a full-time writer. She and her husband, Stan, have four children.

THE SOMERSET & RYDER FAMILIES

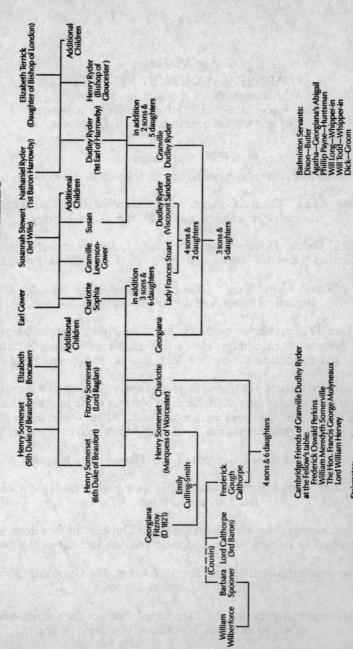

Badminton Servants:
Dixon—Butler
Agatha—Georgiana's Abigail
Phillip Payne—Huntsman
Will Long—Whipper-in
Will Todd—Whipper-in
Dick—Groom

Cambridge Friends of Granville Dudley Ryder
at the Fellow's table:
Frederick Oswald Perkins
William Meredyth Somerville
The Hon. Francis George Molyneaux
Lord William Hervey

Stairmates:
Andrew Anderson
John Henry Rennard

For My Editor
CAROLE SANDERSON STREETER
Who had faith in me and in this project
and who shares many of my golden memories
of an August research trip in England

With Appreciation to
To the Flavells, my friends and hosts in Cambridge,

Alan Kucia, Trinity College, who unearthed Granville Ryder's
signature in ancient tomes in the Wren Library,

David Smith, Domus Bursar at King's College, who showed me
Charles Simeon's rooms and the roof of the Gibbs Building,

Michael Halls, King's College Archivist, who brought me
original sermons and letters by Charles Simeon,

Jane Waley, Harrowby MSS Trust Archivist, who organized
material from Sandon Hall's five muniment rooms, which
led to finding Granville's love prayer in his own hand,

Stanley Bywater, Secretary to His Grace, the Duke of Beaufort,
who gave unstintingly of his time on our tour of Badminton House,
of whom the Compass innkeeper said, "The finest of English
country gentlemen, the kind they don't make anymore."

Lady Frances Berendt, Lord Harrowby's daughter,

Lord Harrowby, the sixth Earl, who both took a personal
hand in my research efforts,

Their Graces, the eleventh Duke and Duchess of Beaufort, who
received us in their home and took gracious interest in the book,

The wonderful staffs at the British Library, the Guildhall Library,
and the London Library,

My many friends on the "sceptered isle set in a silver sea"
to whom gracious hospitality is a way of life.

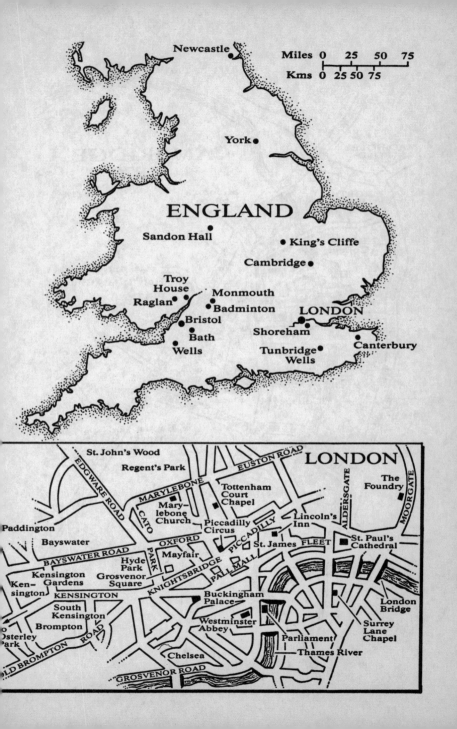

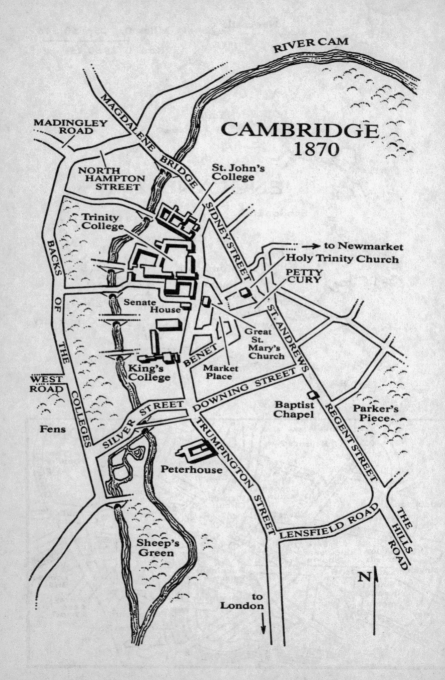

· 1 ·

LADY GEORGIANA SOMERSET, younger daughter of the sixth Duke of Beaufort, frowned into her gilt-framed looking glass. "Agatha, you may remove these odious feathers from my hair." She was surveying the three ostrich plumes that adorned her shining gold Apollo's knots coiffure.

"But, my Lady, you know Sir George is particularly fond . . . "

"If Sir George is so fond of feathers, he should engage to escort an ostrich to the hunt ball. I'm quite certain I have no intention of playing the role for him," and she plucked the feathers from the elegant topknot. They were replaced by a pearl ferronniére that encircled her head with a delicate gold band and ornamented the center part over her forehead with a cluster of lustrous pearls.

Then, because she was not a young lady given to frowning, Georgiana smiled, picked up her sarcenet shawl and lace fan, and swept from the room in a pale blue cloud of French silk, and a delicate mist of rose petal water. As a matter of fact, she not merely abandoned her frown, but as she made her way to the ballroom, her thoughts of George Agar-Ellis brightened her smile. That he should be such a clodpate as to insinuate that fate had destined them for each other because of the similarities of their names—as if half the babies born in England weren't named George or Georgiana in honor of His Majesty, George IV! And then there was this excessive admiration for Horace Walpole he affected, and the great pains he took to store his mind with the light miscellaneous literature in which the master of Strawberry Hill delighted, so as to forever regale his friends with Walpole's witticisms.

11

These wry thoughts carried Georgiana into the great drawing room where the family was gathering to greet their guests. The green damask walls were hung for the occasion with midnight blue and golden buff draperies, the colors of the Badminton Hunt, to which many attending the ball had ridden that day.

She smiled as she viewed the gracious hospitality laid before their guests. There was nothing her papa, the Duke, loved more than extending the amenities of Badminton House to all his acquaintances, and his daughter enjoyed being part of that tradition. As she walked through the softly lit room, the three-tiered Bristol chandeliers threw back multiple reflections of light and color.

"O Mama, how charming you look." Georgiana kissed her mother. "The new styles do suit you." She admired the Duchess' appearance in a soft rose gown with an off-the-shoulder neckline and a tight band just above her natural waist.

"Yes, my Dear, it does feel odd to have a gown banded at the waist; but I daresay we shall all become accustomed to it soon— even to the tight lacing underneath," she added in a lowered voice, and smiled at her daughter.

"If it's to become fashionable, we shall all have to, Mama. And it was very clever of you to have your hair dressed with fans; it sets off your earrings most elegantly." The Duchess turned her head, causing her diamond and pearl earrings to sparkle with fire like the chandeliers. "You shall put all your daughters quite in the shade." From long habit, Georgiana raised her voice so her slightly deaf mother could hear every word without difficulty, enabling her father also to hear her words.

"No one puts my daughters in the shade—nor my wife neither." The Duke kissed his Duchess' hand as he joined them.

"And how was the hunt today, my Dear?" the Duchess inquired.

"Most satisfactory. We ran the cub to earth near the Cricklade covert. I daresay we should have had him sooner, but that fool of a lawyer from Chipping Sodbury hallooed us onto a fresh fox and it took Payne about half an hour to get the hounds onto the original scent again. But it was excellent sport, excellent . . . "

Smiling to herself, Georgiana moved quietly away as her father's account of the hunt continued. His foxhunt stories could become a bit tedious, even to one who loved the sport as well as she did. The room was rapidly filling. The Duchess' guest list having included a large segment of the Glouchestershire gentry, members of the

Badminton Hunt, and leading members of the various compassionate societies Her Grace patronized, the evening should not want for variety.

But in spite of the fact that she never lacked for partners, Georgiana soon found the ball sufficiently dull to match her earlier mood—dull enough that when George Agar-Ellis made his bow to her, she accepted his hand with a ready smile.

George had a reputation for being one of the most conspicuous youths of the day, and no little part of this could be credited to the efforts of his tailor. The close fit of his claret evening coat was enhanced by padding added to the chest and hips to make his waist appear smaller. His striped silk cossack trousers tapered narrowly to be strapped beneath the instep.

"You distressed us infinitely by your absence in the field today," he said, leading her to the floor where a new set was forming.

"Why, Sir, you surprise me. I understood there was excellent sport."

"Ah, yes, excellent sport indeed, but it lacked that luster which your presence alone can give."

It was fortunate for Georgiana that the set divided just then or she would have had difficulty suppressing her laughter at such studied extravagances. By the time they came together at the end of the room again, she had regained her composure, although her bright blue eyes were sparkling mischievously. The lines formed and the gentlemen bowed to their partners. The quadrille continued, with the ladies' stiffened skirts swinging gracefully like bells across the polished wood floor as they went through the intricate figures of the *grande ronde.*

"May I bring you a glass of ratafia?" George offered, leading Georgiana to a gilt and brocade chair as the music came to a close.

"Lemonade, please. And pray, let us find chairs closer to a window—this is such a warm evening."

As George moved through the crowd to do her bidding, Georgiana surveyed the company. She smiled as she saw her brother, Lord Worcester, lead a lady to the floor. *Henry is always the first crack of fashion and yet he contrives never to look overdressed*, she thought, surveying his Beaufort Hunt evening coat of dark blue lined with buff over a white embroidered silk waistcoat, light blue silk-web pantaloons, white silk stockings, and shoes *brode a jour.*

A small sigh escaped her as George reappeared at her side. "Do you have a headache?" he inquired solicitously, seating himself next to her on the green striped sofa.

"Silly, I never have headaches. I was just wishing Henry would take another wife now that his mourning is well past." Her eye strayed to Sir Thomas Lawrence's elegant portrait of her deceased sister-in-law, hanging on the east wall. "He is only at Badminton for a week and then he goes back to his London establishment. It distresses me to think of him living quite alone in that great rambling residence."

"Indeed, yes," her companion agreed. "A most melancholy affair for your family to have Lady Worcester snatched from this life so suddenly. Why, only seven days before to be at a ball at Court and then to be no more. But it must be of great comfort to you that she died like a heroine, full of cheerfulness and courage to the last." Warming to his topic, he turned to Georgiana and seized her hands, narrowly escaping the disaster of causing his lady to pour the contents of her lemonade glass into her lap. Undaunted, he continued, "She was snatched from life at a time when she was becoming every day more fit to live, for her mind, her temper, and her understanding were steadily and rapidly improving."

Retrieving her hands, Georgiana agreed softly to his effusion, "She is missed by all of us."

"Oh, yes, yes! You speak for all her friends. Long, long will it be before I forget her, or before my mind loses the lively impression of her virtues and of our mutual friendship." Before Georgiana could form a reply to this eulogy, her companion sighed and quoted, "But then, in the words of the incomparable Gray,

Full many a flower is born to blush unseen,
and waste its sweetness on the desert air.

Since her late sister-in-law, a favored niece of the Duke of Wellington, had lived most of her life in the social whirl of the London ton, had had her engagement announced at a ball at Carlton House, had been given away at her wedding by the Iron Duke himself, and then honeymooned in Paris, the quotation struck Georgiana as being hardly *apropos,* but she chose not to argue the point. It was much simpler merely to agree to George's offer to secure another glass of lemonade for her.

She sat back against the cushions of the sofa and fanned herself lightly, surveying the whirling dancers reflected in the floor-to-

14

ceiling gilt pier glass between the windows. Suddenly her attention was arrested by the mirrored image of a tall young man with tanned skin and striking military bearing striding into the room at the far end of the hall. Georgiana turned from the glass for a direct view, but the dancers on the floor momentarily blocked her aim. The set parted and she caught sight of him again. Even from that distance she could see the trim cut of his dark blue coat, his high stiff collar tabs, and meticulously tied white neckcloth.

As the newcomer surveyed the room, a slight frown creased the broad forehead beneath his black locks which parted on the side and curled forward. He looked around the room with a detachment that clearly spoke a sense of superiority.

Caught between admiration for his appearance and dislike of his aloof bearing, Georgiana continued to watch the newcomer. Most puzzling of all was the vague sense that he looked familiar. She wondered whether he was a member of the hunting set or one of the compassionate society members. Neither seemed to suit him.

To her surprise she saw that it was the Duchess he sought. Georgiana followed his progress across the room, but as the stranger bowed over her mother's hand, George returned, followed closely by Frederick Calthorpe. Rising, Georgiana said, "Poor George, you have gone to the trouble of securing me a lemonade, and now here is my partner for the next dance. Pray excuse me."

With a swirl of her silk skirt Georgiana was led to the floor by the Honorable Frederick Calthorpe, the brother of Baron Calthorpe, an old family friend, and George was left to drink the lemonade himself.

When the set came to an end, Georgiana glanced around her; but situated in the middle of the company as she now was, she could catch no sight of the newcomer who had so aroused her curiosity. "It is an unaccountably warm evening for September. Would you like to take the air on the terrace, Lady Georgiana?" her partner inquired.

"Indeed, it is warm. But I should prefer you to take me to my mama, Sir." Georgiana smiled and flipped her fan with just a touch of coquetry which she was far from feeling. Indeed, her overwhelming emotion at the moment was curiosity. And the more elusive the stranger, the stronger her desire to have her curiosity satisfied.

When they arrived at the side of the Duchess, the dark young man had departed. Georgiana longed to ask her mama the man's identity, but the Honorable Frederick hovered near the ladies making small talk. Georgiana was just on the brink of sending him off for another glass of lemonade when her partner for the next dance claimed her and she was obliged to take her place in the set for the *pas de Zephyr* with her curiosity still unsatisfied.

When doing a turn around the floor, she caught a glimpse of the inscrutable visitor, standing near the fireplace with his hands behind his back in his detached manner. It appeared that he did not mean to dance, even though several young ladies were obliged to sit out for lack of a partner. Georgiana was forced to conclude that in spite of his pleasing appearance, his manner must be proud and unpleasant. In that case she should give him no more thought. With a toss of her head she laughed at a mild witticism from her partner and was swept around the floor.

For some time Georgiana saw no more of the stranger, which was quite as it should be, since she had determined to have nothing whatsoever to do with such a starched-up person. Just before time to go in for supper, Georgiana paused for a brief chat with her elder sister, the elegant Lady Charlotte Sophia, when she saw George approaching. Georgiana turned slightly only to see herself approached from the other side by the stranger. Unlike his earlier air of apparent hauteur, he was now looking at her with an expression of unseemly familiarity. Lady Georgiana lifted her pert little chin, took the arm of Lady Charlotte, and turned sharply.

"Georgiana, may I have the honor?" George asked, bowing over her hand with a flip of his tails.

In spite of the injury another dance with George was sure to do her slippers, Georgiana accepted and moved to the center of the floor just before the stranger reached her. A quick glance over her shoulder revealed a dark head bowing over Charlotte's hand, and Charlotte smiling radiantly. Georgiana caught only one further glimpse of the couple during the dance and was left with a strong impression of the elegant picture of Charlotte's blond, beflowered hair, and white gauze dress next to her partner's handsome darkness.

Having partnered George for the supper dance, Georgiana was obliged to accompany him into the dining room where the gentle strains of Pandean Pipes floated lightly on the air. Georgiana tried to match the festive mood as around the room candles burning in the crystal-draped chandeliers turned the fluted columns amber gold and caused flickering shadows to play hide-and-seek among the fruit, flowers, and gamebirds of the Grinling Gibbons carvings. But she felt her spirits oddly suppressed, and more than once her attention wandered from her escort as she sought the stranger she had determined to ignore.

The supper table held a fine assortment of dishes and Georgiana suddenly found that an evening of dancing had sharpened her appetite. She accepted servings of haricot of mutton, veal olives, brown soup, and macaroni pie. She was, however, just about to refuse the ragu of pullet and sweetbreads when George gave a slight tug at the narrow frill on his shirt cuffs and said, "I should advise you to refuse the ragu, my Dear. I find ragu of sweetbreads taken at a late hour can be quite as unsettling to the digestion as a fricasee."

Georgiana allowed the footman to place a serving of ragu on her plate and added, "Jensen, after you've served this around I should like a portion of the fricasee of chicken."

"Very good, my Lady."

The brown soup was followed with fish, which Georgiana refused, as she did the almond pudding with coconut and the blanc mange; but the floating island which replaced the pidgeon pie she accepted after George turned it down.

"I understand it was always the habit of Mr. Walpole to retire at an early hour," she chided her partner. "I'm surprised you stay so late."

"If Mr. Walpole had had such inducements at Strawberry Hill, he might have found himself with greater stamina," George replied gallantly. And then he added with just a touch of archness, "But because one admires a man's literary taste and style, one need not go to extremes."

"My sentiments precisely, Sir." Georgiana winced at her own words. In spite of his taste for the overblown, George was a pleasant companion. She wished he didn't bring out such unaccountable acidity from her, and she resolved to behave in a more ladylike manner in the future.

Tea would be served later in the drawing room. Now, the strains of the orchestra announced that the ball was resuming with a country dance and Georgiana was certain that George was considering the impropriety of asking her for a third dance. "Oh," she cried suddenly, "I see Mama and my sister just going into the garden to take the air. Pray excuse me, Sir. I must speak to them."

17

Not waiting for a reply, and praying fervently that the Duchess was not standing somewhere in plain view of Mr. Agar-Ellis, she slipped quickly through the open French window. Just in case George might be thinking of following her, Georgiana sidestepped from the light of the long windows into the shadows cast by the formal shrubbery of the south front lawn. But instead of the fresh, open space she expected, she bumped soundly into a solid muscular chest. Two strong hands gripped her arms firmly to support her. "Steady as she goes, Georgie," said a deep masculine voice, with a hint of a smile in it. "Now that's more like it. In the old days, you were always throwing yourself at me, as I recall."

Immediately concerned for her dignity, Georgiana pulled away. "I fear you mistake, Sir. . . . *Georgie?* No one has called me that for years."

"Indeed, not for nine years, I should hope. Not since I went off to serve His Majesty in the Royal Navy."

With an almost audible click, memory slipped into focus and Georgiana suddenly realized why the intriguing stranger had seemed so familiar. "Gran! How extraordinary! Imagine you the scrawny boy who lashed me to the cherry tree and then forgot to come back until after luncheon."

"Not at all! I'm certain I couldn't have done that. I may have lashed you to the cherry tree, but I would never have forgotten you. And I was not scrawny. But I distinctly remember you coming under the repeated scorn of Miss Primrose for smudges on your face and rips in your lace."

"A gentleman would not recall such things, Sir," she replied, placing her hand on the arm he offered. "But tell me what you are doing here." They began strolling along the garden path.

"I found life in the Navy didn't suit. So I sold out."

Georgiana gave a small trill of laughter. "You sold out and here you are? Just like that?"

"More or less, yes." He paused. "No, there's more to it than that. Ever since the defeat of Napoleon, naval work has been largely a matter of patrol duty, and I didn't want a job that was just putting in time. But worse, I found that I had exchanged an exacting father for an exacting superior officer. The final straw was realizing the pointlessness of promotions that weren't really earned."

"And only something you've earned yourself has value?" She

18

didn't mean to argue with him; she was just trying to understand.

"I have been taught that one must strive for things of true value, unlike the simple inheritance of money and title that is natural to our rank."

"Yes, but . . . " His stormy look made her change her mind and swiftly shift conversation topics. "But fancy Mama not informing me of your homecoming. Surely your mama would have written the news to her."

"Perhaps my lady mother thought to bring the news herself. They are to arrive tomorrow. I came straight here from Southampton after only a brief stop to visit my tailor in London."

"And now that you've sold out of the Navy, what will you do?" Georgiana remembered to speak a bit more loudly, as her cousin shared the Duchess' tendency to deafness. They turned their steps back toward the house, the light falling from the long dining room windows making golden stripes on the lawn.

At her question, Granville became withdrawn and aloof. For the first time since their abrupt encounter, Georgiana saw the coldness which she had interpreted as arrogance in the ballroom. "That remains to be seen," he answered curtly. "With Sandon having taken his seat in Parliament now, and our honorable father serving as President of the Council, our family is not lacking for useful employment. There may be no place for the younger son."

They strolled in silence for a few moments, Georgiana wondering at the sharpness of his words—so unlike the Granville she had known as a boy.

"Well, if you find life too boring, there's always compassionate work." She spoke lightly, thinking a turn to the topic of the religious activities in which both their families took an active interest might enliven the conversation.

But the subject seemed to darken her companion's mood even more. "And just which one would you suggest I put my energies into?" His tone was very near a taunt. "To be certain, there's no end of possibilities. Let's see, I might turn my talents to The London Orphan Asylum for the Reception and Education of Destitute Orphans, Particularly Those Descended from Respectable Parents; or The General Benevolent Institution for the Relief of Decayed Artists of the United Kingdom; or The Association for the Refutation of Infidel Publications; or perhaps I could use my naval training in The Institution for the Cure of Various Diseases by

Bandages and Compression; or maybe you could recommend The Cloathing Society for the Benefit of Poor Pious Clergymen of the Established Church and Their Families?" The list had taken them to the top of the path. Turning sharply he added, "Or better yet, why not The Friendly Female Society for the Relief of Poor, Infirm, Aged Widows, and Single Women of Good Character Who Have Seen Better Days?"

Hearing the aversion in his voice and knowing him to be in earnest, Georgiana dared not give rein to the laughter she felt bubbling up inside her. "There is certainly no doubt about the variety of possibilities," she managed, with only a hint of the humor she felt at hearing his list of inflated titles. "But you must allow that many of them do accomplish their purpose."

"Perhaps, but I can't help wondering how many are subscribed to by people who are as destitute, decayed, and infirm spiritually as the people they would try to help are physically and economically. That would certainly be the case if I were to add my name to the lists."

At these words, Georgiana's desire to laugh died. What did he mean? Spiritually destitute—Granville? Impossible! Perhaps she had misunderstood. But she was certain that he had indeed said that, and meant it. It was obvious he was deeply troubled. And that troubled her.

There was no opportunity to explore his meaning further, however, as Lord Lauderdale, her brother's closest friend, appeared in the entrance, caught sight of the strollers, and came to claim Georgiana for the dance she had promised him earlier. "Lord Lauderdale, I believe you know my cousin, Granville Ryder, newly returned from service in His Majesty's Navy."

The gentlemen exchanged bows. "I ride out before breakfast," Georgiana said over her shoulder to her cousin, as she was borne back to the music and lights of the ballroom.

When the dance was at an end she rapidly surveyed the room for a glimpse of Granville. Since his height placed him several inches above every other man in the room, it should not be difficult to see him.

But he was not there. And she had not had a dance with him, nor a chance to pursue their conversation. His final words continued to plague her—did Gran feel himself spiritually inadequate? She had never known her cousin to be inadequate in anything, nor had she

20

ever had reason to think any member of the Earl's family to be lacking in spiritual commitment.

Could something have happened in the Navy to turn him from his faith? The thought struck her like a knife. Not Gran. Not the dearest companion of her childhood to whom she could always turn. . . . Life was at its best when her Aunt Susan visited Badminton, bringing her sons with her. When Gran was there, Georgiana had no worries; if she skinned her knee, he would bandage it for her rather than make her face the recriminations of Miss Primrose; if she was late for luncheon, he would make an excuse for her; if she was afraid of a jump, he would take it first or find a way around it for her.

She smiled at the memory of the misdemeanor she had confronted him with earlier in the evening—of leaving her tied to a tree. True, Gran had forgotten her, but it had actually been his brother Sandon who had tied her up and then borne Granville off to the house. And the memory had always been dear to her, because when Gran did return for her, his contrition had been so genuine and his care for her so tender.

Surely those days weren't gone forever, her companion irrevocably lost to her? The harshness and self-recriminations she had glimpsed in him tonight were unbearably out of place in her Granville.

Tomorrow most of the guests would be gone and she would talk to him. She must understand what had happened. She must help him.

· 2 ·

THE AIR WAS crisp and golden with September as Georgiana walked
to the stables the next morning. Although she could have made her
way inside the house directly to the stableyard behind, she preferred to use the east exit and walk across the great green expanse
of lawn laid out in the time of the Fifth Duke by Capability Brown,
the most fashionable landscape architect of the day. The cream-
stuccoed Cotswold stone of Badminton House reflected the rays of
the early morning sun. It was going to be a glorious day. If
Georgiana had been a few years younger she would have broken
into a skip, but the Duchess' well-drilled lessons on proper deco-
rum for young ladies had done their work.

Before going to the stables, she decided to walk up the hill to
visit the kennels. She waved to the children playing in the lane
beside the servants' stone cottages and continued along the stone-
walled walk between the twin fox statues at the entrance of the
kennels. A riotous yapping told her the Beaufort Hunt hounds had
seen her.

"Good morning, Payne," she greeted the new huntsman, who
was preparing to walk the hounds in the park.

As he returned her greeting, Will Todd and Will Long, the two
whippers-in, appeared with leashes. Cutting short his greeting to
the young mistress, Payne turned sharply to the servants. "What are
those for?"

"To put on the 'ounds, Sir," the whippers-in replied. "We
always couple up the 'ounds when excercisin' in the park for fear of
their runnin' riot among the deer."

"Stuff and nonsense," the huntsman replied. "They won't run the deer while I'm with them."

"Quite right, Payne," Georgiana agreed. "If the hounds aren't obedient to your voice in the park, I can't imagine the chaos there would be during the hunt."

She moved into the pack to be greeted by her favorites. "Good morning, Flyer," she said to a sturdy Belvoir tan hound who returned her greeting with a lively wagging of his tail. Whirlwind, a badger pie, received a pat on the head and a brisk scratch behind his ears. Potentate, the most famous of the Beaufort hounds, wasn't to miss out on his share of the attention; but he stood a little aloof from the pack, waiting for the young mistress to come to him, rather than vying with the others for her attention.

"They're looking fine, Payne," she said.

"Yes, Miss. Powerful, full of bone, and with ready tongues, just the way the Duke likes them." The pride in his voice was clearly justifiable.

After watching the pack head for the park under the huntsman's competent command, Georgiana left the kennels and turned toward the stables at the back of the house. The unadorned stone buildings were ornamented only by a fox weathervane on the small Wren cupola, but the soft cooing of doves living in the eaves and the scent of new-mown hay embellished the scene to perfection.

Georgiana stepped from the bright early morning sunshine of the stableyard to the cool dimness of the stone-floored stables and walked down the row of mahogany stalls with a leather halter hanging by each gate. The sounds of horses rustling and munching their hay and the smell of clean straw, horsehide, and leather never failed to evoke memories of her earliest childhood. And this morning, memories of long-ago rides with her Cousin Granville were especially sharp in her mind.

A soft whicker greeted her at the stall of a white Arabian mare. Georgiana drew a sugar lump from her pocket and the horse nuzzled her palm. "Hello, Mayflower." She ran her hand over the mare's satiny neck. "Are you ready for a run?"

"She's everything she should be, Miss, in fine mettle. You'll be wantin' me to accompany you?" The groom stepped forward and led Mayflower out of the stall and into the cobbled yard before tossing a gleaming leather sidesaddle on her back.

"Not this morning, thank you, Dick. Has Mr. Ryder been down

yet?"

"Would that be Mr. Granville Ryder? That young scamp what was al'ays tearin' off on my 'orses a few years ago?"

Georgiana laughed at the apt description. "The same, Dick. But you'll find him much changed, I believe." She placed her foot in the groom's cupped hands and he tossed her into the saddle. "If Mr. Ryder chooses to put in an appearance, you may tell him I've gone to the park." She hooked her leg firmly over the saddlehorn, smoothed the gores of her clarence-blue riding skirt, and adjusted the veil floating from her narrow-brimmed top hat.

She had merely to raise the reins in her hands and apply the slightest pressure of her heel for Mayflower to move briskly across the stableyard and through the ivy-covered entrance into Badminton Park; its ten-mile circumference made the park one of the largest in England. Once inside, Georgiana and Mayflower were free to give rein to their spirits. Almost before she was bidden, the little mare broke into a smooth flowing canter which carried her rider at a clipping pace over the brown earth trail between beech and lime trees turning gold and orange beneath a bright autumn sky.

After several minutes of exhiliration, Georgiana checked her mount and proceeded at a gait that allowed her rider to take in the beauties around her. The grass still grew a rich summer green, clumps of Michaelmas daisies burst forth in lavender and yellow mounds, and wood doves cooed from the trees. Mayflower's slower pace allowed Georgiana's mind to drift back to the evening before, but she staunchly refused to pine over the odd behavior of her cousin. With a lift of her chin she lectured herself: *If it pleased the Honorable Granville Dudley Ryder, younger son of the First Earl of Harrowby and cousin to the Lady Georgiana Somerset, to spurn dancing with all the guests except Lady Charlotte at the Duke of Beaufort's Hunt Ball, and to be moody in company with his cousin, and to spurn her invitation to ride out with her this morning, she was sure it was nothing to her—no matter how much she had determined on a visit with him.* With each thought, her nose lifted a tilt higher into the air.

"Hullo, how about a race to the lake?" A voice from just beyond her on the trail broke her reverie.

"Granville! How did you get ahead of me? Dick said he hadn't seen you in the stables." She sternly commanded her voice to sound more surprised than pleased.

"I shouldn't think he saw me. I saddled up myself. You know, I believe old Tom Thumb remembers me." He patted his mount's glossy chestnut neck.

"Saddled up yourself? What a singular thing to do when Papa employs thirty-three stablemen."

"I wanted to be sure I still remembered how. Nine years is a long time to be away from horses. How about that race? I never knew you to refuse a challenge!"

They were off at a gallop, their horses' hooves striking the firm earth solidly and patches of gold and shade flying by. At the edge of the lake, they pulled up sharply and engaged in a friendly but heated argument over who had won the contest.

"Of course, I won; I always did, if memory serves," Granville said.

"Memory, Sir, does not serve. And no gentleman would defeat a lady anyway," she retorted.

"Oh, bosh! You didn't have to be treated like a lady all the time when I last knew you."

"Need I remind you, Sir, that was nine years ago? I was a mere schoolroom miss then. It has been three years since I made my come-out. You should think me very ramshackle, indeed, if I had not grown up in that time."

"And you have become a very elegant young lady." His grin was the most like the Granville of the old days she had yet seen. And his mild compliment gave her a pleasure she didn't wish to contemplate. "Shall we dismount and walk a bit, or do you desire to ride further?"

"It *was* my intention to ride to the end of the lake," she replied. Granville expressed his agreement with the slightest nod of his curly beaver hat and they moved ahead together. Here the path was wider and permitted riding side by side, giving Georgiana ample opportunity to survey his dark brown frockcoat and white Marseilles waistcoat above fawn knee smalls and gleaming black leather top boots with dark brown turnover cuffs. How could anyone who looked such a piece of perfection possibly feel the doubts he expressed last night? Surely she had misunderstood.

The willows bordering the lake were turning yellow, and their graceful branches lapped the water, repeating the arch of the long-necked swans gliding near the shore. The sun sparkled on the water, fish jumped at low-flying insects, and waterfowl called to

25

each other at the far end of the lake. After a few moments of riding in a silence broken only by the soft plod of hooves and the chirping of the sparrows in rustling maple leaves overhead, Georgiana said, "You must tell me about your life in the Navy. It was as if you dropped from the earth when you went to sea. We have had no communication from you."

"Surely you didn't expect any?"

"Oh, not to myself, of course, but through our mamas."

"I daresay with all the honors heaped upon Sandon and Father; and with all her compassionate work to see to, Mama could have had little to say about a younger son at sea."

"Do you mean to say that you didn't communicate with your family?"

"Oh, certainly, my mother and I wrote, and I even wrote to my father, and with quite alarming regularity at first, until I realized how deficient he found my efforts. When I wrote home as a middy, I was informed upon receipt of the next mailbag that my letters were badly formed. Learning my lesson well, I waited for a settled day before attempting another, so that no swelling wave would damage the precision of my penmanship. Unfortunately, perfection was beyond my reach. I was warned by reply mail against blotting my page."

"But you were so young."

"No excuse, my Dear; imperfection is not to be tolerated in the young or it will grow into evil vice in adulthood." Again she heard the bitter note she had detected the evening before.

"But surely things got better as you grew older?"

"What became better? My penmanship? Ah, yes, I fancy it did—I sweated over it enough. But I never managed to please my father, if that's what you mean. When I wrote to inform him that I had received my lieutenancy the reply was, 'Fine, fine, but why did it take you so long?'

"Not that I ever held my father to be unfair," he added quickly. "He was always quite right—I cut a poor figure in comparison to his goals for me."

Georgiana wanted to argue that Granville had never cut a poor figure in comparison to anything, but she knew her defense would be meaningless to him, so instead she said, "Well, *now* you must tell me all about it. You must have had some very successful adventures since you distinguished yourself by becoming a lieutenant." Georgiana expected to see Granville's warm smile and to be regaled with stories of drama on the high seas, but instead the shuttered, withdrawn look that seemed to be with him so much of the time descended like a shroud.

Perplexed over how her intended compliment could have gone awry, she tried again. "I didn't mean to imply that it was all a lark, but that you obviously did well in difficult circumstances. Won't you tell me about it—such a life is so far removed from anything I know of, I should find it very instructive."

"Your servant, Madam. No gentleman could refuse to grant such an earnest request from a lady. But if she is looking for tales of valor on the part of the gentleman, I fear she will be sadly disappointed."

"I am sure you are far too modest, Sir. But if you wish to speak of sea life in general rather than of personal experience, pray do." Then her carefully held pose crumbled and she burst into a tinkling laughter that made Mayflower prick up her ears and toss her head. "Easy girl." Georgiana patted her mare's neck. "O Gran, don't be so high in the instep. You dropped out of sight as completely as if you'd been dead for nine years. Now you simply must satisfy my curiosity over what it was like. Were you beaten?"

"No, no, nothing like that. Nelson's humanitarian example has much transformed life at sea for the volunteer. I never saw a serious flogging. Running the gauntlet and starting were both abolished before I joined up."

"Starting?"

"Beating with a cane or rope's end by the bosun's mate."

Georgiana shivered. "Oh, I'm so glad you didn't have to suffer that, Gran." Then she giggled and placed her hand on her stomach. "But tell me true—were you ever seasick?"

In the bright September morning in Badminton Park, with a fine mount under him and his cousin's charming companionship, Granville seemed to relax and his conversation became more open. "Not in the way I'm sure you mean; but whenever bad weather required sealing the gunports on middle deck, bad ventilation would cause weakness and sometimes putrid fever among the crew. Fighting the enemy is not the severest part of Navy life—the war of the elements is.

"It's well known that the man who faces a Frenchman or Spaniard with intrepidity does not always encounter rocks and shoals with the same feeling. And the entrance to the English Channel is

27

one of the most hazardous landfalls in the world."

Georgiana nodded in understanding, trying to apply these impersonal words to what must have been her companion's daily existence. What in his experience had so changed the carefree young man she remembered? Certainly, much could be assigned to simple growing up and maturing, as changes in her own demeanor were; but she felt the alterations in Granville's personality were much deeper than that, and she wasn't at all sure they were for the good. Maybe if she could lead him to talk about his early experiences she would find a clue. "Do you think it was because you went in at such an early age?"

"Was *what* because I went in at an early age?" He drew back as if she had touched an open sore.

"Oh, I meant, was life in general harder?"

"I think I should have preferred it to be harder than it was. When the sons of noblemen—lads of the ruling class, as we were referred to—are put into the profession, their paths, on the whole, are made very easy for them in the way of advancement. To become a lieutenant, one must spend three years at sea—two as a volunteer, one as midshipman—pass an examination in practical seamanship, attain the age of twenty, and have an appointment bestowed upon him. It's all very natural and orderly and seems in no way to be connected to personal ability—it happens whether one has earned it properly or not."

Georgiana gave a puzzled laugh. "But Gran, why must everything be earned? Why can't one simply accept the good with the bad? Besides, no matter what you say about automatic promotions and the Navy's humanitarian reforms, I'm persuaded you worked very hard and acquitted yourself superbly, as well as submitting to some very harsh discipline."

"Perhaps, but I was well prepared for living by regulations. The number of times my father called me to task for failure to replace a book on its proper shelf, or for wearing my jacket crooked, or for giving a mumbled reply—I must say there were times when Navy discipline seemed almost lax by comparison."

They rode for some time in silence as Georgiana tried to extract the meaning under her companion's words. "But maybe it just seemed that way because you started it all when you were only thirteen."

"That, dear Coz, was rather a late start. Nelson went in at

28

twelve. But I will say, that of all the ordeals with which the naval officer is faced throughout his career, that of joining his first ship is probably the sternest. Nelson's father took him as far as London and put him on the Chatham coach to face it alone. At least my father accompanied me to Southampton.''

And then, for the first time, Georgiana at last caught sight of the flickering smile of amused remembrance that she had been hoping to evoke. "I will admit that of all the trepidations of my first night on the *Malta*, the greatest challenge was mastering the complicated business of turning into a hammock. But one soon learns that a hammock is by far the most comfortable of all sleeping berths on board ship. And, of course, I received the usual christening of having a plate broken over my head and being cobbed for having the impudence to bring my name to sea.''

"Cobbed?''

Granville shook his head. "Forgive me for mentioning it—not a proper subject for the ears of a young lady.''

"Oh, good. Now you're getting to the interesting bits. Tell me what cobbing is, or I'll—I'll . . . ''

"Yes?'' he challenged with an upraised eyebrow.

"I shall tell my papa about your leaving me tied to the cherry tree.''

"And he will order me cobbed again, no doubt, by the head groom?''

"Most assuredly.''

Granville returned her mischievous smile. "In that case, my lady, I submit. Cobbing consists in stretching the victim over the edge of the table and vigorously applying a dirk scabbard, a long ruler, or a knotted napkin to the part of the anatomy thus conveniently exposed.''

"Oh, my!'' Georgiana giggled at the picture drawn so vividly in her mind. "I think I should consider the slate quite even for any mistreatment I received at your hands.''

The recounting of Granville's life at sea had carried them to the end of the park. Ahead were the thatched-roof stone cottages of Little Badminton, covered with rambling red roses in late bloom. Along the stone wall bordering the park was the round ice house with its cupolaed roof, and stone walls so thick the ice kept all summer.

Georgiana heard the doves coo, the sheep baa, the little stream

29

babble, and she smiled. Then, noting the height of the sun in the sky, she said, "It must be past ten o'clock. Breakfast will be served soon—let's hurry." She turned toward the top of the park and set Mayflower at a canter.

When they arrived back at the house, the grooms were just pulling an empty traveling coach bearing a familiar coronet into the stableyard.

"The Earl and Countess of Harrowby have arrived," Granville commented without a smile.

Seeing the shuttered look on his countenance, Georgiana rode near her cousin. "Gran, assuredly my Uncle Harrowby is not an easy person, but why do you hold him in such dread?"

Granville gave her a stiff smile. "Coming into his presence is always something like being doused by a sudden, cold shower, or brushing unawares against a hedgehog." He paused to look at his cousin. "Georgie, don't look so stricken! What a fool I am to distress you with my petty complaints. Don't pay them any heed. And be assured I meant no disrespect to my father. He is one of the most highly esteemed men in the nation."

She forced a smile. "I'm not distressed, Gran, just very interested. I feel as if we need to get entirely reacquainted, as if we met as strangers only last night. Pray, do go on. . . . "

He sighed. "The prospect of meeting my father makes me feel like a small boy again, when I was weekly required to present myself and stand rigid before him while Nurse reported on my behavior, my progress in lessons, my duty in prayers. When she said that I acquitted myself satisfactorily, my father would demand, '*Satisfactory?* I do not want to hear of satisfaction; I want excellence! Your charge is a Ryder. Why does he not excel like his brother?'

"There was never an answer to that. I still don't have one. Worst of all was when she would try to excuse me for something on the ground of my deafness. I didn't want excuses; I wanted to earn his favor." Granville was silent for a moment. "That is, when I wasn't vacillating between determination to succeed and the decision to give it all up for lost. Mostly, though, I was determined to be worthy of my father's approbation.

"But I never was."

· 3 ·

WHEN GEORGIANA AND Granville entered, the family was gathered
in the dining room, serving themselves breakfast from a lavish
assortment of covered dishes on the sideboard. The Duchess,
looking fresh and radiant in a chintz morning dress with a wide
whitework collar, came forward. "Good morning, my Dears. Don't
bother changing from your riding dress. As you can see, my sister
and her husband have just arrived and we shall be all family at
breakfast. I trust you had a pleasant ride?"

"Quite delightful, Mama," Georgiana replied and Granville gave
a small bow in assent.

"Granville, my Dear, how tanned you are!" cried Lady
Harrowby, after kissing her son and receiving his kiss in return.

"Yes, Ma'am. No matter how unfashionable, it's entirely un-
avoidable at sea."

"But it's quite handsome on you, my dear Boy."

"And you, Ma'am, look no older than you did the day I left." He
stood back and surveyed his mother who was obviously pleased by
her son's words. "I think perhaps you look younger. It must be the
relief of not having had me to plague you all these years."

The Countess laughed. "My dear Boy, you will turn my head.
Now I shall surely blossom with my son at home."

"But come now, here's your papa."

Lord Harrowby turned from his conversation with the Duke and
Lord Worcester to approach his son. The Earl's hair was as dark as
his son's with only touches of gray at the temples. His forehead was
creased in a perpetual frown from his almost continual headaches,

31

his mouth drawn tightly at the corners, making his features appear even sharper than they were.

"It is good to see you, Granville. I trust you had a pleasant journey from Southampton." He shook hands with his son.

"Yes, Father. Thank you. And your work is getting on well in Parliament?"

"I have been constantly in London for the last seven months doing nothing. Events there have been none." The Earl frowned even more, then turned to take his seat at the long table where a footman had already placed the plate Lord Harrowby had filled at the sideboard. Others followed his example and moved to the table.

Georgiana was seated next to Lord Harrowby, who was continuing the topic begun by his son's question regarding Parliamentary activity: "They continue to foment controversy over the elevation of my brother Henry to the bishopric of Lichfield and Coventry. And Lord Liverpool continues to hold back on the *Conge d' elire*."

"But on what grounds does the Prime Minister refuse to grant the royal permission to elect a bishop? Liverpool has always insisted that ecclesiastical appointments be justified by merit rather than by influence, and who could possibly merit the position more than Bishop Ryder?" Worcester asked.

"I cannot understand Liverpool's position. As I said last week in the House of Lords, 'If Dr. Ryder is not fit to be a bishop, Lord Harrowby is not fit to be Lord President of the Council.' "

"And how was that received?" the Duke asked.

"As was to be expected, a chorus of 'Hear! Hear!' from our supporters and a rumble of grousing from the opposition."

The Duchess set aside her piece of toast spread with golden marmalade. "And has His Majesty taken a position?"

Harrowby answered with a disgusted guffaw, "How can a man who can't decide which suit to wear for the day determine who is fitted to be bishop? Especially since so much of the dispute centers on such things as Bishop Ryder's public reading of prayers—as if it is a shocking lowering of episcopal dignity for a bishop to approach his God in humility."

The acidity underlying the Earl's outburst left the party concentrating uncomfortably on their breakfast plates until the Duchess observed, "From my earliest youth I have been admitted a good deal behind the curtain, and have known the motives of those who were active in politics. Often I have known that what was done on right principles was misunderstood and misrepresented. From such experiences, I am led to believe that a thing may be viewed in a different light by persons of a different party without their being either knaves or fools."

"I'm sure you are right, Sister," the Countess said, handing her teacup to the Duchess for a refill. "But I must share my husband's forceful sentiments. Just look at what Bishop Ryder has accomplished in the dioceses of Gloucester. He has faithfully served a population of over a million souls, and his church-building society in Birmingham gained fifteen thousand pounds in subscriptions.

"But far beyond his material accomplishments is the fact that he has truly experienced the redeeming power of Jesus Christ—such a shocking thing for a bishop to believe in a personal God." Her voice was heavy with irony. "And then when his opponents discovered his readiness to set forth the great fundamental doctrines of the Gospel—well, it is all quite a bumblebroth."

The Duchess handed the refilled cup back to her sister. "I do pray that he will receive the appointment. No one could deserve it more. Bishop Ryder was the means of bringing me on in the path of life. It seems that of all the Christians I have known, he resembles his blessed Saviour the most."

The men then turned the conversation to a report that the Duke of Wellington had said that Sir William Knighton, the King's physician and private secretary, was managing His Majesty's affairs very well and getting him out of debt very quickly; also, that the ministers were in most matters well satisfied with their sovereign, other than in his procrastination over the elevation of Bishop Ryder.

Although Georgiana found these firsthand glimpses of life at court, from one so close to the crown as Lord Harrowby, most interesting, her attention soon strayed to the far end of the table. Her sister Charlotte, seated next to Granville, was breakfasting in a fetching morning dress of sprig muslin. Georgiana was too far away to catch the conversation, but she could hardly miss the private look that passed between them as Charlotte laughed at something Granville said to her.

Before Georgiana's mind could linger long on this, however, the conversation next to her again caught her attention and she was once more transported to events at the center of government.

Harrowby was saying to Worcester, "Wellington spoke to the King concerning Beau Brummell's Consulship in France and the

King made objections, abusing Brummell, saying he was an abominable fellow who had behaved very ill to him."

"The old story, always thinking of nothing but himself—*moi, moi, moi,*" Worcester spoke with disgust at the King.

"True, but after having let His Majesty run out his tether of abuse, Wellington at last extracted his consent," Harrowby concluded.

"Excellent!" Worcester replied. "The Beau is a deserving fellow—there is much more to him than the dandy his detractors make him out to be. Making cleanliness fashionable was no small accomplishment in itself."

"I fancy you are much to be credited with the decision," the Earl told Worcester. "The Duke said he had no acquaintance with Brummell and only entered into the proceedings to oblige you, my Lord."

Georgiana heard the news with great satisfaction. Her brother, who had served as aide-de-camp to the Duke of Wellington in the Peninsula and was now a Member of Parliament for Monmouth, was establishing himself in the world of politics as well as in the family tradition of country sporting life. If only he would take a wife.

To Georgiana's left, the ladies were discussing the efforts of their friend William Wilberforce to make goodness fashionable. . . . "Oh, yes, I am sure Mr. Wilberforce's Society for the Mitigation and Gradual Abolition of Slavery will meet great success as all his endeavors have done." The Countess of Harrowby's brown eyes sparkled as she moved on to new topics. "I have recently subscribed to The Society for the Relief of Distressed Widows and renewed my membership in The Society for Returning Young Women to Their Friends in the Country. I shall also sponsor The Royal Humane Society for Persons in a State of Suspended Animation. And what of your sponsorship of The Society for Promoting the Enlargement, Building, and Repairing of Churches and Chapels?"

"Funds for the chapel we desire to build in Wales are lagging sadly." The Duchess shook her lace-capped head. "But we have had our greatest success with the local chapter of Mr. Wilberforce's Society for Promoting the External Observance of the Lord's Day and for the Suppression of Public Lewdness."

"That is a victory indeed, and it enjoys great prosperity in

London, as well," Lady Harrowby added with pleasure. "Only last week we were at dinner with Wilberforce and he recalled that when the Society was founded, a friend laughed in his face, agreeing that there was indeed a great deal of debauchery and very little religion, but that in a wealthy nation it would never be otherwise. The only way to reform morals, his friend contended, was to ruin purses. He promised a speedy return of purity of morals in our own homes if no one had a shilling to spend in debauchery out-of-doors; but it seems that Providence has seen fit to grant that it be otherwise."

Georgiana's plate had long grown empty and her coffee cold when Dixon, the butler, appeared to inform the Duchess of the arrival of Mr. Agar-Ellis. She looked at her daughter for guidance. Georgiana started to shake her head, then looked across the table where Granville and Charlotte were deep in conversation. "Please ask him to wait in the octagon room; I'll join him shortly."

The Duchess nodded at Dixon and he departed with a bow.

Georgiana ran quickly to her dressing room where Agatha helped her change from her riding habit into an afternoon dress of soft lavender gray with a padded *rouleau* at the bottom. And a few moments later she entered the octagonal vestibule.

George, who had been waiting in the company of the footman on duty, rose from the wooden hall bench and bowed deeply over Georgiana's hand. "Even in so light and charming a room as this, where nothing distracts the eye from the proportions and the beauty of the plasterwork, you are the finest ornament, my Dear."

Georgiana smiled at the young man in a belcher tie, striped waistcoat, and yellow pantaloons. "Thank you, George. I see you are in fine mettle today. My mama is engaged with the recent arrival of her sister's family, so I am receiving you for her."

"I am sadly disappointed to hear that your mother is occupied. I had hoped to invite her grace and your charming self to accompany me on a ride. I am excessively pleased with my new pair of match greys—I am persuaded you have never seen a pair of sweeter goers. May I prevail upon you to take the air with me?" George bowed deeply again.

Georgiana consented and, with a fleeting thought of Granville's head bent attentively toward Charlotte, she even went so far as to allow her maid to fetch her poke bonnet trimmed with ostrich plumes.

They drove through Badminton Park, where a few hours earlier

Granville and Georgiana had ridden, and out into the ancient village of Little Badminton with its dovecote dating back to the Battle of Hastings. The road wound between cottages of Cotswold stone, their floral-riot gardens enclosed by low walls at the very edge of the narrow road. As soon as they were clear of the village, George dropped his hands and the greys sprang to a sharp canter beneath the leafy trees arching clear over the road. They drove under an ancient arched bridge built by the Romans, and along the road to Acton Turville. Cows lay contented in green pastures, their stone barns ringed with trees.

And here and there the scenery was accented by glimpses of the narrow Avon River as it wound through green fields beginning to show their autumn hues. Overhead lacy branches dropped an occasional golden leaf on them which inspired George to rapturize in the words of Thomas Gray, his idol's favorite poet:

"Beneath those rugged elms, that yew-tree's shade,
Oft did the harvest to their sickle yield.
Let not Ambition mock their useful toil,
  Their homely joys, and destiny obscure;
Nor grandeur hear with a disdainful smile,
  The short and simple annals of the poor."

Georgiana, surveying the trees that had called forth such transports, remarked, "I believe they are oaks and beeches."

Her companion's rhapsodizing at an end, Georgiana settled into the corner of the seat, a position which allowed her to study the driver while he concentrated on handling the reins in his expert way. George James Welborne Agar-Ellis, in spite of his exaggerated affectations, was a kind and considerate companion; and by his frequent and studied attentions to herself, he seemed to be making it quite clear to Georgiana that she would soon be called upon to voice her opinion of him. Indeed, unless she was much mistaken, the situation would soon call for not merely an opinion, but her pronouncement on his suitability as her life's companion.

There was no doubt as to his suitability in matters of family and class; and even though his appearance and social intercourse bespoke a certain shallowness of mind, she knew that to be far from the actual truth. Besides his study of Horace Walpole, he was compiling a monograph on historical inquiries respecting the character of Edward Hyde, Earl of Clarendon, Lord Chancellor of

England, and at the same time writing a fictional work which he called *The True History of the State Prisoner*, but most often referred to as *The Iron Mask*. Further, his *Catalogue of the Principal Pictures in Flanders and Holland* had been published last year and his publishers were already talking about bringing out another edition.

No, she couldn't fault his family or his mind or his manners—at least the sincerity of them; but still, Georgiana could not feel happy at the prospect of receiving an offer from Mr. Agar-Ellis. Whatever her answer, the results would be unhappy. Giving a final blow to his feelings seemed almost as unpleasant as the thought of spending the rest of her life with him.

Ultimately, her decision would rest on the fact that, whatever other qualifications he possessed, George lacked the one quality absolutely essential in a life's mate; for all his outward adherence to the doctrines and practices of the established church, he did not share her faith in a personal God. Georgiana had often seen the pain her mother had endured when members of their social circle snubbed her Evangelical activities and labeled her "an enthusiast." Georgiana could not settle for a husband who did not share her beliefs. But that did not mean they couldn't share a pleasant ride.

As George turned his head to smile at her, she asked him, "How is your work on the letters of Horace Walpole progressing?"

"How obliging of you to inquire." Georgiana felt that if it had been possible to do so on the seat of a phaeton, he would have made a deep bow. "Collecting the letters of one who carried on so wide a correspondence is no small task, but I am determined to prevail. I have recently acquired a delightful missive which he wrote to Miss Mary Berry and another in Walpole's own hand to the Countess of Upper Ossory; but I fear the task is far, far from complete. I am determined, however, to bring to the world a complete edition of the incomparable letters of this Prince of epistolary writers. Presented in chronological order, the series shall form a lively commentary on the events of the age."

"Those are admirable goals, and I heartily wish you well."

"My lady is too kind. Your regard is one I hold near to my heart. And as for my humble literary efforts, I attempt, as always, to do my part diligently, judiciously, and without the slightest ostentation."

"Your sentiments are indeed worthy, Sir." Georgiana was very pleased with herself that she had managed to conduct the entire exchange with a perfectly straight face.

· 4 ·

AT THE SAME time George's match greys were stepping through Badminton Park, breakfast ended in the dining room inside Badminton House. The company rose and the Duchess led the way from the room to take her sister and elder daughter for a turn around the gardens, where the younger Somerset daughters were enjoying a break from the tyranny of an aging Miss Primrose and the schoolroom. Granville was handing Lady Charlotte her light cashmere shawl and receiving a very pretty smile in return when the Earl approached his son. "I shall await you in the library." Harrowby turned on his heel and left the room by the side door.

With all his feeling of being a small boy called on the carpet returning in full force, Granville escorted the ladies to the terrace and then made his way through the Red Room to the library.

Beneath the portrait of John of Gaunt, fourteenth-century founder of the Somerset family, a fire burned on the grate to prevent any possibility of dampness infecting the extensive and valuable collection of the Badminton library. The polished dark woodwork and the richly embossed leather bindings of the books glowed from the sun shining through the beveled glass of the long eastern windows. But the glow failed to reach Granville's spirit.

The Earl, dressed conservatively in a frock coat with a velvet collar, black knee breeches, silk stockings, and buckled shoes, sat in a high-backed Chinese Chippendale chair to one side of the fireplace. Granville, feeling uncomfortably out of place in his riding attire, stood stiffly before his father, his hands clasped behind his back, a level gaze focused just above his father's eyes.

"Sit down, Granville." The Earl rubbed his temple briefly with the fingers of his right hand.

Granville would have preferred to stand, but he sat. "Have you a headache, Sir?"

"It's nothing." The Earl hastily removed his hand from his brow and cleared his throat. "Well, Sir. You are no longer in His Majesty's Navy. What do you propose to do now?" The fire chased any hint of chill from the room, but not the chill Granville felt in his father's voice.

"I don't know, Father," he answered levelly.

The Earl drummed his fingers on the arm of the chair. "You *don't know* what you want to do?" The tone was tart. Never a lenient parent, the Earl was obviously provoked at his son's indecisiveness. "You were, Sir, in a position where you could be sure of employment when you wanted it, and you could be sure of rising high. I do not understand how you could turn your back on this. It is as incomprehensible as if Sandon had suddenly renounced his succession to the earldom and resigned his seat in Parliament.

"It is indeed heavy to me that my son should have failed to uphold the tradition of young men of his class who enter the Navy and show themselves to be of good stuff, who put their hands to the plow, never looking back, who bend to the task with a will, contrive to master the intricacies of their profession, and win credit both for themselves and for those humbler officers who taught them. You have failed to prove yourself worthy of your class and of your office."

"Perhaps, Sir, the problem lies in striving to prove something that doesn't exist."

"Nonsense. You are a Ryder. Now, what do you intend to do about it?"

"I had thought of taking on some of the estate duties, Sir, with Sandon in London now." The mention of his brilliant older brother, now filling the seat for the family borough of Tiverton in the House of Commons, was indeed a misstep, serving further to raise his father's intolerance at Granville's lack of focus.

"And do you intend to take your proper place as a member of the family in compassionate work?"

"Sir?" The Earl had lowered his voice, causing Granville to lean forward and request repetition of the question.

Replying in considerably greater volume than necessary, Lord

39

Harrowby thundered, "Compassionate work. What do you intend to do about your responsibility there?"

Granville paused so long the Earl started to repeat the question again, but Granville held up his hand. "I heard you, Father. I have given the subject considerable thought—perhaps the Duke of Gloucester's Marine Society. I understand there is interest in founding a Royal Lifeboat Institution to improve safety at sea. But . . ."

"But?" Lord Harrowby cut impatiently into the pause.

"But I should like first to feel that I am, as you say, worthy of doing religious and compassionate work, Sir."

The conversation at an end, the Earl rose, bowed briefly to his son, and strode from the room. Granville sank into an armchair near a window. It was not the curt tone of his father's words that stung him to the quick, but their truth.

By choosing to leave the Navy, he had admitted to yet another failure. Since his earliest days, he had been surrounded by people who shone like stars in the firmament. His father, as President of the Council, was one of the most influential men in England; his Uncle Henry, the first Evangelical clergyman to be appointed to the bishopric, was now stirring the nation in controversy over further elevation; his elder brother, Dudley, Viscount Sandon, who had always been able to outrun, outride, and outfight him, was making such a success of his career in Parliament that he was being talked of as the next Lord of the Admiralty; his cousin, Henry, the Marquess of Worcester, had earned a special place in Wellington's affection as Aide-de-camp and was now serving in Parliament.

And this list didn't begin to touch on the renowned charitable work of all the members of both families. But all *that* he could cope with; he had little doubt of his ability to carve a niche for himself in the world. The thing he found overwhelmingly deflating was the spiritual confidence of those around him. How could they be so sure they were right with God—sure of their acceptability to Him?

From earliest days he had striven to be a good, obedient son, to do all that man and God required of him. But how could he ever know when he had done enough, when he was good enough for acceptance by God? When could he know if he merited salvation?

He had found no answers in the Navy. Where would he seek them next? *God, if Thou art here, show me how to find Thee. I'm groping in the dark; give me the light of Thine assurance.*

He sat long, gazing across the lawn toward the park until the sound of carriage wheels on gravel stirred his reverie. He stepped to the window, admiring the fine pair of match greys pulling the phaeton in the drive; but when he saw the elegant young man Georgiana had danced with the night before escort her from the carriage with an air of solicitude, a frown creased his forehead.

As Georgiana glimpsed her cousin in the library window and saw his troubled look, all pleasure she had felt in the ride with George vanished. She took hurried leave of him and went in search of her mother whom she found just entering the yellow drawing room which the Duchess used as her private parlor.

"Are you occupied, Mama?"

"Never too busy for you, my Dear. Come in." The Duchess and her daughter sat in a pair of yellow upholstered chairs before a carved mahogany cabinet made by Thomas Chippendale. "My sister has gone for a short lie-down and I thought I might attempt a bit of correspondence—I'm always so behindhand with it. But I had much rather talk with you. You look uneasy, Dear. What is it?"

"It's Gran. We were such close companions as children, and now, I find I hardly know him. And he seems much troubled too. This morning we rode in the park and he said all manner of nonsensical things to me about his inability to please his father. But the worst was last night when he hinted at feeling spiritually inadequate. How can that be? He is everything that is most amiable—can't he see that he has no need of improvement to be acceptable to God or to his father—or to anyone else?"

"My Dear, even the vilest sinner has no need of improvement to be acceptable to God."

Her mother's theological answer irritated Georgiana. "Yes, yes. I know! But why can't Gran understand that? Oh, I most desperately want him to be happy. He was such a lighthearted boy—why can't life remain so? Why must everything get so complicated?"

"One cannot forever remain childhood friends—no matter how dear. And irritations that seem small at the time, when often repeated, can add up to a powerful influence—a harsh, demanding father, a brilliant, overshadowing older brother, a difficulty in hearing that puts one at a slight social disadvantage . . . as I so well know," and the Duchess opened the hand she held to her ear to exhibit the small, shell-like hearing device that had been invented for her by her friend Charles Simeon—a great convenience because

41

it could be held in her palm.

But Georgiana wasn't interested in Mr. Simeon's inventiveness. "Oh, I'd never thought of all that—it must be awful—never feeling you're quite—well, quite up to snuff." She rose and began walking around the room with small, jerky steps. "But that's ridiculous! Can't he *see* what an absolutely superb person he is?"

"No, my Dear. None of us can truly see ourselves. Your cousin sees himself in the mirror his father has always held up to him and measures himself by his brother's achievements. Even before you were born, I recall seeing Granville toddle along after Sandon, absolutely adoring him. But Sandon had no time for him, found him irritating—especially since Gran's slight deafness obliged him to repeat things."

"But Gran is worth a dozen of Sandon in so many ways!" In her agitation Georgiana's voice rose to a high pitch.

"Yes, Georgiana, you and I know that, but Granville doesn't. Of course, the fact that he's so oblivious to his charms is one of the most winning things about him; but it leaves him even more vulnerable."

"I still don't understand why this should cause a spiritual problem. Gran has been raised in the way of true Christianity as carefully as I. . . . " She choked and turned her back to her mother. "I couldn't bear to see Gran . . . " She was unable to finish.

"It must be very difficult to feel accepted by one's Heavenly Father if one doesn't feel satisfactory to an earthly father. . . . But, Georgiana, you need to realize that spirituality isn't as easy for everyone as it is for you. I thank God that from your youngest days faith has been your gift—for yourself and to help others. But many people, like Granville, have to struggle to find their own place. If you would help your cousin, you must have two things—"

"Yes, Mother?"

"Faith and patience."

Georgiana grimaced. "Patience?"

The countess smiled. "Not easy, especially in youth. But I have never forgotten the lesson I learned from Mr. Simeon when I was tempted to impatience with the behavior of others: 'Let us sit upon the seat of love instead of judgment,' he said. Can you find it in your heart to do that, Daughter?"

"Oh, yes!" Georgiana gave her mother a brilliant smile. "Things are always so much clearer after I talk to you—it's no wonder life has been uncomplicated for me, with a mother like you."

The Duchess returned her daughter's kiss. "Now, run along and dress for dinner, Dear."

While at Badminton House, the Beauforts compromised between country and city hours and dined at six o'clock in the evening. Georgiana dressed for dinner in a pale green percale dress with bouilloned sleeves which were puffed to resemble the surface of a simmering pot. "Aggie, you may do my hair with the green grosgrain ribbon and yellow crepe flowers." Georgiana sat on the small bench before her dressing table and sprayed a breath of Hungary water over her white shoulders.

Agatha hurried to do her mistress' bidding. A few minutes later, after turning this way and that before a tall pier glass, to observe the effect of the scallops of Mechlin lace adorning her gored skirt, Georgiana left her room with a smile on her lips, her mind focused on all the good she should do for her cousin.

Her campaign was hampered, however, by the seating protocol that placed the eldest Ryder son present, Granville, next to the eldest Somerset daughter, Charlotte. So throughout the first course, Georgiana attended to her brother whom she was partnering. But her mind was fixed on the couple across the table. And the more Granville and Charlotte laughed and chatted, the more Georgiana's irritation rose. If her cousin preferred Charlotte's light banter, then perhaps she wouldn't tell him what was on her heart.

Since they were dining *en familie*, there were to be only three courses. The first course of soups at the end and foot of the table were being replaced by fish and saddle of mutton when Granville turned from his conversation with Charlotte to address Georgiana. "And did you have an agreeable afternoon, Georgie?"

Her irritation at him showing only by the tilt of her chin, Georgiana forced her brightest smile. "Quite delightful, thank you, Sir. Mr. Agar-Ellis' new greys are high-steppers, indeed, and he is a whip of the first rank. And our Gloucestershire countryside—quite incomparable." If he was to find solace in Charlotte, she should do the same in George.

Charlotte then required her partner's attention and Georgiana forced herself to attend fully to her brother, Henry, who was saying to Lord Harrowby, "It is Wellington's judgment that the fact that the people of England are very quiet may explain the character of

43

English religion."

"Do you take that to mean that the Duke believes the English are religious because they are quiet, and not quiet because they are religious?" The Earl's perpetual frown accompanied his words and no one ventured an answer.

From the head of the table the Duke replied, "I could wish some of the dissenters a little quieter in their religious enthusiasm. But it does seem that the democratic character of the nonconformists trains their members in administration and public speaking."

"Indeed, I have observed that also," the Earl agreed. "But most fortunately, it is not necessary to go to the extreme of dissension for these happy effects. I find those of our Evangelical Anglican beliefs maintain a serious and unselfish attitude toward public affairs which makes them the most valued of public leaders. They use their wealth conscientiously to good and noble purposes; and they care nothing for popularity but strive to do what is right. . . . "

The Duke motioned for the footmen to clear away the first course before continuing. "Quite right. Our friend William Wilberforce is a case in point. I suppose it wouldn't be an overstatement to say that no Englishman has ever done more to evoke the conscience of the British people and to elevate and ennoble our public life."

"You are quite right, my Dear," and the Duchess smiled at her husband. "I certainly feel for Mr. Wilberforce an affection that surprises even me, and which always mixes itself with my anticipations for the happiness of a future world."

The Earl accepted a slice of gabena fowl from the footman; then, with one bite held on his fork midway between plate and mouth, he turned all his attentions to discussing the work of his colleague. "I have just last night concluded my reading of Wilberforce's *Appeal to the Religion, Justice, and Humanity of the Inhabitants of the British Empire in Behalf of the Negro Slaves in the West Indies.* If it can receive a wide readership, there can be no doubt of the outcome of his efforts to achieve freedom for these downtrodden peoples."

He paused for a sip of wine, but no one ventured to interrupt his discourse, so he continued, "Of course, the most important fact of his work is that he builds it solidly upon the firm foundation of Scripture: 'Woe unto him that buildeth his house by unrighteousness, and his chambers by wrong; that useth his neighbor's service without wages, and giveth him not for his work,' from the Prophet Jeremiah, and 'Do justice and love mercy,' from Micah. But you must read it for yourselves to savor its power and righteousness."

Worcester turned from attending to a comment by his sister and said, "Yes, but Wilberforce is getting much opposition from his old friend Canning who repeatedly warns him to stay silent for fear of rocking the delicate balance in the West Indies. Wilberforce, of course, refuses to be warned."

"Yes, I'm sure opposition only makes him speak more forcibly."

Worcester continued, "But Wilberforce needs a clearer strategy. Canning is sure to outgeneral him in Parliament."

Harrowby cleared his throat, "Indeed, I hope not. Quite apart from the right of the matter, Wilberforce takes everything too much to heart. He once told me he believed that but for the all-atoning blood of Jesus Christ, he would be condemned everlastingly for his failure to rescue the slaves from bondage."

"Nonsense!" Worcester said. "He hasn't failed. The fight continues."

"Yes," the Earl agreed. "But when poor health strikes his feeble constitution, he is wont to be a victim of depression." The footman offered mashed potatoes trimmed with small slices of bacon, broccoli, and Jerusalem artichokes, and the Earl turned to his food.

While the conversation continued at the other end of the table, Georgiana took a serving of carrots and turnips and of light suet dumplings; and then, because she was feeling a twinge of remorse for the abruptness of her earlier reply to Granville, she turned to speak to him. But her softened feelings were short-lived when she found the intended recipient of her graciousness absorbed in a tale Charlotte was recounting about Fred Calthorpe's new hunter.

So she turned instead to Lord Harrowby and asked him about the achievements of The British and Foreign Bible Society of which he was president. "The work progresses, my Dear, but it is hindered by rigid churchmen who fear that the circulation of the Bible without the prayer book will encourage the growth of dissent."

"What we need are more Evangelicals like Bishop Ryder in high church office," Worcester said, returning to a favored family topic.

"I believe it will happen soon," Harrowby replied. "With men like Wilberforce and Simeon urging the appointment."

"If Simeon is supporting him, surely the Duke of Gloucester is too?" asked the Duchess, who had been following the conversation.

"Indeed, the entire Cambridge group is most active in its support," the Earl agreed. "But many high churchmen are skeptical of giving him this greater scope for his energies."

"The Bishop's best recommendation is his own attractive personality," Lady Harrowby said of her brother-in-law. "As well as his keen mind. I'm assured the clergy of his present diocese were not disposed to welcome him warmly at first; but many of the prejudices against him vanished when they discovered he was a better scholar and divine than they themselves."

"Excellent fellow," agreed the Duke, "and thoroughly loyal to the church, even if he is a low churchman."

Several footmen entered the room bearing silver salvers displaying a variety of ices to present to the company.

"I suspect his vigor may put the fear into some of his peers, that similar dedication might be expected of them." Lord Harrowby selected a raspberry ice. "He rarely preaches less than twice, often three times on a Sunday, besides weekly church lectures. . . . "

"True," said Lady Harrowby with enthusiasm. "Oh, sorry, my Dear, did I interrupt you?" Then before the Earl could reply, she continued, "As well as spending his Sunday afternoons instructing the children in the Gloucester National School."

"Well," the Duke said, "coming from one of the first families in the nation don't do him any harm neither."

The Earl of Harrowby raised his wine glass in acceptance of this tribute to his family, then added, "But I suspect his support from Cambridge will be decisive."

"When I was a young man at Oxford, that was the center of Evangelical activity; but due largely to Simeon's work, the focus seems to have moved to Cambridge," the Duke observed.

"If I were a young man today, Cambridge is where I should wish to be," the Duchess said, her warm brown eyes shining in the candlelight as brightly as the stones that adorned her amaranth pink turban. "Think of coming under the tutelage of Charles Simeon. What splendid young men he is instructing! I almost believe I am sorry you didn't go there, Henry," she said to her eldest son. Then turning to Granville, she inquired, "Have you thought of taking residence at Cambridge?"

Before Granville could reply, his father spoke, "I shall secure a position for Granville in the Home Office."

Granville slowly raised his white linen napkin to his mouth and regarded his father for several moments. No one spoke. Then Granville lowered his napkin and said, "I shall go to Cambridge."

· 5 ·

IN SPITE OF the skiff of late January snow covering the college courts and clogging the traffic in the narrow Cambridge streets, Granville was settled in time to matriculate for Hilary term. His second floor rooms in G staircase were just to the right of the gate of Trinity College inside the Great Court. A visit to the establishment of Elliott Smith, the furniture man close by Trinity Gate, had served in a few hours' time to provide the bed, sofa, chairs, tables, and carpets requisite for furnishing a gentleman's rooms. The furniture, sturdy if well-used, had provided comfort for many a gownsman before Granville, as it would for many after him, with each turnaround securing a tidy profit for Mr. Smith.

Granville crossed the larger of his two rooms, furnished as a parlor, and pulled the deep red moreen curtains across the window looking out on Trinity Street. The curtains' color told their age since, as all college curtains, they had begun life a soft gray. When that shade was faded beyond recognition, they were dyed scarlet-red, and as age advanced, the shade of red deepened and darkened. The price of the draperies was thirded down from tenant to tenant at two-thirds cost, until in due time they reached zero. Where, by rights, Granville had argued unsuccessfully, the price should have remained. But by no means, they then took an upward course and the process began all over again at the seller's valuation.

Granville shook his head at the dilapidated condition of his window hangings and turned toward the dressing room where his gyp, the college-provided servant, had laid out the black satin knee breeches and white silk stockings that were *de rigeur* for dining in Hall. But his progress was interrupted by a knock at his door.

47

"Hullo, Andy," he greeted the gownsman who occupied the rooms just above his. Andrew Anderson was a Sizar, an impecunious scholar working his way through Trinity. Although Granville found his stairmate abnormally studious, his company was not unpleasant. "Come in, I'm just getting ready for Hall, although I must say, eating dinner in midafternoon is something my stomach is not yet accustomed to."

Andrew, who was in his third year at Trinity, agreed that he had found it so at first. As he also had to change before dining, he wouldn't come in. . . . "Just stopped by to ask if you'd care to attend Simeon's conversation party tonight. Now that everyone's getting settled into term, there should be a good group of Sims on hand," he said, referring to the followers of Charles Simeon's counseling.

"Very thoughtful of you, Andy. I might just do that. Been intending to drop in one night anyway. Perhaps I'll see you after Combi." That would give him more time to make a final decision about the Simeon matter. But Combi must come first, as the consumption of port in the combination room, with its double flow of wit and wine, was a necessary conclusion to Hall.

Granville had gone to Cambridge with high hopes of quickly solving his spiritual dilemma. But the time slid by pleasantly, each day bringing a new amusement with lighthearted friends. When he thought about his problem in moments of introspection, he tended to put it aside, as something he would consider later.

But there was no time for self-examination now. Granville made progress on his toilette so far as to have removed his jacket and boots before the next knock came at his door.

His gyp answered the knock and ushered Freddie Perkins into the room. Frederick Oswald Perkins sat next to Granville at the high table in Hall and they had become good friends through sharing the long hours of boredom produced by the formal service.

"Somerville's turn to host Club tonight. Should be good sport." Freddie threw himself into a soft chair, doing violence to his formal attire and knocking his stiff, flat hat askew. "Just laid in two dozen more port. Told me so!"

"I'm thinking of giving it a miss tonight, Freddie. I've been invited to attend Charles Simeon's conversation party."

Freddie sat bolt upright, his face looking as thunderstruck as if lightning had passed through the room. "Shouldn't do that, Gran.

Not the thing at all. You'll find it devilish boring. Bad *ton*."

"I hadn't thought of going for purposes of raising my estimation in society," Granville replied, achieving a perfect crease in the waterfall he was tying with his stiffly starched cravat.

"You can't be thinking of doing it for *amusement!* " Mr. Perkins looked even more shocked than before. "It really won't do. They drink tea. And talk—" he stole a quick glance upward as if to see if he were being overheard—"about God. Oh," his face broke into a wide grin, "bamming me, ain't you?"

"Not at all, Freddie. I had thought of attending for purposes of enlightenment." Mr. Ryder slipped a black academic gown trimmed with gold lace over his other garments and donned the soft cap that proclaimed him to be a nobleman before moving to the door.

"Sounds cork-brained to me." Freddie shook his head as he followed his friend out the door. "You'd best come to Merry's with me—he serves the best claret at Trin."

Granville laughed off his friend's protestations and strode across the green grass of Great Court, past the renaissance fountain and into Hall where he paused to inscribe the buttery book, "The Hon. G. Ryder," and toss his gown and cap on a table provided for that purpose. Then he took his seat at the far end of the long room with Freddie and other friends.

At the table William Meredyth Somerville was telling the Hon. Francis George Molyneaux and Lord William Hervey of his plans for the evening. "The usual schedule, I daresay, whist to ten, a moderate supper, then we'll declare Club officially closed and allow deeper gaming—more to the sporting taste."

As he tried to determine his course for the evening ahead, Granville surveyed his surroundings. The Hall of Trinity could easily have modeled for an ornate version of Hrothgar's mead hall, or so it seemed to Granville, with its high, dark, beam-vaulted ceiling and long rows of benched tables. But no ancient Danish king could ever have dreamed of such intricately ornate carving, enriched with deep red, blue, and gold paint as decorated both ends of the long narrow room. Nor could Hrothgar's Heorot Hall have boasted the glories of stained glass that filled every window.

From the top of his long table, beneath the blazoned arms of Trinity supported by rampant gold lion and silver unicorn, Granville looked out across the warm glow of candles lining the tables.

As his eye followed around the shape of the room, he saw that the bay alcoves to either side of the Fellows' dias gave the room the proportions of a cathedral—or more precisely, the shape of a cross. And the image brought forcefully to his mind the spiritual turmoil he had attempted to discuss with his cousin last fall, but had kept so firmly submerged since coming to Cambridge. The introspection he had avoided by concentrating on new friends and new experiences suddenly pushed its way to the forefront and he knew he would have to deal with it soon. . . . Why did even the shape of the room have to mock his spiritual dilemma? Couldn't he at least eat his dinner in peace? Surely Hrothgar had the better part—to be haunted by Grendel, a monster of form and substance, rather than by the shades that followed him.

In the interval between terms, a pair of blackbirds had made their nest atop the ornamental carved screen at the far end of the room. Attracted now by the crumbs dropped by the dining gownsmen, the small dark birds fluttered about in the alcove windows, flew to the top of the wainscoting behind the Fellows' table, and then the braver of the two hopped onto the table right in front of Granville. But in his present mood, the sight failed to elicit the amused smile usually brought forth by the college pets. In the stained-glass window to his left, a white dove descended to announce Christ's acceptance by His Heavenly Father. The common English blackbird approaching Granville could only signal rejection for him.

All right. He would go to Simeon's party. It seemed unlikely that any counseling could help him find rest of soul, but he would hear what the venerable man had to say. After all, he was a particular friend of Granville's aunt, the Duchess, so it would be churlish of him not to pay a call.

At the end of Hall, gownsmen strolled back across the court to the social room they called Combi. "Draw the curtains," Lord Hervey called out to the porter on duty in the room. "We don't want to attract the attention of the townies on the street."

"Those stones they threw last time came devilishly close to shattering the windows." Frank Molyneaux tossed his cap and gown on the table near the door.

"Hope they try it . . . maggoty lot. Like to draw their corks!" Freddie flung himself into a chair with a force that moved it at least two inches closer to the wall and took a glass of the heady port wine that was being passed around. "Hear, hear," he raised his glass,

50

"drink to gown." He put his glass to his lips, then stopped, "I say, Gran, you ain't got a glass."

Granville shrugged, picked up a glass of the fiery Black Strap port, and joined in the toast to the superiority of gown over town.

The bumpers were refilled and toasts went around again, this time drinking the health of everyone present—some twice. A large bowl of creamy milk punch had just been presented to the company when Granville's stairmate appeared at the door.

Granville groaned and shook his already light head. He couldn't meet Charles Simeon reeking of port. Besides, it would be much too bad to break up Somerville's party now. "Thank you for coming by, Andy, but I'm sure you shall get on very well without me."

"Well done, Gran," Freddie said when Andrew Anderson's back disappeared down the hall. "Rackety notion, that. Knew you didn't mean it. Couldn't have!"

The party moved on to Merry Somerville's rooms where they were joined by a number of other guests. For a couple of hours, the playing of whist sedately occupied the gownsmen, interrupted only occasionally by the call for breaking out one more cool bottle of port from the sawdust-packed locker under the window.

"Ah, now *that's* port, alcoholed and talkative," William Hervey said, as he laid his cards on the table to savor his drink more fully.

From an adjoining table Frank raised his glass. "Port is the Englishman's wine. If not, how could we have beat the French?"

"A law of life—for health and constitution," Somerville agreed.

Granville sipped his wine. No one commented on his silence. Even in his short time at Cambridge, his reputation was established—older, quieter, more contemplative, one inclined to take life seriously. Although not popular qualities, they were accepted in a nobleman's son returned from service in the Royal Navy.

Somerville's gyp announced that supper was laid out in the next room. Their host, who made no secret of the fact that his kitchen bills were frightful, had provided roast lamb and salad as the centerpiece, and down the table as many dishes as Lawrence, their cook, could crowd in from the college kitchen, crowned by a fine Stilton cheese.

At ten o'clock, Club officially ended and, as their host had promised earlier, they could get on to more serious gaming. Two faro banks were set up and six or seven gownsmen at each table began placing their bets, some with carefree insouciance and others

51

with earnest solemnity. Granville took a place at the nearest table. "Stakes, Gentlemen," directed Somerville, who was presiding as banker at this table, since he had put up the largest stake.

The players signaled their bets by placing chips on the layout of the spade suit across the table. For a moment Granville sat abstractedly as the question flitted through his mind, *What am I doing here?*

"Come on, Granny, are you playing or not?"

Hastily, Granville placed his chips on the six and waited for the dealer to turn up his cards.

"Two of hearts," Somerville announced. This card was *soda* and had no bearing on the bets.

Somerville turned up another card and placed it face up on his right. "Jack of spades. Jacks lose." He triumphantly scooped Lord Hervey's chips into the bank.

The next card would win the turn. Granville glanced carelessly at the table; not a gamester at heart, he found the whole thing a bit of a bore. "Ten wins," the banker called, and handed a stack of chips to the grinning Frank Molyneaux. Since neither card turned up had been a six, Granville's bet stood. He could let it ride or cancel it by placing a copper on top of his chips.

The deal continued, and Granville, who had not coppered his bet, lost on the turn of the second card. The gyp was handing around drinks again, somewhat unsteadily, Granville noticed, as if he had already handed rather too many to himself. His bald head, shining with perspiration, seemed to wobble precariously on the thin neck sticking out of his high, stiff collar.

With studied casualness, Frank staked two rouleaux of guineas on the turn of the next card. Granville would have liked to decline hazarding anything. He was not a lucky punter and was already feeling a bit dipped. Although a noted leader, the Earl of Harrowby was not a wealthy man and the large sums he donated to worthy causes diminished his own bank account. His son's allowance was not large.

"Dash it all, I'm no gamester," Granville muttered and wondered briefly what was taking place now in Mr. Simeon's rooms in the Gibbs Building. Yet, in response to a sharp nudge from William seated next to him, Granville placed his bet.

He continued to play cautiously for a while, then grew bolder presently as the atmosphere captivated him and he began to relax. He won a little, lost a large bet, refilled his glass. As the fumes of cheroots mingled with the claret, his absorption increased, and so did the size of his wagers. "Ten chips on the Queen."

Money and chips clinked metallically, and occasionally a player's dog, lying obediently at its master's feet, would rumble a low growl as his sleep was disturbed by a scraping chair, a sharp cry of "Split," as a dealer took all the bets on a rank, or a moan of "Dipped again. Gyp, refill," as an unlucky player drowned his losses.

Dawn was rimming the sky with gold when Granville and Freddie made their way to their rooms. "Pockets to let and the quarter ain't half over!" Freddie laughed loudly in the still morning air.

"Freddie, you're foxed," Granville attempted to quiet his companion.

"No, I ain't. Trifle bosky, maybe. That don't signify. Thing is how I'm to get more of the ready from my trustees."

They parted company at Freddie's staircase and Granville went on, concentrating on being quiet so as not to disturb the elderly John Henry Rennard, the bachelor clergyman, Trinity fellow and vice-master, who occupied the rooms below Granville; nor to let the devout Andrew Anderson upstairs know the outcome of his misspent evening.

Too far gone to engage in conscience-searching, Granville pulled off his boots and rolled into bed without a thought to the harsh looks such behavior would draw from his gyp on the morrow. Or, far more serious, the harsh scolding he would give himself.

· 6 ·

THE SUN WAS at its apex when Granville awoke to the certainty that he had never before known what a headache was. At his rather unsteady ring, Creighton appeared with what should have been his master's *morning* coffee and, as silent witness to the lateness of the hour, the post.

Granville picked up the letter and blinked to clear his vision. A London postmark. Ah, yes, his aunt had promised to send him an account of their proceedings when they removed to Town. But the handwriting was not the Duchess'.

January

Dear Coz,

I think it is not very civil in you not to write to me first, but, however, as you never do anything I like, I should not be surprised at your not beginning our correspondence.

I am depriving myself of a walk to write to you, but you must not become puffed up taking the credit to yourself. As my mama is engaged in making calls, I sat down to fulfill her promise of writing to you, though I fear I shall not entertain you as well as she. I will only say that I have grown quite a fine lady, for I have been out almost every evening lately; have seen the *School for Scandal* and *Robinson Crusoe;* and to complete all, I believe that soon I shall have the honor of admiring the much celebrated dancing of La Trainon at the opera.

But, alas, I have no ball to give you an account of. Monday

54

evening, when I thought myself secure, I received a note from Lady York to say that Lord York was taken so ill of a fever that she was obliged to put off the dance till the twenty-second, when most probably Papa and Mama will be out of Town, so my expectations on that side are disappointed.

But you mustn't think me all frivolity. I am reading a most excellent volume published by J. Downing in Bartholomew Close entitled *Acquaintance with God*. I should be happy to send it on to you, but as you are in the saintly company of such men as Charles Simeon, I refrain from sending coals to Newcastle.

Papa & Mama desire their love to you.

My pen is so bad that I absolutely cannot write any more, and if you are not satisfied with this, you are an ungrateful and perverse boy; however, at all events I am

Yr. affect. cousin,
G. Somerset

P.S. I with you would send me word soon how you are.

Granville sipped his cooling coffee as charming images of his cousin flitted before his vision and he examined his unaccountable pleasure in calling forth her voice. And also, his unaccountable, if churlish, pleasure in hearing that she had attended no London balls. The idea of Georgiana passing her time dancing in the arms of London's society bucks, and various pinks of the ton, was not a pleasing thought to him.

But what would she think if she knew how he was spending his time? *"Send me word soon how you are,"* she had said. And the knowledge that she expected to hear of his time spent in academic pursuits and company with godly men was bitter to him. How was he? What could he possibly reply to her?

He stared long at the letter, his mouth tightening a little like a man in pain. Even if he had abandoned his halfhearted attempts at gaining merit in God's eyes, perhaps he could at least gain estimation in his cousin's.

On the following Friday, with the vision of Georgiana fixed firmly in his mind, Granville held fast to his determination to attend Mr. Simeon's party, in spite of the strongest protestations Freddie Perkins could put forth:

"But Gran! Can't have considered. Never know what you may

come to. Look at me! Always swore I'd join a regiment rather than go to Cambridge, but I passed those cursed smalls—can't think how I did it. Careless of me. So here I am, with a deuced crammie on my back hounding me to study all the time. Now what if it'd been religion? It really won't do."

But when resolved on a course, Granville was quite unshakable. He had been told that all who accepted Mr. Simeon's invitation were accustomed to arrive punctually, directly after dinner, so as to avoid commotion in the room after Simeon had taken his seat. Indeed, when Granville arrived at ten minutes of the hour, sixty-nine gownsmen were already seated on chairs and benches arranged for the occasion around the parlor and some were occupying even the recesses of the windows.

Upon being introduced to the venerable minister who had been guiding students for almost forty years, Granville was immediately aware of his cordiality, suavity, and courtly polish. Mr. Simeon bowed to his guest and had just concluded noting down, "The Honorable Granville Ryder, Trinity" in his memorandum book in which he recorded the introduction of any stranger, when they both became aware that Granville had stamped his bootprints in yellow gravel upon Mr. Simeon's dark carpet.

The offender was led back into the passage and asked, half playfully, "Mr. Ryder, what more could I do than put down such an array of mats as you here see, in order to give a hint or to afford the means of preserving my carpet from the yellow gravel which my visitors' shoes catch up?"

Granville smiled and returned Simeon's slight bow. "Sir, I do apologize for my unthinking slovenliness."

Simeon's famous affectionate smile, which appeared more in his eyes than on his mouth, and seemed to soften even his pointed nose and chin, accompanied the offer of his hand. "My Brother, I do love to see a clean carpet."

When Granville had cleaned the bright buff gravel from his shoes, he took his place on a bench near the door, which was cleared for him when Andrew motioned for several gownsmen to move closer together.

Mr. Simeon took his usual place on a stool by the right side of the fireplace, in full view of the young men around him. He rubbed his hands together, seeming to indicate an overflowing of placid gladness, just like a child clapping its hands as a mark of glee. Two servants began to hand tea around, and the conversation party was officially opened. The students on their crowded benches quietly sipped their tea as every eye was turned to Mr. Simeon and every ear tuned with expectancy to the wisdom he would impart.

It soon became apparent to Granville that the questioning function was largely in the hands of a few. By a kind of tacit understanding, it seemed that the conversation was to be as much as possible left to Simeon himself. Also, one or two members served as spokesmen for their more nervous friends.

Granville noticed a thin-faced young man tug at the sleeve of a questioner, and whisper in his ear a question that the latter presented, dealing with the propriety of the serious student spending time in exercise and recreation.

"I always say to my young friends that your success in the Senate House exams depends much on the care you take of the three-mile stone out of Cambridge. If you go every day and see that nobody has taken it away, and go quite round it to watch lest anyone has damaged its farthest side, you will be best able to read steadily all the time you are at Cambridge. If you neglect it, woe betide your degree. Yes—exercise, constant, and regular and ample, is absolutely essential to a reading man's success."

Mr. Simeon's guests laughed appreciatively at their host's drollery; and many, who had experienced the truth of his advice, nodded in agreement. Indeed, a brisk walk to the three-mile stone was just the tonic to clear a brain befuddled by too much concentration on a Latin epic.

The gownsmen who filled the room were largely candidates for Holy Orders—younger sons like Granville whose older brothers would be inheriting the family estates. For them the church would provide a living. They were sent up to Cambridge to prepare for the ministry with classical studies and mathematics. From a fellow-feeling for these young men who, like himself in 1782, were put into the pulpit without the remotest idea how to set about preaching, Simeon had conceived the singular notion that spiritual grounding was needed by men who would be ministers of the Word of God. Simeon took it upon himself, at first much to the consternation of the Fellows of the University, to provide this instruction.

The questions turned to the theological and Granville, listening earnestly, found much to think upon. "How long and uphill and often very bewildering is the road to God in most men's experience," Simeon said. Just then, the sound of carriage wheels on the cobblestone street beyond the screen of King's courtyard reminded Granville of his friends, tonight gathered in Frank Molyneaux's rooms for what was sure to be a repeat of last week's revels. Granville wondered if assuredly, his struggle was not up a far steeper hill than most, due to his desire but inability to make himself eligible for salvation.

He looked at the others in the room, contrasting them mentally with his livelier friends. Which did he want to be like? Which *could* he be like? It seemed he didn't truly fit in either group, just as he hadn't truly fit in the Navy, in spite of his outward success there, nor did he fit in his family circle of political and compassionate achievement. Simeon's gentle voice penetrated Granville's reverie:

"We may as well try to examine microscopic insects with the naked eye, as try to see divine truth without faith. Men see themselves too near; they see divine truth too far."

True, thought Granville, *far too far for me to reach*.

"Our best works afford cause for humiliation; all our actions afford this. But our worst deeds afford no ground for discouragement in seeking mercy. No, not our mightiest sins."

No discouragement? Easy for him to say. He doesn't know how many times I've failed.

"But he who believes in Jesus Christ shall be saved by grace." Mr. Simeon accompanied his statement with an animated gesture which, even though somewhat exaggerated, compelled attention and respect.

There was present a clever young clergyman who talked dogmatically, in an attitude of setting everybody to rights. He asked many flippant questions of the respected preacher. "Mr. Simeon, Christ told the rich young ruler to sell all he had and give to the poor. Do you teach this?" His gaze was directed at the delicate gold, marble-topped tables which were prize possessions of Simeon's, because they had been bequeathed to him by a deceased friend.

Mr. Simeon said quietly, "Young man, have you learned the difference yet between the spirit of wisdom and the spirit of knowledge?"

The challenger was silenced.

Granville allowed his mind to wander as the company explored a theological technicality, and then was brought sharply back when he heard the speaker say, "The truth is, we will be seeking for some goodness in ourselves, or for less sin in ourselves, as a ground of hope with which to come to Christ. We think we must *do* something for salvation. It is the spirit of pride. We *will not* allow ourselves to be saved by Christ alone.

"But remember, it is not what you do yourself. 'It is God who works in you, inspiring both the will and the deed, for His own chosen purposes.'

"And now, may the grace of God and of Jesus Christ our Lord go with you."

The hour was up. Granville would have liked to hear more, but Simeon was on his feet. "I love these little conversation meetings; they diffuse a spirit of love amongst us. I would I could have them oftener, but I must be glad to do just what I can. These meetings seem to me somewhat a foretaste of heaven," and he dismissed his flock.

It was said of Simeon that all Cambridge was filled with the belief and love of the truth which he preached. Although Granville knew many an exception to that rule among his friends, he examined its application to himself. After some moments of consideration while he walked slowly back to his rooms, he concluded that the closest he could come to that application would be to say that he would love to believe that what Simeon preached was the truth. But he knew such halfhearted acceptance wasn't enough.

Later, when he tried to pen an answer to Georgiana's letter, he knew that would not be enough for her either and he crumpled his blotted writing paper in disgust.

Why should it matter so much? None of his friends worried about such things. Freddie Perkins, Merry Somerville, Frank Molyneaux, William Hervey, none of them wasted time in despondent soul-searching, and they seemed to be better off for the lack thereof. What he needed was to relax, forget the standard set by his family, forget the expectations of his golden-haired cousin, forget the dejection in his own soul, and enjoy his university days as they were meant to be. After all, he didn't feel any better after the evening at Charles Simeon's; and if such a virtuous act as spending a whole evening talking about religion didn't help, what would? Why should he bother?

The relief of his thoughts flooded his tense body and a smile crossed his face. Relax, give up the struggle, accept things as they were. That was the ticket.

· 7 ·

GEORGIANA SAT AT the writing desk in the yellow parlor, the morning sunshine flooding through the long windows and filling the room with a cheer that she was far from feeling. Summer was now past and she had received no reply from the letter she sent Granville months ago. Through all that time she had suffered many emotional ups and downs, wavering between compassion for his struggles and pique at his ignoring her. And always, the slight fear that his silence meant he didn't care. At the times when that emotion controlled, she saw again his tanned darkness bending toward Charlotte's ivory paleness; and though she dearly loved her sister, she knew the bitter taste of jealousy.

But through all the ups and downs and fears, one thing remained. No matter what Granville might or might not feel for her, she cared deeply for him. And no matter what the future might hold, even if they were destined never to be more to each other than dear friends, she longed for his happiness and spiritual wholeness.

"Oh!" With a cry of frustration Georgiana looked at the blot of ink she had allowed to fall from her quill onto the piece of parchment stationery. Crumpling the crisp paper and determining to keep her mind on the task at hand, she bent over her letter-writing. Since she had no idea how Granville felt about her, it was imperative that her tone be light, that she make clear she was writing as her mother's emissary, and that she impart her information as briefly as possible.

It took two more sheets of the Duchess' costly paper before Georgiana was pleased with her efforts. She read it over once more, then sat long again, a frown creasing her forehead. She couldn't sign

60

a letter to her Granville with nothing more than her name. Memories of that evening almost a year ago brought back his troubled countenance and she longed to offer him solace. But at this distance in time and space, and with so many uncertainties. . . .

At last she penned a final line, dusted it with sand to dry the ink, folded the paper, sealed it with a wax wafer, and entrusted it to the Royal Mail.

Several days later Granville and Freddie were taking morning coffee in Granville's rooms when they were disturbed by a loud knocking on the outer oaken door. They gyp crossed the room quickly and opened the portal to admit Revesby, Freddie's tutor.

"Come along, time for chapel, Perkins." The intruder held out Freddie's academic gown.

"Dash it all!" Freddie ran his fingers through his tousled locks. "When's a fellow supposed to relax? Bad *ton*, getting out early. Deuced unfair—Ryder don't have to."

"As you well know, Sir, Mr. Ryder is the son of a nobleman, and therefore exempted from attending lectures, exercises, and examinations. None of which applies to you, Mr. Perkins, who are required to earn your degree."

"Afraid he's right, Freddie," Granville said.

"That's fine for you to say! Your crammie ain't encroaching," and Freddie shot Revesby a baleful look.

"I flatter myself that Mr. Peacock knows his place. Not that he wouldn't bearlead me if he could. Now be a good chap and go along, Freddie."

"Well, I don't like it above half." Freddie grumpily shrugged into his academic robe. "Tell Merry I'll work on the bonfire before Hall," and with that parting shot he was shepherded off to compulsory chapel and lectures. As the door closed behind them, Granville gave a silent cheer for the Elizabethan code which allowed the university to confer the MA degree upon the sons of peers with the only requirement being six terms of residence. In the Navy, he had rebelled at the process of automatic advancement for sons of noblemen; but now that he had decided to relax and abandon his efforts at earning his credit in the spiritual realm or the secular, he was willing to accept the privileges of his rank.

He had, however, put his name down for several lectures on philosophy, mathematics, and the classics, and with the beginning of Michaelmas term he resolved to attend them with sufficient regularity to enable him to follow their content, yet not with such slavishness as to cut up his peace.

And since his decision to give up his spiritual struggle last term, his days had been filled with a sort of peace—or at least enough activity to keep him from worrying about the condition of his soul.

Just as last spring, the days of the new term were filled with sporting events and the nights with card parties. Hervey accepted a challenge to race his tilbury pulled by a high-stepping bay against Somerville's blood grey, in a dash along the narrow roads crossing the fields outside Cambridge; another day everyone drove to Royston to view a mill between a prize student of Gentlemen Jackson and the Champion Molyneaux, an event which, as well as attracting gownsmen, drew all the Corinthians from as far away as London; and then, a cockfight in Wellingborough between a noted Wednesbury grey and a much-touted red pyle which Somerville declared to be, "Not nearly up to snuff," but was highly favored by Frank Molyneaux because of the similarity of its coloring to his own. That outing required an overnight stay and drove Freddie's conscientious crammie nearly to distraction. And, of course, at the end of each event, in the best tradition of sportsmanship, the defeated team stood drinks for everyone.

It all left very little time for serious endeavors at academia or for spiritual growth. And, except for an occasional strained look about the mouth or an unaccountable furrowing of the brows, there was nothing to show that Granville Ryder had a care in the world.

Only in times of quiet contemplation, when he returned tired and empty after an evening's revels, did Granville have times of continued spiritual struggle. At such times, he often found himself comparing his present state with the contentment and assurance he had known as a boy. Once he even looked in a book of religious poetry and came across lines by his mother's favorite poet, William Cowper, that sent him into long moments of soul-searching.

> Where is the blessedness I knew
> When I first saw the Lord?
> Where is the soul-refreshing view
> Of Jesus and His word?
> What peaceful hours I once enjoyed!
> How sweet their memory still!

But then a new amusement would require his attention and the spiral would begin again.

Today, the passion that gripped every loyal Trinitarian was the challenge issued by St. John's to see which college could build the biggest bonfire in the open fields beyond the Backs. The gregarious Merry Somerville had the lead in defending Trinity's honor, and for several days crews had been at work scouring the surrounding countryside for firewood. Since early morning, sentries had been set at the selected spot to guard the mountain of wood that now grew under the Trinitarian efforts.

By noon, Freddie's enthusiasm for the event reached such consuming proportions that Revesby threw up his hands in despair and joined in the scramble for firewood on the theory that the sooner the wretched pile was built the sooner he could get his charge back to his books.

Feeling uneasy about the wasted time, however, Granville attended his early afternoon lectures and then translated two poems of Hesiod, so that after Hall it was with the exuberance of a clear conscience that he joined in the bonfire festivities. The sun was setting, leaving only a thin ring of orange light at the edge of the darkening sky that covered the fens, when Granville drove out in his phaeton to join Freddie and their colleagues for the lighting of the fire.

Cries of, "Sear and scorch!" were raised around the pile as Merry approached with a blazing torch. He circled the huge conical pile of wood three times before he stopped, bowed low to the company, and with the ceremonies due to the occasion touched the torch to the base of the pile. A great cheer rose as the flames crackled, caught blaze, and soared upward through the wood.

Across the fields, dots of blazing light showed that Caius, John's, King's, Peterhouse, and the other colleges were similarly engaged. Sounds of clinking glass and boisterous laughter mingled with the snap and crackle of the flames, as flasks and bottles were produced from the gigs and carriages the gownsmen had driven out in. In several small groups ringed around the light of the fire, gamesters began rattling the ivories.

"A pair of sixes!" Merry called to those in his circle, their faces lighted by the wavering orange light of the flames. Bets were placed and the ivories rattled again. Granville's slow smile parted his lips. This was like many a night spent in his early days at sea, gathered around the light of lanterns on deck where the roll of dice provided one of the few entertainments available. He could almost feel the sea swell below the boards as he placed his bet.

The punters became more and more engrossed in the sport until the cry of, "Town!" brought them to attention. In the constant state of warfare that existed between town and gown, the bonfires provided a perfect occasion to test the relative strength of their forces.

"A mill!" shouted Freddie, who was no more than two sheets to the wind from the liquor he had consumed. Others joined the cry and set on the advancing townsmen. Granville had no desire to take part in a fracas he considered to be inelegant at best and childish at worst. But no such considerations held his friends back, as caps flew in the air and the sound of running feet signaled the arrival of gownsmen from other bonfires.

Granville stood aloof, surveying the affray much as he had surveyed the Duke's ballroom little less than a year ago. And now, as then, his appearance of austere hauteur was due not to any inherent snobbery, but to the intensity of the inward struggle from which he could never truly escape. The longing for spiritual tranquillity that he had for several months kept subdued beneath a superficial concealment of pleasure now surfaced with a raw ache, as the scene before him suggested an image of hellfire to his tender conscience. The flames leaped even higher, belching clouds of black smoke; and whenever the hungry tongues reached a branch filled with pitch, a small explosion would fill the night with a shower of sparks, causing Granville to flinch as if he had been burned.

As the mayhem increased, the brawling figures were silhouetted against the orange flames like grotesque demons in a ritualistic coven. . . . Like Granville's own demons which taunted him— *You'll never be worthy. Everytime you try to master virtue, you slip further into weakness and vice. You came to Cambridge hoping to gain merit, but you've lost self-respect in a constant round of gaming and brawls. Look at you!* Imaginary fiends leapt at him from the fire.

The blazing fury beckoned him to join in the revel, to abandon restraint, to embrace the freedom of the moment. He took a step toward the flames, then paused. The choice was clear: The frenzied figures writhed in gaiety—he could join them or retreat; the infernal flames leapt like hellfire—he could go forward or turn away. The satanic fervor reached out to snatch him—he could submit or escape.

The scene was no longer a simple college festival, but the embodiment of the struggle he had waged for years. How simple it would be to submit, what a relief to join his friends, how easy to give up the contest.

And then he thought of Georgiana—her caring, her faith in him. He turned his back on the flames and focused his thoughts on this cousin. All desire to join the carousing evaporated.

But no more was his struggle ended than a sharp cry made him turn again to the fire just in time to see a burly townsman break a heavy cudgel over Freddie's head and his friend sink bleeding to the ground. As the coarse assailant raised his weapon for another blow—which would likely be fatal, Granville rushed into the fray. Moving with the speed and grace gained from years of military training, he caught the man's raised forearm and brought it down hard across his own upraised knee. The cudgel dropped from the ruffian's hand and he set up a howl, "Broken me arm 'e 'as! What's a swell like you got with interferin' in a man's sport?" The man lunged at Granville who sidestepped neatly, tripping the attacker as he did.

Before the man could right himself, Granville grabbed Freddie by the scruff of his coat, pulled him from the mill, and shoved him into his phaeton. In the relative quiet of his carriage, Granville hastily staunched Freddie's bleeding wound by making a compress of a handkerchief, and drove back to the college, leaving the roaring fire and violent fisticuffs behind them.

Hauling the semiconscious Freddie up the dimly lit staircase, Granville was able to gain his room without attracting the attention of the vice-master living on the ground floor, or of the college porters who would no doubt be making their way out to the fields soon to break up the violence. By the time Freddie began coming around, Granville had him propped in a chair before the fire, had rung for Creighton with orders for hot water and bandages, and was removing Freddie's cravat.

Mistaking Granville for his assailant, the rummy Freddie surged unsteadily to his feet, flailing with his fists. "Come on, raise your maulies!"

"Freddie, please try not to make more of a cake of yourself than necessary." Granville pushed his friend back into his chair.

Freddie flopped heavily into the cushions. "I say, what happened?" He blinked to clear his view of the room.

"It seems that some people have decidedly strange notions of what constitutes an evening's pleasure." Granville dabbed at the cut on Freddie's head that was still oozing blood. Creighton, holding the basin of water, was beginning to take on a pronounced gray hue, as the water in the basin turned increasingly brighter red with repeated dippings of the cloth.

"Give me that before you fall into it," Granville ordered, taking the basin from the gyp who tried not to show his relief, "and see what you can do about repairing Mr. Perkins' coat. I hardly dare hope his neckcloth can be rescued. And then I think some strong tea would be in order."

The gyp gathered up the ravaged garments and bowed his way out of the room.

By the time Granville's ministrations were completed and Freddie's equilibrium was somewhat restored by the tea tray Creighton produced, the night was well spent. Rather than take Freddie across the court to his room, Granville tucked him in his own bed and stretched out on the sofa himself. It seemed little more than a matter of minutes until the bell of St. Mary's tolled six times, sounding surprisingly close in the heavy morning air.

"Can't they muffle that thing? Deuce of a headache," Freddie sat up and moaned, holding his head.

"Well, we aren't likely to get any more sleep now. Let's go for a walk to clear our heads," Granville proposed.

Freddie rose somewhat unsteadily to his feet. "Come on, Boy," he called to the drowsy spaniel who had stayed by his master's side throughout the fracas. Boy crawled out from under the bed in an attitude of sorely put-upon obedience.

Granville stared at the dog for a moment. "Why you don't keep that mongrel in the stables I don't understand."

"It won't do. Animal worships me. Sulks when I'm gone," Freddie protested, then brightened as Granville grinned at him and his dog. "Oh, you're roasting me, aren't you?"

The two early morning strollers were the only moving figures about, as they crossed Trinity bridge spanning the Cam. All of the previous night's revelers had gone to their beds to sleep off their overindulgence. Granville and Freddie paused to watch the slow, smooth waters flowing inkily beneath them in the predawn light. A lone duck glided past, in search of an early snail.

As they reached the footpath beneath King James' elms along the Backs, they quickened their pace but continued in silence, breathing deeply of the fresh, moist air that still retained a slight smokiness from last night's bonfires. The fallen leaves were moist from autumn rains and a thin mist clung to the ground. Tree branches over their heads took on a delicate beauty as the gray sky gave way to a spreading pink glow of dawn. It would be a fine day. Granville stopped and held up his hand to motion his companion's silence. Freddie put his hand on Boy to silence him likewise. For some moments they stood attending to the tiny rustles and scurries among the leaves and branches—small animals making hurried attempts to gather their autumn food stores before the arrival of winter.

If life could always be pure and clear and simple like this moment, Granville thought. He felt he could stand there for hours, just breathing and listening as he so often had on board the *Owen Glendower.* But the fresh air and exercise had cleared Freddie's head and awakened his appetite, and so they retraced their steps more briskly than they had come. Boy, now fully awake also, bounded ahead of them, a russet streak among the brown and amber foliage.

Back in his room, Granville gave two sharp pulls on the bellcord hanging by his bed. Creighton entered bearing brass cans of hot water for the young gentlemen's ablutions, and steaming pots of coffee with milk for their refreshment. He then exited with equal equanimity, bearing two pair of boots, their shine dulled by the recent excursion through damp grass and leaves.

The young men washed quickly, then turned to the coffee awaiting them on the small round table in the middle of the room.

"My gyp's stealing again," Freddie commented, as he two-handedly poured coffee and milk simultaneously into his cup. "Sack of coals a week, regular as can be . . . tea, sugar, pocket-handkerchiefs. Caught him red-handed. Said he only borrowed 'em."

"Why don't you change gyps?" Granville was now pouring his coffee—black.

"No odds at improvement. All alike." Freddie shrugged.

"Literally a den of thieves, huh? Suppose they're only living up to their name."

Freddie took a sip of coffee and scowled to show his innocence of any knowledge of his friend's allusion.

"*Gyp*, from a Greek word signifying a vulture." Granville stirred a spoon of sugar into his cup.

"Well, Creighton's the best of good fellows. You're lucky to have him. Still, don't hurt to keep one's valuables tucked away."

As if on cue, the rotund form that was the good fellow Creighton returned with the morning post. On top was a letter to Granville bearing a ducal crest and franked by the Duke of Beaufort. As Freddie was occupied feeding snips of toast to Boy, Granville opened the letter straightaway without apology.

September

My Dear Cousin,

I shall endeavor not to be angry at you for your lack of communication, as, indeed, I am sure you must be much occupied by your studies. But I must say I do not think it very obliging in you not to inform my mama of your health.

However that may be, as it is Wednesday morning, I am faithful to my promise to my mama to help her with her correspondence and have got my pen in hand to write to inform you that we shall descend upon you in a fortnight's time. We shall stay at The Rose where Mama and Papa are to attend a meeting of Mr. Wilberforce's Society for the Mitigation and Gradual Abolition of Slavery Throughout the British Dominions, to which they are so much attached. Their daughters are longing for some stimulating society, which I trust Cambridge might supply. Cannot you round up a simple country ball or rustic fair for our entertainment?

Which is the earnest request of (if she may presume to call herself so)

Your Ever Affecte Cousin,
G.S.

The letter fell to the table, its reader torn between despair and delight. Only hours before, he had been longing for the quiet joy of his cousin's companionship, but the pleasure of her visit was blotted out by the disapproval he knew his way of life would arouse in her.

· 8 ·

No MATTER WHAT his internal conflicts, when Granville went to The Rose the following Friday to welcome the new arrivals, his spirits climbed at the sight of the Duke looking so sedate, exactly like a Duke should. And the warm greeting Granville received from the Duchess and her daughters was pleasant indeed.

The Rose Tavern, frequented by Pepys in the previous century, and now often host to foreign royalty visiting Cambridge, was known as a center of gossip and political intrigue. But this evening it was alive with a different tenor of anticipation as it prepared for the speech William Wilberforce was to make from its balcony. Even in the Beauforts' private parlor, the bustle of preparations in the courtyard below could be heard.

"Thank goodness we have seats reserved for us on the dias," Her Grace said, observing from the window the crowds beginning to gather. "It's going to be a terrible squeeze. Of course, that will make it more of a triumph for Mr. Wilberforce."

"What of tomorrow—have you arranged any entertainment for us, Gran?" Georgiana offered him a biscuit to accompany the tea he was drinking. "Mama and Papa are obliged to attend their Abolition Society meeting all day and Charlotte and I shall be frightfully dull if you don't rescue us."

"I have procured an invitation for our party to the concert at the Black Bear to be given by its Music Club. They are quite famous for their performances of Mozart, Haydn, and Purcell."

"I'm sure that will be simply delightful for Mama and Papa," Charlotte spoke up. "But Georgiana and I are quite sated with such

69

formal entertainments. I'm longing for more rustic pleasures."

Granville felt at a loss as to what to suggest in the way of bucolic entertainment that would be suitable for ladies. A cockfight or prize mill would hardly do. "Well, perhaps a drive in the country, and er, a picnic?"

"That would be just the thing. We could drive into the fields and observe the harvest—with your permission, Mama?" Georgiana sought her mother's approval.

"Certainly, my Dear. I'm perfectly complaisant as to Granville's capability of providing whatever escort is necessary." She glanced out the window, "But the courtyard is filling rapidly. Perhaps we should make our way downstairs before it becomes impassable."

The ladies retired to don their hats and gather their shawls and gloves.

When they were alone, the Duke asked, "And how is your reading progressing, Nephew?"

Granville hesitated. Should he put a good face on it for his uncle? "I'm afraid it's rather—er, uneven, Sir," he admitted after a pause.

The Duke laughed and slapped his knee. "Well chosen word, my Boy, if it's anything like it was in my day. I quite concur with the idea of encouraging young noblemen to attend university to set the tone for the lower orders; but it seems that the policy of conferring degrees without requiring examinations is an open invitation for young men to be fast."

The entrance of the ladies rescued Granville from further comment.

By the time their party was seated on the raised area reserved for members of the Abolition Society, the gathering crowd reached beyond the inn and was filling the street. And they were none too early, for only a few minutes later Mr. Wilberforce appeared on the balcony. He was flanked by Charles Simeon, the spiritual founder of the Evangelical party, and Isaac Milner, Wilberforce's spiritual father and old schoolmaster, who had become the intellectual chief of the movement. The preliminaries were simple: A prayer by Simeon and an introduction by Milner. Then both retired to leave the platform clear for their distinguished friend.

Wilberforce's small frame, clad in black knee breeches and frock coat, seemed like a slender but bent cylinder of a candle supporting the flame of his lustrous face with its bright eyes and shining white hair. But when he began to speak even his striking appearance was overshadowed by the charm of his voice, which years ago had won for him the title of Nightingale of the House of Commons. The appeal of his smile, the music of his voice, and the intellectual and spiritual force of his words produced an impact that his hearers could never forget.

"Let me declare to you at the beginning that the mainspring of our philanthropic movement is faith in the Gospel of Jesus Christ which proclaims liberty to the captive and the opening of the prison doors to them that are bound." The speaker's voice was bold and impassioned with the inspiration which deep feeling alone can breathe into words. Although his health was failing, his power to move an audience was not.

But even with such a gripping scene before him, Granville's mind turned in upon itself, as Wilberforce's words burned his conscience and forced an application to his own life, as well as to the slaves on whose behalf Mr. Wilberforce was speaking. *The Gospel of Jesus Christ proclaims liberty.* . . . As yet he had found nothing but bondage in his own strivings. Each time he had determined to turn his back on what his uncle had so rightly termed a fast life, he had found himself a captive in his prison of pleasure. He longed for freedom from the guilt of sin.

And yet he truly believed in the Gospel of Christ. Was he so unworthy that Christ wouldn't open the doors of his prison? Wilberforce continued:

"The Abolition Society has sometimes been criticized for being as much religious as it is political, but I declare to you that England's destiny lies safest in the hands of men of clear Christian principle, and that submission to Christ is a man's most important political as well as religious decision."

Applause resounded from the courtyard, led by the Society members. This man, whose single-minded efforts had led Parliament to abolish the slave trade in 1803, and who continued to work with all his strength for the abolition of slavery itself, now spoke forcefully for the interim measure of Amelioration, of bettering the condition of the slaves to keep their hopes alive until the final objective could be achieved.

"And so we must follow our call to right wrongs and establish justice in the name of Jesus Christ wherever our destinies take us. At this hour in history, it is incumbent upon us to fight against the degradation of that odious state of slavery which not only corrupts everything it touches with its plague-spots, but also taints everything within the reach of its very atmosphere. . . ."

Each word drove Granville lower as he contemplated the degradation to which his own personal state of slavery had brought him. It was useless to argue that his dissipation was not as severe as that of his friends, that he was drunk less often, that he gambled less deeply, that his association with lightskirts at Newmarket never went past flirtation. Granville knew that a God who said, "Be ye perfect, even as I am perfect," would never find him acceptable. It was a relief to Granville to turn his attention once more to the impassioned orator.

"Let our exertions in the cause of the unfortunate slaves be zealous and unremitting. Let us act with energy suited to the importance of the interests for which we contend.

"Justice, humanity, and sound policy prescribe our course and will animate our efforts. Stimulated by a consciousness of what we owe to the laws of God, and the rights of the happiness of man, our exertions will be ardent, and our perseverance invincible.

"Our ultimate success is sure; and ere long we shall rejoice in the consciousness of having delivered our country from the greatest of her crimes, and rescued her character from the deepest stain of dishonor."

The Society members were on their feet. Those in the courtyard were tossing their hats in the air and all within the reach of Mr. Wilberforce's voice were cheering and applauding, pledging themselves to rid England of this ignominious blot. And Granville, standing with them, wished ultimate success in his own personal struggle was as sure. He knew that the conflict was no longer one on which he could turn his back.

His campaign to make himself worthy of salvation, however, had to be postponed at least temporarily, for the next morning he was pledged to take his cousins into the country. Enlisting the help of Freddie and of Meredyth Somerville with his tilbury, Granville stowed in his phaeton a hamper filled by Lawrence from the college kitchen, and they left to call for the ladies at The Rose.

Servant lads were sweeping the courtyard, clearing away evidence of last night's stirring meeting, as Georgiana and Charlotte joined their escorts, looking fresh for their rustic outing in simple gowns of printed cotton and natural straw bonnets. Granville presented his friends to the ladies and noted with some displeasure the inordinate amount of time Somerville spent in bowing over the hand of Lady Georgiana. But Freddie spoke for him, "I say, Merry, you planning to dawdle here all morning?"

"No, indeed. I intend to escort this lady to a view of the fairest fields the county offers." And offering his arm to Georgiana, he led her to his two-wheeled gig. "The finest the carriage shops of Tilbury could produce, but none too fine for my lady," as he handed her into the vehicle.

As Granville's phaeton was larger, the remaining three rode in it. They were quickly clear of Cambridge's narrow streets and into the fresh, bright countryside where they saw golden fields of ripened grain rimmed with green and rust hedgerows, interspersed with clumps of autumn-hued trees.

Near the tiny village of Haslingfield, they pulled to a stop beside a "fair field full of folk," just as might have inspired Langland's *Vision of Piers Plowman* in medieval times. The field of wheat rippled in the breeze in waves, and except for its color Granville could have thought he was on the Quarterdeck on the open sea. The wheat was being harvested by a crew of laborers hired for the season to aid the men of the farm. And working beside them, with skirts tucked into their apron strings to keep them out of the way, were the laborers' wives and older children, bundling the freshly scythed stalks and tying them into sheaves. Younger children romped and chased across the stubble, playing hide-and-seek behind the sheaves. Sharp cries of laughter mingled with the songs of birds in the hedgerows beneath the bright, blue sky.

When the tinkle of harness bells and the heavy plod of workhorses' hooves signaled the arrival of the flatwagon, several of the harvesters left their cutting to walk beside the wain and toss the golden bundles of grain onto its low bed. And then one worker at the side of the field near Granville's party began singing an ancient song of harvest.

Come sons of summer, by whose toil
Wear the lords of wine and oil.

The melody was taken up by others around him, and soon the whole field was ringing with song:

By whose tough labors, and rough hands,

73

We rip up first, then reap our lands.
Crown'd with the ears of corn, now come,
And to the Pipe, sing Harvest Home.

Her face shining with delight, Georgiana clasped her hands and cried, "Oh, they're far finer than any choir I've ever heard! Let's eat our picnic in that shaded spinney so we can watch their progress."

Making their way to the small woods, the picnickers found themselves working in rhythm to the harvesters' song as they spread their rugs on a carpet of leaves and unpacked Lawrence's hamper. Georgiana's exuberance continued as she quoted from Gray's elegy between bites of Scotch eggs:

Oft did the harvest to their sickle yield . . . .
How jocund did they drive their team afield!
Let not ambition mock their useful toil,
  Their homely joys, and destiny obscure;
Nor grandeur hear with a disdainful smile,
  The short and simple annals of the poor . . . .
Far from the madding crowd's ignoble strife,
  Their sober wishes never learn'd to stray;
Along the cool sequester'd vale of life
  They kept the noiseless tenor of their way.

The attendance being danced on his cousin by Merry Somerville was too like that of the ingratiating George Agar-Ellis for Granville's comfort. And now Georgiana was quoting the favorite poet of Horace Walpole, Ellis' idol. A cold light filled Granville's eyes, and for one of the few times in his life, he issued a setdown. "I didn't know you had a turn for the sentimental, Georgie."

"Oh, but what charming sentiment she expressed, and so charmingly spoken," Merry said, as he leaned forward and lifted her hand lingeringly to his lips.

"I've had quite enough to eat. Would you care for a stroll, Charlotte?" Granville got to his feet and held out his arm.

"I should love it," and Charlotte rose gracefully. "But pray, save some of those delectable jam tarts for my return," she called over her shoulder.

Georgiana gave her sister a frown that clearly said she should do

74

no such thing for anyone who smiled so beguilingly at *her* Granville.

Granville and Charlotte walked to the edge of the wood where they stood watching the harvest scene before them. "How very curious! What can they be doing, all gathered in the center of the field around that last little patch of wheat?"

"I'll tell you," Freddie said, as he and the others came up behind them. "Ain't lived in Kent all my life without learning a few rustic Banburies. It's unlucky to cut the last sheaf—final refuge of the Grain Spirit and all that—he's likely to get a duster up over having someone hack about at his domicile."

"Surely they don't *believe* that. . . . This is the nineteenth century, not the ninth," Georgiana protested.

Freddie shrugged. "Maggoty idea, but there it is. Probably some corkbrained notion of the Romans. When country folk take something into their head, it stays there."

"Surely they aren't just going to leave the wheat? That would be so wasteful." Charlotte moved closer to the field for a better view.

As the harvesters encircled the standing wheat, the picnickers also moved into the field to see what was happening. A tall, muscular man walked to the center of the circle, grasped the stalks with one arm and whipped a cord around them to form an uncut sheaf. Then, as he stood back, a group of harvesters gathered in a wide half-circle before the sheaf, threw their sickles at the standing bundle, and it fell to the ground.

The tall man then jumped forward, held the sheaf of wheat above his head and shouted at the top of his voice, "I havet! I havet! I havet!"

From all around the harvest ring came the cry, "What havee? What havee? What havee?"

And the shouted reply was, "A neck! A neck! A neck!" Cheers and shouting followed, for with the cutting of the final neck of wheat, the harvest on that farm was finished.

The infectious enthusiasm was irresistible. Georgiana led her friends in rushing forward to join the festivities with the farmers. The neck, whose communal cutting could now bring bad luck to no one, was tossed on top of the load, and the women and children dashed off to the wood and hedgerows to gather flowers and tree boughs to decorate the last load of the harvest.

Georgiana and Charlotte ran with them and began making garlands of fall crocus and Michaelmas daisies. The men followed a bit more slowly, but soon they too had shed their coats, waistcoats, and cravats and, in rolled-up shirtsleeves, were cutting branches of oak and ash.

His arms full of dark-green ash branches laden with bright orange berries, Granville strode across the stubblefield, oblivious to the fine golden dust dulling the high polish of his boots.

"Gran, wait!" With a yellow and purple garland looped around her neck and held aloft in her arms, Georgiana ran to Granville. "Isn't this famous? I'll remember this day all my life."

Granville's slow smile came from deep inside him. "Just a few days ago, I was longing for a simpler, purer life. It seems I've found it—at least for a day."

Georgiana grinned at him saucily. "So do you apologize for calling Thomas Gray sentimental?"

"Certainly not. Gray is sentimental, but I'll allow him perfectly appropriate for the occasion," and he grinned back at her.

"That's much better. I can't bear to see you sunk in the dismals. You've been quite out of countenance ever since we arrived. I thought perhaps you didn't like our coming."

"What a fiddle, Georgie. You're just trying to get me to tell you how happy I am to see you looking so beautiful."

"Oh, are you? Am I? How very delightful to hear!" She skipped a few strides ahead. "Still, I think something is amiss. But never mind, I shall worm it out of you later."

Georgiana stood on tiptoe and tossed her garland around the neck of the lead bay horse who shook his head, making his harness jangle like a bell. The women were now producing scarlet ribbons from their apron pockets and tying them to the harness and the frame of the flower-decked wagon as the men, Granville with them, began climbing atop the load. When the men were settled on the wain, they produced the small horns they had brought for the occasion.

With a triumphant shout and a blast from the horns, the wagon moved ahead. The women ran and danced alongside, singing and laughing; and the children, with cups of water from a nearby stream, began showering wagon and revelers alike, showing their appreciation to the rain that first watered the crop, then held back to allow them to harvest it.

Across the field and a short distance down the road, the wagon lumbered to a stop before the barn that had been cleaned and adorned with garlands of flowers for the harvest supper. "Will ye

76

join our horkey?" The man who had led the cutting of the last sheaf approached Granville with an open smile, and an invitation to the harvest supper.

"Is it all right? We didn't do any work to earn our supper."

"Oh, aye. I'm the lord of the harvest, and what I say goes."

While Granville and Merry went back to the woods to bring their carriages around, Freddie joined in with Georgiana and Charlotte and some of the younger men carrying victuals from the laden wagons sent down from the squire's house. Workers carried crisp brown sides of roast beef and mutton, trestles of sausages and buns, steaming platters of green, gold, and orange vegetables, and an endless number of plum puddings and apple pies from the wagons to the long, groaning tables inside the barn.

Near the door of the barn, several of the women were gathered around the neck of wheat, fashioning it into the shape of a doll with hair and hands made of wheatears.

" 'ere, now, is the frock we used last year," and one woman produced a slightly tattered white dress that would have fit a young girl. The doll was stuffed inside the garment and other women produced colored ribbons to decorate its hair and wrists.

Just as the first red streaks of sunset marked the sky, the completed kern-baby, symbol of the wheat spirit and guarantor of good harvests to come, was hoisted on a pole by the tallest and strongest men of the party and all followed it into the barn where the feasting was officially begun.

As Granville worked his way through a plate heaped as high as that of the hardest-working laborer, and washed it down with mugs of cider, his mind took a serious turn. He thought of Jesus' Parable of the Harvest, some who worked all day, some who worked half a day, and some who worked for only one hour before sundown—and yet all received equal wages from the Master, the same Master who later, as the Lord of the Harvest, invited His friends to "Come and dine."

Granville looked at his companions, Georgiana, Charlotte, Freddie, and Somerville. None of them had worked for even an hour before sunset, and yet they had been graciously invited to come and dine. Perhaps not all rewards had to be earned. . . .

But just then the musicians struck up a merry tune. A bonfire had been set in the paddock to provide light for the country dancers who whirled and clapped in its golden light to the simple melodies provided by two fiddles and a mouthharp.

"Sir, I refuse to stand upon points and allow you to snub me at yet another dance," Georgiana accosted her cousin.

"Did I do that?"

"You most assuredly did. I'll allow to having been quite outshown by my sister, but you should have taken charity on a wallflower and done the polite at any rate."

Granville led Georgie into the set, spun her around, then bowed to the lady behind him, and danced around the circle before the steps brought him back to Georgiana. "What a bubble! I couldn't get close to you for your admirers. And you were far too occupied with your beaux to notice what I did."

"I noticed enough to know that you danced with Charlotte twice."

"So I did." He grinned at her with a twinkle in his eye. "And a very graceful lady she is too."

Just then the music came to an end, giving Georgiana an opportunity to stamp mischievously on Granville's toe before she gave her hand to Meredyth Somerville for the next set.

The pleasure of her minor triumph was destroyed, however, as Georgiana saw the hurt look on her cousin's face, the same look she had seen earlier when Merry Somerville had kissed her hand, spurring Gran to invite Charlotte on a stroll. And then her conscience stung her even further when she saw that Granville had not turned to Charlotte this time, but chose instead to bow over the hand of an awkward country lass who had thus far been left out of the festivities. The maiden blushed with pleasure at his attention and her plain face broke forth with a smile that made it almost pretty.

Georgiana became so engrossed in watching the small scene on the sidelines that she missed a step and had to apologize to her partner. But then her thoughts returned to earlier times. That was so like Gran. He would always do or say something to make another person feel good—no matter how much he might be hurting himself. She recalled childhood scenes when he had received such severe setdowns from his father or rebuffs from his older brother that it brought tears to her eyes; but seeing her hurt, Granville's concern would be all for her. "Pray, don't let it distress you, Georgie. I shan't make such a muddle of things next time and it will all come quite right."

And no matter how many times such occasions were repeated, he never lashed back, but always continued trying to please.

A short time later, with her softened feelings glowing in her eyes, Georgiana saw to it that she was in a position to be handed into her cousin's carriage. And when Freddie, taken by the charms of one of the country girls, elected to remain behind, Georgiana smiled with pleasure at this opportunity to be alone in Granville's company. Perhaps at last they could have the serious talk she had desired for months. She was tired of the cousinly banter they always seemed to fall into as a carryover from earlier days.

The carriage moved quietly down a country lane flooded with golden light from the harvest moon. After a few moments of casual chatter about the day's activities, she came to the point. "Granville, you must forgive my directness, but you know I've never had any patience with roundaboutation. I told you earlier I believed something to be amiss with you, and I am determined to know what it is."

"Why do you say that?" he hedged.

"Gran, don't tease me. I told you I have no patience for it. I've been in your company very little since you returned, but even on those few occasions, I can see that you are unhappy a great deal of the time."

He made no reply to that, but she needed none. The look in his eyes spoke clearly.

"Gran . . ." It was so hard to put her feelings in words, and she was afraid of seeming prying or pushy.

He turned to her. That simple movement gave her courage. She took a deep breath and plunged. "Gran, do you have faith?"

He turned away and Georgiana held her breath, fearful of having shut the door that had just opened between them. Then he spoke and she saw that he had turned away to concentrate on her question, not to dismiss her.

"Faith? You mean do I believe in God? As certainly as I believe in life."

Relief flooded over her. "O Gran, that's wonderful! I was so afraid. . . . But if that's firm, nothing can be really hopeless."

But his next words shattered her joy. "It's *me* I don't believe in. How can I ever be good enough? What *is* enough? Must I live forever on the brink, looking to heaven but never able to reach it?"

"O Gran. . . ." The pain and hollow desperation in his voice choked her. She longed to have answers for him, but none came.

"Georgie, I'm sorry." He squeezed her hand briefly. "Don't let it worry you."

She managed a smile, but couldn't get any words past the lump in her throat. All she could do was place her hand in his and pray that the specters be kept at bay.

When they arrived back at The Rose, it wasn't a specter of evil that came between them, but the thoroughly solid pair of hostlers leading away a shiny black carriage with a familiar pair of matched greys.

"Groom!" Georgiana called out. "Is that Mr. Agar-Ellis' carriage?"

"Yes, Ma'am. 'e arrived 'ere not more'n 'alf an 'our ago. Must of cantered 'alf the way from London—'is 'orses is in a fearful lather."

"Well, see that you cool them properly, then." Georgiana dismissed the stablehand and turned to Granville. "Isn't that famous! I haven't seen George for donkey's years."

Georgiana more sensed Granville's frown than saw it. "Don't be silly—George is just an old friend."

At first she was hurt by Granville's failure to reply to her soft words; but later, in her room, she realized he hadn't heard her.

· 9 ·

As DETERMINEDLY AS if he had heard that the captain of his ship were considering replacing Lt. Ryder's command with an upstart, Granville strode into the vestibule of Holy Trinity Church the next morning at the hour appointed to meet the Duke's party. It was his full intention to wrest Georgiana from the clutches of that mushroom Agar-Ellis, if it meant breaking his arm.

Fortunately for the proprieties in the house of God, Granville was outflanked by the Duke himself, who was listening intently to George report the latest word from London—that Wilberforce was toying with the idea of Britain buying the slaves' freedom by a treasury grant. And Georgiana, her hand resting on her father's arm, was hardly in a position to be forcibly removed.

At the opening strains of organ music, Granville bowed stiffly to Charlotte and escorted her to the second of the two front pews reserved for the Beaufort family, right behind Georgiana sitting between her father and Mr. Agar-Ellis. Of course, it could as easily have been said that Georgiana was sitting with her father as with Agar-Ellis, but Granville did not see it that way.

The elegance of the white church with its rows of pillars rising to sharply apexed arches, and its Gothic stained-glass windows looking like bejeweled hands pointed in prayer, was entirely lost on Granville whose strong jawline was set even more ruggedly than usual and whose eyes were like steel.

Even the animated preaching of Charles Simeon from the high pulpit, the full sleeves of his robe flowing majestically as his gestures gave emphasis to his words, made little impression on Granville.

81

"While ye were yet *without strength*, in due time Christ died for the *ungodly*."

And at the last word, Granville's cold stare and wrathful thoughts focused on the carefully pomaded head of the young man in front of him.

"Are we in a state of *guilt?* God has provided a substitute and a surety for us, in the person of His dear Son. Are we in a state of *weakness?* God has provided all needful strength for us, in the operations of His Holy Spirit.

"If ever we have access to God, it must be through Christ and by the Spirit. It is for this end that the Spirit is given; and this end He will accomplish, in all who implore His aid."

The preacher, fully into the power of his message, removed his pince-nez and leaned forward over his tasseled pulpit with a sweeping gesture that arrested even Granville's wandering attention.

"The first thought which occurs to men is that they must do something to merit and to earn salvation." At that moment Georgiana turned her head slightly to look at George and Granville failed to mark the rest of the speaker's words.

"But, if we consider the condition of our first parents after the Fall, we shall see how vain must be such a conceit, how fallacious such a hope. What could Adam and Eve do to recommend themselves to their offended God?"

Simeon paused, the absence of sound again focusing Granville's mind on the speaker; then Simeon gestured, with a long, thin finger that seemed pointed straight at Granville.

"What could you do to merit the gift of God's only dear Son, and the influences of the Holy Spirit?"

The question was enough for Granville. The anger he had directed at George Agar-Ellis he now turned on himself. Indeed, he knew himself to be in a state of weakness and guilt, just as the preacher had said. And he recalled those phrases that his distracted attention had caught, *Men must do something to merit and to earn salvation. What could you do to merit the gift of God?* Caught up in repeating to himself the few phrases that had penetrated his consciousness, Granville failed to hear the concluding answers.

"God of His own mercy and grace has given us a Saviour, and without Him we can do nothing acceptable to God.

"We must be indebted altogether to the sovereign Grace of God which first gives us to will and then to do of His good pleasure.

"Just as the gift of a Saviour sprang altogether from the sovereign Grace of God, so must salvation in all its parts."

The Duke and his party had been invited by Christopher Wordsworth, Master of Trinity and brother of the poet, to dine at the Master's table before leaving Cambridge. But the classical proportions of the richly paneled room, and the gleaming elegance of crystal, china, and silver on the long polished table, made no impression on Granville, as Mr. Agar-Ellis held forth on the scholarly work he intended to accomplish at Cambridge, researching the years Horace Walpole spent at Trinity, "holding fellowship with her venerable books."

Granville, however, was certain that the object which had brought George to Cambridge in such a lather was not the venerable books read by Mr. Walpole, but the presence of Georgiana Somerset. And he would have been willing to wager a pony that George would not remain long once she had departed.

Easily stirred by his topic, George continued, "It is remarkable how nothing that transpired in the great world escaped Walpole's knowledge or the trenchant sallies of his wit, rendered the more cutting by his unrivaled talent as a raconteur.

"Oh, how piquant are his disclosures! How much of actual truth do they contain! How perfectly his anecdotes trace the hidden and often trivial sources of some of the most important public events!" In an excess of emotion, the speaker waved his napkin, narrowly missing a long-stemmed wine goblet.

"Indeed. To be sure," the Duke replied calmly, and then turned to their host. "And what of the progress on your new court?"

More extensive accommodations for students, thereby reducing the numbers required to live in lodgings in town free from college discipline, had been Wordsworth's most fervently fought campaign since becoming Master. "Ah, you mean King's Court, as it is to be called, since His Majesty has been so generous as to contribute one thousand pounds to its building. I wish your grace could have been with us last month when the cornerstone was laid on the King's birthday. The band, stationed just inside the gate, played "God Save the King" and led the procession to the site, where we heard both Latin and English orations. Then the band played "Rule Britannia" while the King's representative laid the first stone. The festivities concluded with prayer by your humble servant."

The Duke raised his glass to the Master. "Most stirring, I'm sure." But George, not to be long deterred from his topic, persisted in his conversation to Georgiana and Charlotte. "As great beauties yourselves, you ladies will assuredly agree that if the irresistible court beauties of the first three Georges have been compelled to yield to ungallant liberties of Time and to the rude destruction of Death, it is a delight to us to know that their charms are destined to bloom forever in the sparkling graces of the patrician letter-writer."

He turned from one lady to the other to collect their smiles. "In his epistles are to be seen, even in more vivid tints than those of Watteau, those splendid creatures in all the pride of their beauty, pluming themselves as if they could never grow old. . . . "

At the far side of the table, Granville was having a quiet conversation with the Duchess. "And what is the news of your family, Aunt Charlotte?"

"The news most likely to make you stare comes from your Cousin Worcester. He has informed us of his intention of offering for Lady Jane Paget."

Granville puzzled at the tone in which the Duchess pronounced this information. "Am I to understand that you wish them joy?"

"Of course, I do. We all do. Worcester's happiness is among my fondest wishes and deepest concerns."

"Then why do you speak with such a lack of enthusiasm?"

"Precisely because my son seems to lack enthusiasm." She sighed. "I had thought he was developing a tendre for another. Ah, well—" her voice trailed off.

"But what of you, Granville? We have had no opportunity to talk and I had so hoped for a quiet coze. I shall, of course, report to your dear mama and papa in my next letter. They shall be delighted to hear that you are looking so well. In fine fettle, I suppose you young people would say, although in my day we would have blushed to use so coarse a phrase. But enough of that. . . . Have you found what you came to Cambridge in search of?"

Granville met her searching gaze levelly. It would be useless to try to cut a wheedle with her; he could feel her penetrating blue eyes reading his mind. "I have not. But I am determined yet to do so."

"Indeed, I am sure you shall." The Duchess gave him an encouraging smile. "When an officer of His Majesty's Navy has set his course, he is not easily deterred."

Monday morning Granville stood waving as the Beaufort coach rumbled out of the cobblestoned courtyard of The Rose. "Don't forget—you promised to come to us at Christmas," Georgiana called out the window, just before one of the liveried outriders cut her off from Granville's view.

He had two months before Christmas hols and he was determined that not a moment would be wasted. Any attempts he had made at gradual reformation had failed; this should be a revolution. Already a plan was forming in his mind: he would put himself into the hands of his tutor for reading; daily chapel attendance should be readily accomplished; one hour given to Bible study before breakfast and another after Combi—or should he refrain from attending the easy joviality of the combination room? And prayer—how much time should be given to that? How much time *could* be after one had read the daily allotment from the prayer book? Mr. Simeon's conversation parties and services at Holy Trinity—of course, attendance would be unfailing; compassionate work—well, after its hotly contested beginnings, there *was* an auxiliary branch of The British and Foreign Bible Society at Cambridge. . . .

He walked slowly back to Trinity, through its Great Gate, across Great Court with its clock tower on the right by the chapel and the Nevile Tower and statue of Queen Elizabeth on the left, through the arch to Nevile's Court with its loggia running around three sides. It reminded him of the long, columned walkways in the cloistered monasteries he had visited in Italy. For a moment he imagined himself walking there in sandaled feet, his hands clasped devoutly, his head bowed in prayer. . . .

With a thoroughly unmonastic stride, he crossed the court and bounded up the stairs of the Wren Library. In all his months at Trinity, he was still something of a stranger to the long narrow room with its tall windows and pale wood pendants of Grinling Gibbons carvings ornamenting the dark paneling of the room. But now he was determined to develop more scholarly habits. He browsed for some time in the stacks running along both sides of the room until a small volume bound in gold leather took his eye. He drew it out and held it in his hand—*Acquaintance with God*. Where had he heard of that? Perhaps his father had a copy. He started to replace it on the shelf, then remembered. Georgiana had mentioned this in one of her letters. She said she was reading it with great enjoyment. He took the book to a small table in a private alcove.

As he scanned the chapter headings, the title "Impediments to Heavenly Mindconcepts" caught his attention. If there was anything he needed it was a heavenly mindconcept, so he might as well be forewarned of the impediments. He began reading:

> God says, "Hear today"; we harden our hearts and say, "Tomorrow." Neither Time nor Grace are in our Power, yet we often act as if we could command both. This is our way, our Sin and our Folly.

Granville sat up straighter and squared his shoulders. Well, he was done with saying "Tomorrow." He was determined to face the problem today.

> Worldly-mindedness is another great enemy to acquaintance with God. The world is God's grand rival for our Hearts, therefore the Love of it is called Enmity to Him. If then we would cultivate friendship with God, we must not hug His Enemy in our bosoms. . . .

The faces of Granville's friends rose before him: the tall, lanky Merry Somerville with his easy smile and gregarious way, who seemed villainous only when he appeared to be competing for Georgiana's favors; Frank Molyneux and William Hervey, their red and black heads close together as they sang slightly off-key in Combi; the sometimes caper-witted Freddie who was his closest companion. Certainly, they lived the careless, here-and-thereian life of their class, but it was difficult to cast them in the role of God's enemies. Well, they should have to be made to understand. Somehow, they must understand the fault was his, not theirs. He wouldn't hurt his friends.

Avoiding contact with anyone who might be passing through the courts, Granville made his way back to his rooms. Relieved to find it empty he flung himself on his bed. The gloom that his new resolution had held at bay now overtook him. He had always failed before. . . . He would fail again. . . . So why try?

But before he could sink any further in the dismals, the door flew open—he had omitted to close the heavy outer oak door which would have prevented intrusion—and a jovial voice broke on his solitude, "Famous mill on Pease Hill. Shame you missed it, Gran.

I'd have come for you, but wasn't time once it got started." Freddie flopped into the nearest chair and propped his feet, muddy boots and all, on a small, spindle-legged table.

"It was top-of-the-trees—caps flying everywhere, women watchin' from second-story windows—we put on a good show for 'em. Handy with my fives, if I do say so." He held up his slightly bruised fingers and paused long enough in his narrative to look at his friend. "I say, you in the sullens?"

"Precisely, but I am determined to extricate myself—from the sullens of sin."

"I knew it. Shouldn't of gone to church yesterday. Depresses you every time. Won't do."

In spite of himself, Granville grinned at his friend. "That's easy for you to say, Freddie. You haven't a soul to wrestle with."

"Have too," and he moved his hand around searchingly on his chest. "Right here somewhere, sure of it. Just more concerned with my stomach right now, that's all. Late for Hall."

Granville was quiet during the meal, gathering his willpower for the task he had set himself. The prospect was not pleasant, but surely the most arduous effort would seem as nothing once grace was earned. At the conclusion of Hall, force of habit carried Granville toward the Combination room with his friends until his conscience smote him. Before turning away to his own room, he made one last attempt to explain to Freddie.

How far short of success he fell in making his friend understand, became evident when he heard Freddie tell Molly, "Gran ain't comin' to Combi. Gone off after some female."

"Female? You mean a light skirt? That don't sound like Gran. He's not in the petticoat line. You must be mistaken."

"No. No mistake. Her name's Grace."

But two who did understand were those who shared his staircase: Anderson, the poor but scholarly divinity student upstairs, and John Henry Rennard, the elderly bachelor clergyman whose presence downstairs had, more than once, been a curb on Granville's activities. He now turned to them repeatedly for counsel and they were unflagging in their encouragement. "You judge yourself too hard, Granville."

Rennard seconded Andy's statement, "My thought precisely. You see yourself much too low. Now have some more coffee and let us begin again on this passage."

Obediently, Granville took a sip of the weak coffee and applied his attention to the open Bible before him. Three nights a week, for three weeks in a row, the stairmates had met in Rennard's rooms after Hall seeking to discern a true sense of the divine excellency of the things of God's Word. The flame of the oil lamp flickered, then burned more steadily as Rennard turned it up and the study continued to the end of the chapter.

"Excellent." Rennard closed his Bible and reached for another volume. "My brother has sent me a volume of sermons by the American preacher Jonathan Edwards. I want to read a bit to you that you may increase your thankfulness that your mind and your steps have been turned to the spiritual. Edwards gives a stirring picture of what the godless have in store for them."

He increased the oil flow to the lamp one more turn so that it sent long shadows across the room, and read in dark tones that surely could not have been exceeded by the Puritan preacher himself:

"Your wickedness makes you, as it were, heavy as lead, and to tend downwards with great weight and pressure towards hell; and if God should let you go, you would immediately sink and swiftly descend and plunge into the bottomless gulf. Your healthy constitution, your own care and prudence, your best contrivance, and all your righteousness, would have no more influence to uphold you and keep you out of hell than a spider's web would have to stop a falling rock. . . ."

Granville shifted in his chair. Was this meant to comfort him? Comfort one who was already so painfully aware of his own unworthiness in God's eyes? Comfort one who knew how little progress he had made on the path to righteousness?

Rennard looked across the table at his two listeners, curled his thin lips in a half smile, and continued with a slight nod:

"The God that holds you over the pit of hell, much as one holds a spider or some loathsome insect over the fire . . . looks upon you as worthy of nothing else but to be cast into the fire. He is of purer eyes than to bear to have you in His sight. . . .

"O sinner! Consider the fearful danger you are in. 'Tis a great furnace of wrath, a wide and bottomless pit, full of the fire of condemnation, that you are held over in the hand of that God whose wrath is provoked and incensed as much against you as against many of the damned in hell. . . ."

A log in the fireplace snapped and sent a shower of sparks onto the hearth, causing Granville to start in alarm. The reading continued, but Granville needed to hear no more to be convinced of God's displeasure with him.

And late that night, after a painful time of tossing and turning, Granville finally fell asleep, only to find his dreams filled with the images Rennard's voice had invoked: Granville saw himself hanging by a slender thread with flames of divine wrath flashing about it, ready every moment to singe the string and burn it asunder. The heat of the flames scorched him, the acrid smell of smoke filled his nostrils and stung his eyes, and as he looked upward at the unraveling cord, his mind filled with terror. Only one thread as frail as a spider's web, held him from eternal doom.

A cry tore from his throat as a flash of lightning leapt at the thread. Sweating profusely, Granville sat up in bed, clutching his bedclothes. Then, with a great rush of released breath, he realized that the rumble of thunder shaking his windowpane was the sound of a November storm, not the voice of divine judgment.

But as he crossed the room to shut his window against the coming rain, he knew that someday, however far distant, he must face the eternal Judge. And he knew with equal certainty that there was nothing he could lay hold of to save himself; nothing to keep off the flames of wrath. Nothing that he had ever done or could do would be enough to persuade God to spare him for one moment.

· *10* ·

THE NEXT MORNING IN CHAPEL, however, it was not the heat of the flames of hell that enveloped Granville, but the numbing coldness of a universal void. He shivered in the frigid iciness of a world without God. The rain outside made the chill dinginess of the chapel even more penetrating, as Granville took his seat in the long, narrow room with its black-and-white marble floor and the indistinguishable picture above the altar. Even the stained-glass windows high in the white walls were dim and obscure, for they received little illumination today from the gray sky behind them.

It was all as cold as Granville's heart, and it matched the sterile words of the devotional being delivered to the sleepy, sullen gowns-men. All was meaningless ritual. If there was a personal God, why would He hide Himself? Of all places, He should be in chapel. But if this cold ritual of religion was God, or if the vengeance-seeking, flame-throwing figure of his last night's dream was God, Granville could well do without Him. He could find more meaning in a good horserace.

And a few days later, that is exactly what Granville set out to do. The frost-tipped, sun-gilded air making his horse step even higher, and pull his perch phaeton even more briskly than usual, Granville joined his friends enroute to Newmarket. At the junction with the London road, the carriageway was choked with traffic.

"Whole world going racing." Freddie, beside him on the carriage seat, flashed his open smile. "Glad *you* are, Gran. Missed you. Not cut out to be a monk. Told you so."

"Yes, you did, Freddie. Who you backing today?"

90

"Merry says Rubini. Won a pot at Epsom. You thinkin' of havin' a flutter?"

"I might hazard a bit if anything takes my fancy."

Then a familiar tilbury pulled alongside them and Freddie leaned out to pass a flask of blackstrap to Merry and Frank Molyneaux. When they returned the drink, Merry raised the ribbons and left Granville and Freddie in the dust.

"I say, you gonna take that?" Freddie cried.

Gran took up the challenge and sped his chestnuts forward, the many capes on his dun-colored driving cloak rippling in the breeze as he dodged the heavy traffic on the narrow road. Frank Molyneaux looked back and waved his curly brimmed beaver hat with a shout, just as Somerville cracked the whip and his horses shot forward with a jerk that almost unseated his companion.

If Granville's way had not been blocked by a large barouche carrying two exceedingly elegant ladies, he would have given Merry a good race; but instead he accepted defeat gracefully and raised his hat to the ladies who appeared to be escorted only by their groom.

The irrepressible Freddie went further in his greetings, and, holding to the side of the phaeton, stood and executed a deep, sweeping bow, much to the amusement of the ladies.

The little town of Newmarket was so packed it was nearly impossible to negotiate their way up High Street toward the clock tower. "Bad ton, all the hoi polloi these races attract." But Freddie didn't seem to be worrying about his social standing as he waved again to the ladies in the barouche. "Would you ladies care to join us for some liquid refreshments at the Bushel?"

Granville raised his eyebrows at such forwardness, but the "ladies" showed no inclination to stand on points. Granville was beginning to doubt the correctness of that appellation.

"I'll take the one in yellow, if it's all the same to you, Gran," Freddie said, hopping down from the phaeton as soon as they pulled up in front of the inn.

Granville gave instructions to the stable lad, then joined Freddie. On closer inspection, he knew he had not been wrong to question the standing of their female companions; but they were extremely pretty little ladybirds. Clad in a peacock blue pelisse with an openwork white ruff accenting her golden curls that peeked from beneath a feather and ribbon-trimmed bonnet, the female Freddie had just handed down from the barouche approached Granville.

"I'm Clarissa. It's very kind of you and your friend to invite us to take lunch with you. We brought a hamper for later. You'll have to let us return the favor."

Granville extended his arm. Freddie's invitation for a cold drink had suddenly expanded into a meal, but, Granville reflected, he was rather hungry and it was still two hours till post time.

Unfortunately, all the private parlors were already bespoken, so they were forced to take their luncheon in the public rooms. But the inn offered a fine cold collation of meats, cheeses, and jellies, and their companions weren't in the least dismayed at being obliged to dine in such a squeeze.

"I say, this is Fifi." Freddie introduced his dark-haired companion who, Granville discovered, was not so young as a first glance at her ruffles and curls would lead one to believe. Nor, he suspected, was her French lisp as genuine as she would have one credit.

"I've just had a grand idea." Clarissa fluttered her eyelashes at Granville, who preferred not to look much lower since the removal of her pelisse had revealed a shockingly low-cut gown. She reminded him of the "ladies" who had thronged the port cities.

"Well, don't you want to hear it?" Clarissa's slightly nasal voice and a touch on his arm brought Granville back to the present."

"Yes, yes, of course." He wasn't as sure as he sounded that he really wanted to hear her, but innate gallantry forbade insulting even one of such low station.

"Why don't we all go to the racecourse in my barouche? There's plenty of room and it's nonsensical to take an extra carriage."

Granville would have declined, but Freddie's acceptance of the proposal was immediate; so shortly the party made its way across Newmarket Heath where Clarissa's groom wrestled manfully with the Herculean task of parking the barouche amid the crush of revelers, picknickers, and sporting men thronging the trackside. "Oh, good, Jason. Just a little further up, if you can. I simply must see my favorite win." Clarissa directed her groom.

"You ladies planning to sport the blunt?" Freddie asked as he examined his racing card.

"I'm seemply wild about ze races!" Fifi's pink feathers and yellow flowers bobbed atop her high-poke bonnet. "Zey are so exziting, no? And so much more exzitement if one has ze small wager, no?"

"Well, come on then, let's go have a flutter." Freddie led the way to the betting post where wagers were struck. It was obvious the ladies had no intention of wagering any of their own funds, so Granville and Freddie did what was expected of them and placed their companions' bets with their own money.

"All mine on Gimcrack!" Clarissa ordered. A few minutes later, Granville handed her a ticket and pocketed one of his own.

"I shall take Rubini, az you suggested, Freddie." Fifi was all smiles and flutters.

They were returning to their carriage when Merry and Frank Molyneux hailed them, "There you are! Thought we'd lost you."

Clarissa and Fif were delighted to have their party enlarged by two more handsome young men, especially since they had brought a large hamper of port. Molly was offering a share all around, pouring while holding spare glasses under his arm, when a trained dog act caught Fifi's attention. "Oh ze darlings!" and the group followed her pink feathers to where three French poodles in little pointed hats were rolling balls and jumping through hoops.

The dog act was followed by a strolling band which was going in the direction of Clarissa's carriage. When they arrived back at the barouche, they watched a pair of jugglers in red-and-yellow striped costumes with red pompoms on their shoes and bells on their hats, entertaining those nearby and collecting pennies for their efforts.

The first three races drew little attention, as none of their group had money on any of the horses running and the band, jugglers, and port provided plenty of entertainment. But Rubini was running in the fourth.

"Oh, pull ze carriage closer! I must see everything!" Fifi clutched her racing ticket to her ample curves.

The starting gun fired and the thoroughbreds sped down the field in a pack on the far side of the ring before the grandstand. "Oh, which one ez he? Ze glasses, where are ze glasses? O Freddie, eezn't eet fun?" As the horses pounded around the field, Fifi stood up in the carriage and clung to Freddie. "There, zat one—ze jockey with green silks! No? Yes! Yes! Zat eez Rubini!"

By the time the horses reached the curve at the top of the field, Rubini's jockey made his move and the gleaming chestnut horse began to move ahead, passing one, then another of the leaders. "He's doing eet! He's doing eet!" A flash of green silk crossed the finish line ahead of all the rest.

"I won! Oh! I won!" she cried, forgetting her French accent and hugging Freddie with such force that he lost his balance and they both tumbled from the carriage in a spill of yellow flounces.

"Are you hurt?" Freddie scrambled to his feet and endeavored to help Fifi up. "Most awfully sorry and all that. Afraid you caught me off balance, what?"

Fifi took his hand, then sat down again sharply with a small cry, "Oh, my ankle, eet eez in pain!" She raised her skirt to reveal a shapely leg.

"Any trouble here?" A man in a brown-and yellow checked suit who had been standing nearby approached them.

Clarissa answered him, "Nothing we can't handle, thank you." The man looked at her for a moment, then turned away.

"Shall we fetch a doctor?" Granville asked.

"Oh, no, please. I do not weesh to spoil ze party. I will just sit here until eet eez better. I know! Get out ze hamper and you weel all sit wits me and celebrate zat I won." In a few moments rugs were spread on the grass and the party was consuming roast chicken and veal pie. Fifi's appetite was undiminished by her misadventure, but the ruffled skirt remained just below her knee so as not to put any undue pressure on the injured limb. Granville noticed the loudly dressed stranger eyeing them once.

The highly favored Gimcrack was to run in the final race of the day. Although Fifi didn't have any money riding on him, she insisted on being lifted back into the carriage to watch the race, while Clarissa, clutching her ticket for good luck, sat on the top of the seat back with her feet on the cushions for a better view. Granville, who also had money riding on the horse, stood beside her with the glasses to his eyes.

From the moment of the starter's signal, Gimcrack exhibited that he was in every way a champion. "Magnificent piece of horseflesh! Look at the flow of those muscles," Granville said to Freddie who had mounted the box by the driver.

"Champion. Sure thing. Shoulda put a monkey on 'im."

The horses swept around the first curve of the long oval track and already the front-runners were beginning to edge ahead, Gimcrack among them.

"Absolute perfection. Never saw a horse run so well," said Granville as he watched the horses pass in front of them, shaking the ground with their pounding hooves. The cheers of the grandstand reached them from across the track and the shouts from their

94

own side of the course were equally loud, vibrating painfully in Granville's sensitive ears.

"Gimcrack!"

"Come on now!"

"Make your move!"

The band played, dogs barked, carriage horses stomped and whinnied, banners fluttered in the air, all mingling with cries, shouts, and laughter of those holding tickets certain to win.

At the top curve Gimcrack moved to the front of the lead pack, and the roar of the crowd was deafening.

In the home stretch, three horses from the front group moved ahead. Gimcrack was not among them. For a moment it was impossible to distinguish what was happening, "Your whip! Use the whip," Granville growled between clenched teeth.

The cheers of the crowd turned to an angry rumble as a furiously spurred and whipped black took the lead, followed closely by a gray who seemed to emerge from nowhere. Gimcrack and a long-legged bay were nose to nose over the finish line for third place.

"Can't be," Freddie said. "Don't believe it."

"He was pulled." Granville sat down heavily.

"Pulled?" Clarissa tossed her ticket to the floor of the carriage. "How can you tell?"

"Did you see the jockey? He was riding with his whip in his mouth! Can you credit it? I'd like to ram it down his throat."

Granville regretted the money he had lost; but he regretted even more allowing himself to be in a situation where a fool and his money were soon parted. If the wages of sin weren't immediate death, they were at least imminent financial ruin. He wanted to be rid of Clarissa and Fifi as soon as possible and return to the quieter scenes of Cambridge. But Fifi's agonies over her sprained ankle forced him to give up any hope of immediately abandoning them.

"Better go into town. See if we can find a sawbones," Freddie said.

Granville helped Jason stow the picnic hamper and rugs in the barouche and they drove back to town. 'Stop at the chemist's," Granville ordered the groom. "He should know of a doctor."

The chemist knew the location of Doctor Aspery's surgery, and he also knew that the doctor had been called out early that morning to attend the birth of twins and had not yet returned.

Upon leaving the shop, Granville raised his hat to a group of distinguished gentlemen gathered on the sidewalk, then froze, as he turned into the direct gaze of Lord Calthorpe, one of his father's close Evangelical friends.

"How do you do, Sir? A, er, pleasure to see you. I trust my father was well when you left him?" Granville endeavored to put the best possible face on it.

"I believe he was tolerably well. Suffering from his headaches, as usual, unfortunately."

"Yes, to be sure. I look forward to seeing him and my lady mother at Christmas. Will you be at Badminton, Sir?"

"Not I, but I believe my brother Frederick is going for the hunt." Then Lord Calthorpe's eyes narrowed in scrutiny of Granville's sporting attire. "And what brings you to Newmarket, Ryder? Haven't been to the races, have you? Such worldly amusement is not consonant with an upright life. Let the experience of Scrope Davies stand as a warning to you."

Granville's blank look encouraged Lord Calthorpe to continue, and he launched into a cautionary tale. "Davies was a great and liberal favorite at Cambridge in my day, but he was a betting man. He fattened his pockets to the sum of twenty thousand pounds at Newmarket. But, driven by greed and addiction to gaming, he sought to double it and plunged. Then came the evening when he hurried into his rooms and requested his bedmaker's help in packing. 'What is it, Sir?' she enquired. 'Ruin!' he replied, 'I've just lost all I had, and as much more; and must leave tonight. Tomorrow will be too late.' He died abroad."

At that moment the uncomfortable situation was made even more unbearable as Clarissa's shrilly nasal voice called from the carriage, "Gran, do hurry! Fifi here's in excessive pain."

Granville took refuge in a deep parting bow and turned from his father's friend.

Ever since the mention of Lord Harrowby's headaches, Granville's own head had begun to ache abominably. He longed for nothing more than a quiet drive back to Cambridge in his phaeton. But it was clear that his relief must be postponed, as Fifi cried that her ankle was paining her severely, and the slightest jiggling caused pain to shoot clear to her knee.

"Freddie, Darling, you must zecure rooms for Clarissa and me at ze inn for ze night. I cannot possibly travel in zo much pain. I know you would not want me to; you are zo thoughtful."

So Jason drove to the Bushel where Freddie engaged a room for the night, and he and Granville carried the invalid between them up the narrow, curving stairway to the private parlor. Clarissa lagged behind for a moment, but soon appeared, leading a serving wench carrying a tray of cheeses and biscuits with several bottles.

"Put them by the fire," Clarissa directed. "I knew you wouldn't want to set out without some refreshment," she smiled at Granville with half-lowered eyelids.

"Thoughtful of you, but I'm not really hungry. If you'll excuse me, I think I'll see if Merry is below."

But a quick survey of the public rooms told Granville that no help was available from that quarter. The only familiar face Granville saw was the man in the checkered suit who had parked near them at the racecourse. Granville was just debating whether or not to summon a stable lad to ready his phaeton when the arrival of Lord Calthorpe's carriage sent him back inside. He could think of nothing less desirable then meeting his father's close friend in an inn where Clarissa was sure to come and fetch him at any moment.

"Not a sign of Merry. Might as well join you." He accepted defeat, as Freddie, who was drinking wine from the glass Fifi was holding to his lips, obviously already had.

The next morning neither Freddie nor Granville could recall any events beyond drinking the spicy, heady wine Clarissa served. Indeed, through the blur of his fuzzy vision and aching head, Granville could barely gather his wits to remember where he was.

Then, as the scenes of the previous day made their way to his consciousness, he knew. "The duce! Rolled, like a bloody flat." That he should have been suckered by one of the oldest tricks in the book was doubly humiliating and infuriating.

"Been made a cod's head of, that's what," Freddie muttered.

Granville didn't need to check his pockets to know that his purse was gone. But the even worse loss was the pocketwatch his father had presented to him on his twenty-first birthday. He swore under his breath, too angry even to give vent to the words.

"Thing that's worrying me," Freddie made his way unsteadily to the window and opened it for a breath of fresh air, "is how we're gonna pay our shot." He started to leave the window, then turned back sharply. "Oh, there's a piece of luck. Fellow we can borrow from—friend of my father ." He stuck his head out the open window and yelled loudly, "I say, Lord Calthorpe!"

· *11* ·

"Everything must be simply perfect, Dixon," Georgiana swept into the great drawing room ahead of the butler who had been following her all morning, practically at a run, making careful notes of all that the lady desired in preparation for the Christmas holidays.

"That medallion will be the perfect place to hand the kissing bough." She stood in the center of the room, craning her head backward to view the large, plaster centerpiece symbolizing her father's title of Knight of the Garter. "It will be just the thing, and give excellent balance to the room." She held a slim white finger to her cheek, considering. "Yes, that's it! Make it in three tiers just like the chandeliers, only slightly larger. I want it to be the most elegant possible. And when the basic structure is ready, I shall take a hand with the boughs and ribbons. Have you got all that?"

"Yes, Milady."

"Good." Georgiana whirled around to consider the rest of the room. "It must be decked with greenery—holly and ivy over all the portraits." She paused to look at the imposing naval officer over the fireplace. "Be sure you find branches with especially nice berries for Admiral Boscawen; we must do honor to our heroes of His Majesty's Navy."

She paused longer over the next knotty problem. "But what of the late Lady Worcester?" She frowned at the elegant Georgiana Fitzroy. "If Worcester is to bring his new fiancée with him for the holidays. . . . " Dixon's impassive face and poised pen implied that he would in no way allow himself to have an opinion on a matter of such delicacy. "Perhaps if we choose boughs of profuse foliage, it

98

might just shadow the picture a bit."

"Very good, Milady."

"And then we shall require garlands of laurel and bay in festoons from the cornice and mantel. And the other rooms and chapel in a similiar motif—but no mistletoe in the chapel."

"*Yes*, Milady." Dixon's stiff back showed that under no circumstances would he allow so much as one berry of that pagan foilage to desecrate the family chapel.

"Now we must check with Cook to make sure she has all the ingredients for the Christmas pies. If everyone comes we shall be twenty some at table and there must be no shortages."

"*No*, Milady." Even Dixon's impassive face registered the horror of such a thought.

"Pheasant, duck, quail—Papa said they have all been in good supply this season." She ticked them off on her fingers, then paused to lift her printed muslin skirt as she hurried down the scrubbed wooden stairs to the kitchens. "Venison, swan, bustards, peacocks—the gamekeepers have been notified, haven't they?"

"Yes, Milady."

"Good. And, of course, the boar's head. . . . " Her quick steps led them into the vast white culinary center already bursting with scents of baking gingerbread and mincemeat, of roasting pork and beef, and of simmering apples and cinnamon.

Cook was able to reassure the young lady about the food preparations and put both her mind and appetite at ease with samples of jam tarts, chess pies, boiled sweets, and steamed puddings.

Still sucking on a Jordan almond, Georgiana left Dixon to expedite the plans on his pages of notes, while she went to the yellow room to report to her mama. The Duchess sat at a tall marquetry escritoire, her soft green dress and the coolness of the Dutch paintings on the walls setting off the warmth of the yellow flocked wallpaper and yellow striped upholstered furniture.

"Well, Mama, I think we can plume ourselves that our Christmas celebrations shall be complete to a shade."

"I do appreciate your instructing Dixon for me, my Dear. Worcester has me all at sixes and sevens with the pother over his engagement. I no more than have the announcement written for the *Times* than I receive a note from London scribbled post haste that it's *not* to be announced yet; then I receive a long letter telling me about all the fine qualities the lady possesses. This isn't like your brother. You don't think the lady has cried off, do you? I can't bear to see my children hurt, and he did suffer so over his wife's death." The Duchess put her little hand-held reverberator to her ear to hear her daughter's reply.

"The lady would need to have more hair than wit to cry off an offer from my brother. He's the prime prize in the marriage mart." Georgiana kissed her mother, then sat on a tall-backed, petit point covered chair. "Don't worry, Mama. I'm sure everything will be perfectly unexceptional when they arrive."

"Well, I trust you are right." She picked up a letter from the pile in front of her and sighed. "But I am fearful I shall have to abandon my scheme for building my chapel in Monmouthshire. The subscriptions have fallen off shockingly and I don't know what to do about it. One doesn't want to be in a position of actually begging from one's friends, and yet I did have my heart set on the chapel. So many people in Wales are without spiritual guidance."

"But what of the local vicar?"

"Alas, it is a plural living and the vicar is there not above three times a year and the curate is very idle. I had hoped to supply the district with a young man of energy and vision." She picked up another note, the one informing her that Lord Berry would not be renewing his subscription.

"Would Papa . . . ?" Georgiana's thought was unfinished.

"Perhaps he would, my Dear, he is always most generous. Only at the moment, all his attention to our duties in Wales is going to the clearing of Raglan Castle. He feels he owes it to our ancestors as well as to our national heritage. I really don't think this is quite the time to distract him with my project. But my own income is quite depleted, and I can lay my hands on nothing without touching my capital. 'Pockets to let,' as your brother would say."

"Mama, are you still feeding and clothing two hundred families a year?"

"I fancy it was nearer three hundred this year." Georgiana shook her head, thinking of all the misery her mother had relieved in ministering to both the physical and spiritual needs of these people.

"You are too good, Mama. I'm sure something will turn up—you won't be obliged to abandon those souls in Wales. Perhaps The Society for Promoting the Enlargement and Building of Churches and Chapels? After all, our Uncle Harrowby is its Vice-President."

The Duchess shook her head and picked up another missive.

100

"I've contacted them. Their funds are fully committed for the next three years. Unless, of course, I should see my way clear to increase their subscription roles." She dropped the paper with a wistful smile.

"But I am most gratified, my Dear, to hear that everything shall be precise to a pin here." She held out a note, its red wax seal broken to reveal a fine copperplate hand. "Your Cousin Granville informs me that he shall be with us the first of next week, in time for the hunt."

The Duchess laid her hearing aid aside and returned to her correspondence. Georgiana sat back in her chair, holding Granville's letter between her fingers, remembering the night, more than a year ago, when he had reentered her life. What happiness it had brought her to discover that Granville, the companion and idol of her youth, had become the handsome man of the world she always knew he would be. She realized now that, although unaware of it at the time, she had always been waiting. Waiting for her childhood comrade to return. Granville was the touchstone she had held all her other escorts to—and they had all fallen short.

She sat long, a soft smile playing around her lips. But then the smile faded. What of the other side of the question? Had she been the image he had carried in his heart for nine years? Or was she merely a juvenile playmate, amusing, but outgrown like his other toys, to be replaced by more sophisticated companionship?

From that uncomfortable question she shifted her thoughts to their long talk after the harvest festival. She had prayed daily that he would find spiritual solace; but as no letters had passed between them, she had no idea of his circumstances now. She must make an effort to discover the answer to all her questions. She would contrive to spend as much time as possible with her cousin this holiday.

Three days later, when Granville arrived, bringing his much neglected crammie, Mr. Peacock, along with all his other baggage, Georgiana had no more idea of what was in her cousin's head or heart than she had before. Except that it took little perception to know that he was still troubled. The deep furrows in his high brow, and the self-contained silence of the man who had replaced the open, laughing boy she once knew, wrenched her heart and she breathed a prayer for him.

The morning of the Christmas hunt all was astir in the servants' hall long before daybreak, and Georgiana wakened to a great commotion of barking and yapping from the kennels. This would be a special day. She tugged impatiently on her bellpull. She was determined that today would mark a new beginning in her relationship with her cousin. "Agatha, lots of hot water, quickly."

The maid disappeared as quickly as she had appeared and Georgiana picked up her hairbrush and began pulling long strokes through her golden locks. Frederick Calthorpe would be here to occupy Charlotte; George Agar-Ellis was staying in London for the season; neither Merry Somerville nor any of Gran's Cambridge friends were coming—so there would be no interruptions.

Agatha entered with a brass can of steaming water and turned to attend the fire. Georgiana shivered as she dropped her flannel chemise around her ankles and began splashing herself with warm water. . . . Her first goal would be to cheer her cousin up. It promised to be a perfect day in the field. If her best efforts and a day running the Beaufort pack couldn't raise Granville Ryder's spirits, then he must be past praying for indeed.

Georgiana donned her best riding dress of Beaufort Hunt blue and buff. The finely tailored jacket with sleeves puffed from elbow to shoulder, and the long skirt, cleverly divided in the back to accommodate the side saddle horn, showed off her slim form to perfection. "Just a bit more forward, Aggie," she directed, as her maid placed the narrow-brimmed polished beaver hat atop her curls.

"Ooh, my Lady, you look just as elegant as Countess Kaunitz what cut such a figure when she hunted here last month." Georgiana's Abigail sent her off with a smile.

Family, guests, Hunt members, grooms and horses filled the courtyard which Georgiana entered when she went out the north front. Dick, who had been waiting for her appearance, brought Mayflower forward and tossed her into the saddle. From this position, Georgiana could see her father mounted on his favorite hunter, Free-Martin, for which he had refused an offer of five hundred guineas just last week. And there was Worcester on Tom Thumb, wearing green plush and carrying the horn which signaled that he was Master of the Hunt today. Near him on a small brown mare was Jane Paget, the lady whose unclear position in Worcester's affection had all their family astir. Georgiana had met her only briefly the night before, upon the couple's arrival from London, and did not yet feel she could form an opinion of the lady's suitability for the position she aspired to fill.

Georgiana guessed there must be upwards of eighty in the field, all to whom the Duke had granted the privilege of wearing jackets of Beaufort Hunt blue with buff lapels and brass buttons. Some from other hunts added a dash of scarlet in their traditional pinks; others, not members of official hunts, wore riding habits of black or brown; the hunt servants were in green velour.

The pack would be taken to Worcester Lodge, three miles away, in the mule-driven van. But the terriers and small dogs who followed the pack and were so useful in case the fox went to ground in a hole, milled around at the horses' hooves, adding their excited yaps to the snorting of horses, crunching of gravel, and happy calls and laughter of the hunters. The weather was keen with an easterly wind, and there had been frost over the night—conditions which should insure a strong scent for the hounds.

The Duchess and several nonhunting guests took their places in the Badminton coach which led the way out the arched stone entrance into the park, and the company, ready for their breakfast, followed apace. The morning was complete to a shade, except for its most important element—where was Granville? Georgiana reined Mayflower into step beside Charlotte who was turned the other direction listening to Frederick Calthorpe's rather involved but apparently amusing story.

". . . . And you can imagine my brother's shock when he went into the parlor and found Granville had also spent the night with—er, ah . . . " Here Mr. Calthorpe turned as pink as his jacket and suffered an alarming coughing fit.

Charlotte laughed, "Never mind, Fred, I am no schoolroom miss to be shocked by the mention of a bit o' muslin. But *Granville?* Are you sure?"

"Oh, yes. My brother's a high stickler. He'd never have lent money to that loose screw Freddie Perkins. But, of course, the son of Lord Harrowby was quite another matter. . . . "

Georgiana checked Mayflower to a slower pace. The beauty of the day suddenly clouded for her as surely as if a thick gray fog had settled over the park. Well, if *that* was what he'd been about, the Honorable Granville Dudley Ryder deserved to feel troubled and she wasan't about to lift a finger to soothe his feelings.

At the lodge Georgiana joined her mama in playing hostess to their guests, seeing that the servants kept everyone amply supplied with platters of roast ham, game pie, broiled tomatoes, mushrooms, sausages, and glasses of punch.

"Would you care for another slice of pie, Sir?" Georgiana asked a pale, gaunt young man in an ill-fitting habit. She hoped he'd accept—he looked as though he needed it. He did accept, and returned her a kind, intelligent smile for her efforts.

"I say, Georgie, I don't believe you've met Mr. Peacock, my crammie. 'Cock, this is my cousin, Miss Georgiana Somerset."

The lady whirled to face the speaker. "Granville! You surprise me. I thought you had forsaken the field." She made her tones as frosty as possible, then turned her back on Granville to extend her hand to the new man. "So you are my cousin's tutor, Mr. Peacock? Indeed, you have my condolences."

Mr. Peacock flashed the smile which so transformed his impoverished appearance and made Georgiana think that his name might not be quite such a misnomer after all. "Not at all, Miss Somerset. Your cousin is a most courteous charge with a very fine mind."

"Indeed, I have no doubt of it. And so studious as to give you cause to worry for his constitution, to be sure. We must have a long visit later, Mr. Peacock." She changed to a less ironic tone, "I trust you will enjoy your day in the field."

"I have no doubt of it. I understand this may be considered as among the finest fox country in the provinces with some of the finest natural fox coverts in all England."

"That is what we are often told by those from other hunts, Sir. I believe there is no country like it for long, fast runs. It's often said to be the wildest and roughest of the shires. And did you know that fox hunting began here?"

"Here? At Badminton? You astound me."

Enjoying the full back she was giving to Granville, and fully aware that he could hear little of what she said when turned away, Georgiana prolonged the conversation. "That is the tradition. It seems that my grandpa, the fifth Duke, was returning after a disappointing stag hunt when he threw his hounds into Silk Wood for a last run and there found a fox which gave them such a good run that thereafter the Duke decided to hunt the fox exclusively."

"I am entranced to find I shall be walking in the steps of history—or my horse shall be, at any rate." Mr. Peacock put a hand to his breast to emphasize his earnest words.

"Georgie, could we . . . "

Georgiana laughed and continued talking to Mr. Peacock as if Granville hadn't spoken. "Popular belief, however, is not always strictly accurate, but it is a charming story, is it not?"

"As charming as the storyteller. Have you hunted all your life, Miss Somerset?"

"From my earliest days. But Papa was strict—we could not hunt more than three times a week till we were five years old."

"You astound me. And is there no controversy over the—ah, fierceness of the sport?" Mr. Peacock was obviously enjoying the lady's attention and was in no hurry to relinquish it.

"None raised by well-informed people, Sir. Indeed, fox hunting became popular just in time to *prevent* the extinction of the breed, rather than the reverse. Foxes are so well thought of on my papa's lands that servants who sight any on the estate are required to raise their caps or touch their forelocks in respect."

This time Mr. Peacock had nothing to reply to her answer, so Georgiana turned away, anxious to put more distance between herself and her cousin. "You must let us know if you wish anything. Papa wants his guests to have everything they desire."

Giving a final smile to Mr. Peacock, she turned her attention to other guests until the barking of the pack gave notice that it was throwing-off time.

When Georgiana was mounted she moved forward into the riders and suddenly found herself between her father and her cousin. The Duke leaned forward jovially to address them both. "If you won't ride more forward than twenty paces behind the hounds, I think I may promise you something like a good day's sport."

Georgiana laughed at what her father intended as a witty comment. "Indeed, Papa, you outdo even yourself in such moderate demands. But I have no intention of being one of the thrusters in the field.'

"Don't worry, Sir," Granville replied. "I shan't override your hounds."

The Duke laughed, "I credit your good intentions, but I well remember what it was to be young and eager in the field on so fine a morning."

Georgiana was relieved to see her mother approach, as she had no desire to be thrown together with a 'young and eager' man who entertained members of the muslin company, after he had aroused her deepest concern for his spiritual condition. The Duchess, smiling warmly at horses, riders, and dogs alike, made her way through the throng to bid her husband farewell. "Pray, think of me when you are hunting, that I may be a preservation against leaping or imprudence of any kind whatsoever."

The Duke guffawed at her intent words. "Have no fear, my Dear. I am well past the age of showing off. It's these young thrusters you need have a thought for—or rather for my hounds that they won't ride over 'em."

The Duchess smiled at his bolstering words. "I pray you are right, but my blood is chilled when I think of the risks run in the field. Take all imaginable care of yourselves, my Dears—all of you." She stepped back and waved them away.

Payne released the hounds who replied to Worcester's opening cheer with a challenge. In a moment the famous badger pies were throwing their tongues with a charming chorus, and the music of the hounds, which has no equal for those who love the chase, rang through the wood and told of a good scent. Georgiana's spirits soared afresh, in spite of the presence of her cousin whose chestnut mount stayed close to Mayflower.

Within a few minutes of entering the field, the cry that all huntsmen wait for rang out on the clear air, "View Halloo!" The Duke himself was the first to sight fox.

Worcester sounded the horn and the hounds flew to its signal. The moment the hounds were thrown in, the fox was off, running in gallant style across the open country. In a few minutes, Georgiana, riding about midfield caught sight of the fox as he took a flying leap and cleared the fenced brook at the bottom of the field, its bright red brush describing an arc against the green expanse. "Look!" In the enthusiasm of the moment Georgiana turned to Granville and pointed, "Oh, that's the prettiest thing I ever saw!" She spurred Mayflower to a full run and the field of hunters flew forward, urged by the Duke's cry, "Hold Hard!"

It was a run of the kind huntsman dream of and talk about long after, and Georgiana knew the day would live forever in her memory. The sharp air flew past her, her horses' hooves striking the frozen earth in rapid rhythm, the blur of frosty green fields and stretching horses streaking past her vision, and Granville close beside her, as if, in the midst of the racing field they were alone together. Unable to hold the last traces of ill humor in the face of such exhilaration, even against one so deserving of her bad graces, Georgiana gave her cousin a smile.

It seemed that everyone in the field sensed that they were in for a great run and all were riding resolutely, silently, making every effort to save their horses. Silently the pack swept onward; silently the field followed. In the intensity of the run, Georgiana looked straight before her, her vision limited to the eager white ears of Mayflower pricked forward for the slightest signal, and between the frame of ears the fleeting piebald mass of the hounds.

The pack flew over a fence of bramble hedgerows, and a few minutes later, Georgiana lowered her hands holding the reins, leaned forward in the saddle, and Mayflower took the fence as lightly as if she were winged. As soon as Mayflower's four feet were on the ground, she was off again and Georgiana turned just enough to her left to receive a salute from Granville who had jumped alongside her. She smiled with pleasure, knowing that he appreciated the fact that she had not moved in her saddle.

And then, with a yip of confusion, the hounds slowed at the edge of a wood and began running about sniffing the ground.

"Stand still, Gentlemen!" the Duke called.

"Lost him in the gorse," Granville said to Georgiana, the first words they had exchanged in almost an hour of riding together. "He's a stout runner, but a fox like that always makes his point. He'll double around in some clever way to show the hounds he's up to snuff."

Then the splendid chorus of the hounds rang through the covert and put the riders once more on terms. This time the fox was fairly away, but there lay before the pursuers the Brinkworth Brook. Some charged it, some refused, and some went in. Some, their horses nearly spent, dropped out. Lord Worcester and a few followers saved their horses by going over the bridge. Georgiana was among those who went her brother's route, her mind too occupied by other thoughts to choose the stiffer going.

She had exchanged few words with Granville and on perfectly neutral subjects—the sentences could have been spoken to anyone in the field—and yet they were enough to quicken her heart. She could not remain shut to him, no matter how callous his behavior. Feeling a warm glow of righteousness, she decided to adopt the pious position of hating the sin, but loving the sinner. Much pleased with herself, she urged Mayflower forward.

Sun sparkled on small remaining patches of frost, adding to Georgiana's virtuous satisfaction—a glow which lasted until Fred Calthorpe cantered by and greeted Granville who was riding just ahead of her, directly in her field of vision. Fred's salute and bold wink told all that was in his mind as loudly as if he publicly addressed Granville as a care-for-nothing.

Too late Georgiana realized a stone wall loomed right before her. Without any time to gather her mount or even adjust her reins, she closed her eyes momentarily and clung to the saddle. Mayflower landed steeply off balance, took one stride, and then almost toppled over. Georgiana's heart thudded wildly in her throat—she was sure Mayflower would fall, but she sat tight while the mare somehow managed to find her feet.

Georgiana eased their pace and patted her little white horse, "That was very clever of you, Girl. Very clever."

At the village the hounds threw up their heads. Giving them time to make their own cast, Lord Worcester watched closely, and then, with a low whistle, quietly urged them on. Steadily and without flash, they settled on the line again like the serious, working dogs they were bred and trained to be. Riders followed hounds, running hard for the common. There the pack never paused or wavered, for the fox had gone right through.

But on the other side of the common, either because he felt the hounds too close, or perhaps because he met some obstacle, the fox twisted about and sought the shelter of a thick covert. The confusion among the dogs required the riders to pull up. By this time many had fallen back to ease their horses, so that there were fewer than twenty still with the huntsman.

Among the stout ones was Lady Jane Paget, but she had had enough sport. "Henry, I simply cannot go on. I am *not* one of your Tally-ho sort! I am *not* an accomplished fencer! And I *hate* drop-fences! And furthermore, I have mud splattered all over my skirt!" She finished on a high-pitched note nearing hysteria.

Worcester, whose mind was clearly more on his hounds than on his intended, spoke off-handedly, "Quite right, my Dear. Will Long will see you back to the House."

"But Henry, it's *miles*. Surely you aren't so heartless as to send me all the way with a *servant?*" The others turned away, uncomfortable at being forced to hear a private altercation, but Lady Jane's high-pitched voice had great carrying power.

"Henry?" she persisted, forcing him to break off just as he was about to give a signal to the hounds.

"Then stop at the inn for refreshment. I can't be bothered right now," he snapped without looking at her.

The lady was visibly near the exploding point, but whether it would have been tears or angry words to have burst forth, the company was saved from finding out by the intervention of Fred Calthorpe who rode forward and begged the privilege of escorting the lady himself. The relief of those remaining was almost audible as Fred and his charge left the field.

"The longer I hunt, the more I value silence on the part of everyone in the field except the huntsman," the Duke said, not quite under his breath.

Then Worcester's arm flew up with a jerk in a signal that the hounds were running on. Just one faint whimper, then not a tongue was heard, and only the shrill whistle of the huntsman told that the pack was away, and stealing over the turf at a pace which challenged the fastest to catch them.

But because the wind had chopped round to the southwest and was blowing fresh, comparatively few people heard the whistle. So as Georgiana sped across the field, wishing to outrun her troubled emotions, as much as to keep up with the hounds, she was almost alone. But not quite. As if to tease her with the fact that she couldn't outrun herself, Granville pulled alongside her. "Must you be such a hard-goer? I want to talk to you."

"Well, I don't wish to talk to you. You—you—rake!" She dug her heel into Mayflower's side.

Unfortunately, she was obliged to slacken her pace as they entered a spinney, giving him another chance. "Georgiana—"

She hardened her heart against his downcast look. "I heartily hope you are feeling as miserable as you deserve, Sir. I have nothing to say to you."

At that moment they broke from the small wood and were greeted with the beautiful sight of the fox crossing in full view ahead of them by the river. Taking the little red streak as an excuse to escape the emotional turbulence she felt, Georgiana spurred the wearying Mayflower forward.

This time Granville's voice was not a plea, but a demand, "Georgie, stop!"

But she was too set on her own course to attend to the urgent warning of his voice. "Don't! That bank is hollow!"

The words were no more flung on the air than the ground broke away beneath Mayflower, and horse and rider were thrown into the icy flowing water.

In a second Granville was off his horse and running down the crumbled bank. Mayflower churned and floundered, seeking her footing in the slippery streambed, spraying water over the already soaked riders as Granville strove to pull Georgiana from the stream.

"What were you thinking of?" he growled, standing knee-deep in the water beside her.

"I was thinking of putting distance between us!" she sputtered.

"But didn't you hear my warning?"

"I did not, and I don't want to hear anything else you have to say." She shook his arm from around her waist and waded toward the shore, the water pulling heavily at her skirt.

She stumbled on a rock and he reached for her. "I do not need your help!" The effect of her words was spoiled somewhat as she slipped again, this time on the muddy bank, and was obliged to allow him to draw her onto the grass. Mayflower was already shaking herself vigorously, flinging icy drops in all directions.

"Here, let's get this off you," Granville reached for the brass buttons of her drenched jacket.

She pulled back sharply, "I will thank you to keep your hands off me, Sir! I am not one of your—your pamphylians!" Much to her horror, the angry words came out with a strangled sob.

"Have some sense," he ground at her through clenched teeth. "I've no desire to ravish you—I'd far rather throttle you. But I've no desire to see you take a putrid fever, either—so put this on." He stripped off his relatively dry coat and thrust it at her. "Now get that skirt off and wring it out!"

"Sir—"

"Don't get missish with me—I've seen you in your knickers more often than your brother has, and if you don't do it, I will."

The sound of the hunting horn reached them from a distant field and a short, sharp yapping of the dogs told Georgiana that the hunt was over and that she couldn't look for help from any of that party. She obediently unfastened the band of her skirt, but suddenly found herself incapable of wringing it out as her knees gave way beneath her and she sank to the ground.

"Georgie!" Granville was beside her in a second. "Are you hurt?"

Even through the coat, his hand on her arm felt warm, and for some reason that made her cry. All she could do was shake her head.

"You've had a nasty shock." His tone was understanding and reassuring. He picked up her soggy skirt and twisted it until the water ran out in a stream. "Here, that's the best I can do." He handed it back to her. "Can you manage to get it on?"

She nodded, but after a moment's struggle found her fingers were so numb she was obliged to let him do the fasteners. "I'd give my quarter's allowance for a dry blanket," he said. "Blast this wind. We'll take you to the Compass and I'll ride to the house for dry clothes."

"We'll do no such thing. I can ride home as quickly as to the inn. If you will be so good as to give me a leg up." She suppressed a shiver as the chill breeze overmatched the sun's efforts to provide warmth.

Granville made no attempt at conversation on the ride home, as all his efforts were bent on covering the ground in as short a time as possible; and Georgiana, content to let him choose their course, gritted her teeth to keep them from chattering, and concentrated instead on the muddled thoughts that scampered through her mind like a fox chased by hounds. For all of his yelling at her and pulling her clothes about, it was clear that Granville was concerned for her welfare—so why did his avuncular attitude *I'd far rather throttle you—seen you in your knickers more than your brother*—make her want to cry again?

And what of his deplorable behavior reported by Frederick? Why was she so much more deeply hurt by that than if it had been her brother? What difference would this knowledge make in her relationship with her cousin? Could they ever return to the lighthearted companionship they had shared at the harvest festival? Could she forgive him? Did he want her forgiveness?

A chimerical fox waved his red brush in derision and her thoughts went yapping after it. She stretched to understand why this was such a personal affront to her. Then she recalled her thoughts of a few days earlier—how Granville had always been her ideal. That was it. Her idol had crumbled and she felt bereft. There was no one to take his place and she was left with an aching, unfillable void.

A tearing sneeze scattered all her thoughts and turned her mind to nothing but getting to the warmth of her room.

· 12 ·

When Georgiana wakened late the next day, on the morning of Christmas Eve, it seemed that the worst fears of the Duchess, and all who predicted that she would take a severe chill, were proved wrong. The combination of Cook's hot broth, a well-warmed bed, Aggie's receipt of volatile salts in syrup of balsam with oil of sweet almonds, and Georgiana's strong constitution worked such wonders during a good night of sleep, that she wakened with only the slightest scratch at the back of her throat and such little tendency to sniffle that it might be altogether ignored.

And this was indeed fortunate, because even had she been running a high fever, she would have insisted on taking part in the day's festivities. Aggie was full of news when she brought Georgiana's breakfast tray in. "Such comings and goings, my Lady." She fluffed the pillows at Georgiana's back and put the tray on her lap. "Lord and Lady 'arrowby arrived before breakfast, and their coach 'ad no more than pulled back to the stables than that there Lady Paget ordered 'is grace's coach—ordered it 'erself, mind you.

"Well, I can tell you that put Dixon's back up a bit, it did. But then Lord Worcester came in and said to give the lady anything she wanted, just so she left—"

"That will do, Agatha. It's most improper in you to be gossiping like that."

"Yes, Miss. I forgot myself. But there is a message for you."

"Well?" Georgiana set her cup of hot chocolate down and reached for a piece of toast.

112

"Mr. Granville. He begs to visit you at your earliest convenience."

"My, that's very formal of him. I'm surprised he doesn't just barge in without a by-your-leave. Well, then. Bring me my morning dress with the whitework collar and help me arrange my hair." She was irritated at herself for her lack of resolution. Yesterday she had been angry with him, and yet now she couldn't get ready quickly enough to receive him.

The wide sleeves of the printed cotton dress emphasized Georgiana's small waist, and the effect was not lost on Granville when he was admitted to the dayroom off her bedroom. "They said you were unharmed, Georgie, but you look so—so frail. . . ."

"Thank you, Sir. It's all the fashion." Then she turned more serious. "But I am perfectly well. I must thank you for your quick action in fishing me out and, er—wringing me dry." She sat on the sofa and indicated he might sit beside her.

"Georgie, I can't tell you how I felt when I saw you take that dunking. I'm convinced a good share of the fault is mine. If I hadn't shouted at you, you wouldn't have crammed Mayflower—"

"I beg your pardon, I did not cram my horse—that bank crumbled. It was no one's fault."

"As you say. Yet I feel. . . ."

She held her breath at the intensity of his voice. Never a person to do anything lightly, he seemed to be on the brink of revealing a new depth of himself to her. "You feel . . . ?" she encouraged him to go on. Sensing the hesitation in him, she breathed a prayer that at last he might be open with her, that they might have the conversation she had been longing for ever since his return.

He stood up and ran his fingers through his locks, ". . . hunted. I know how that fox felt yesterday. But I am hunted by hounds of failure, profligation, sin.

"You must think me run mad even to talk like this—but I have wanted to talk to you again since we started after the harvest home . . . Why can't *I* find peace? Why is it so easy for everyone else—my aunt, my brother, my—father? Will God never grant me the peace of *knowing?*"

"Granville, your conscience is too tender; you judge yourself too harshly. . . ."

"But that's just it—how does one ever *know?* Rennard and Anderson tell me I must do more; others at the church, that I do too

113

much. Then I abandon hope of ever knowing and I do something unspeakably stupid like—." The words trailed off and he turned away from her. "Georgie, I 'm sorry. That's what I came to say. I felt that your accident was a kind of punishment—on me—for things I deeply regret." There was anguish in his voice.

Standing with his back to her, he couldn't see the radiance on her face. If he was repentant, then all could be freely forgiven. Her hero had risen from the dust, perhaps less heroic, but more vulnerably human, and therefore more dear. She went quietly to him and put her hand over the ones he held clenched at his back. "Then, Sir, you must ask forgiveness and mend your ways."

He grasped her hand tightly as he turned to her. "But that's just it. I have. So many times. And each time the failure is worse."

"I know."

"You know?"

She nodded, "I heard Freddie Calthorpe—his brother . . ."

"Oh, of course. That's what you meant about pamphylians yesterday. Georgiana, I swear to you—"

"It's all right, Granville."

"No, it's not all right. I've never been a bigger fool. But it's not what it looked like, not what you're thinking." He dropped her hand and turned sharply away. "Not that it makes much difference—it might have been."

"Well, it makes a difference to me."

"It does? You care?"

His eyes burned into her and she returned his gaze levelly, looking directly at him—it was so important he not miss a word she had to say that she wanted to give him any opportunity he might need to read her lips too. "Yes, Gran, I care. I care very much."

He drew a long breath, held it, and released it before he spoke. "Then I shall try again."

"Good. You might start by attending to that poor Mr. Peacock. You didn't intend to study over the holiday, did you?"

"Certainly not."

"Then why did you bring your tutor? Not that he isn't perfectly welcome, of course."

"It's customary. Everyone takes their crammies home."

But you weren't obliged to?"

"No."

"Then you didn't really want to get away from it, did you?"

114

Granville was silent a long time. "No, I didn't."

Georgiana smiled, "That's a good sign. Now you must leave this slough of despond and come help me stir the plum porridge."

She led the way to the bustling kitchens where throughout the day every member of the family would put in an appearance to take a hand in stirring this traditional Christmas dish. The big pot of spicy meat broth with raisins, fruit juice and brown bread crumbs was simmering beside the open hearth and Georgiana took an enormous wooden spoon and gave it several vigorous stirs. "You must make a wish while you stir. If the pudding cooks without lumps, your wish will come true." She spoke lightly, but then her face turned serious as she struggled to formulate her wish.

Discarding several attempts at being more specific, she finally returned to the theme she had determined on before the hunt, *I wish Granville to be happy.* She gave a final vigorous swirl to the savory pudding and handed the spoon to Granville. He regarded the contents of the pot for a serious moment, then gave Georgiana a look of such intense meaning as the spoon circled the pot that she was compelled to ask, in spite of her knowledge that wishes were never to be told, "What did you wish?"

Granville gave her his slow smile and raised one eyebrow. "I'll tell you at Easter . . . if you're very good."

She started to protest, but just then Dixon appeared at the kitchen door. "Milady wished to be notified when the kissing bough was ready to decorate."

"Oh, indeed. Thank you, Dixon. You must help too, Gran." And she took off almost at a skip for the servants' hall.

The vast room, hung with copper pans and antlers, was a hive of activity centering around the construction of the magnificent Christmas centerpiece. It was suspended in the middle of the room by ropes running from the fireplace mantle to one of the windows that extended from wainscot to ceiling. One long oak table was piled high with small, gaily-wrapped packages sent down by family members; another was rapidly being covered with red satin rosettes formed by maids who were cutting lengths from bolts of ribbons and tying them cleverly. Three footmen were cleaning away the trimmings of yew boughs, ivy runners, and holly branches that had been used to cover the three concentric circles forming the structure. "Where are the apples and candles, Dixon?"

"Just coming in now, Milady." As he spoke, a kitchen maid

entered with a wooden bowl laden with bright red apples, followed closely by a footman bearing racks of newly made candles.

"Perfect! Gran, you attach garlands of apples with those wires and I'll tie the presents on with these streamers." She picked up a long, shiny red ribbon.

"Yes, Milady," Gran replied with a perfectly straight face, but a twinkle in his eye.

They had worked companionably for some time amid the bustle of servants and the giggles of maids when Georgiana remarked, "Mama told me that two years ago a member of Queen Caroline's court did the most remarkable thing at a children's party—she had a fir tree brought inside the hall and attached candles and presents to it. Princess Fred had told her they always do that in Germany. It was quite the nine days' wonder, but I don't think I should like it above half so well as an English kissing bough." She completed fastening a festoon of rosettes around the large top ring.

Granville laughed, "If the truth were known, Queen Caroline's lady-in-waiting probably didn't have a staff she could bludgeon into all the work of erecting such an elaboration as this. Chopping down a fir tree sounds infinitely easier."

"Do I detect a note of complaint?" she looked at him severely.

"No, Milady. Your humble servant begs forgiveness."

"Well, I should hope so." She stood back to admire their labors. "Excellent. Just one thing missing." She selected the largest, most elegant rosette and used it to hang the final piece of greenery from the very center of the small bottom ring—a large, green clump of mistletoe, heavy with clusters of waxy white berries.

"Quite the most perfect kissing bough I've ever seen," she announced with triumph. "You may hang it, Dixon." The fact that the footmen all blanched at the thought of carrying that magnificent structure to the Great Drawing Room and suspending it from the ceiling went unnoticed by Georgiana as she turned to her cousin. "And now you must excuse me, Sir. I have one more duty to perform which is of a private nature." She turned with a secret smile and hurried to her room.

But Agatha didn't seem entirely pleased to see her. "Are you feeling just the thing, Miss? You look tolerably pale."

"I'm feeling top-of-the-trees, Aggie. But I think I took the stairs a bit too quickly—my head is spinning. And now that you mention it, my throat is rather dry too. I should like a tray of camomile tea.

And I have some writing to do."

"Very good, Miss. And a dose of my receipt too, I should think."

"Oh, very well, if you insist, Aggie." She laughed at her maid's concern and dipped a freshly trimmed quill in ink. Then she sat considering for some time before putting pen to paper.

When they were schoolroom infants, the Somerset children had all been directed by their tutors in the composition of Christmas pieces which they laboriously copied onto sheets of decorated paper in their best handwriting. The polite greetings were then presented to their parents on Christmas Eve. Georgiana had long outgrown the tradition, but she now had a new application for the custom.

Her pen moved slowly over the paper, then went back to make a scratch-out and insertion. There was another long pause before she dipped her quill again, but far too deeply, and blotted her paper. After some time of such uneven effort she laid down her quill with a sigh and took a sip of the tea Agatha had quietly placed on her writing table.

Georgiana's forehead wrinkled in furrows as she read the results of her labors:

> A Christmas prayer I wish for you,
> Of peace and joy the whole year through;
> Of laughter, love, and much content,
> That all may be from Heaven sent.
>
> G.S.

Embarrassed that such a simple rhyme should have cost her so much effort, she started to crumple it up. Then with the gloomy certainty that another attempt would fail to produce much improvement, she took a final sip of tea and recopied the couplets on a piece of parchment elaborately ornamented in scrolled designs of red, gold, and green. When it was finished, she sprinkled it with sand, rolled it into a cylinder, and sealed it with a gold wax wafer.

She rose wearily and rang for Agatha. "Aggie, please take this to the drawing room and place it in the small drawer on the lower right of the Pieturadura cabinet." She handed her the parchment.

"Yes, my Lady," And the maid bobbed a curtsy, leaving Georgiana alone.

If she didn't change her mind, she would give the poem to Gran tonight. But for now, her head was aching and she felt she must have a nap before the evening's festivities. . . .

"Most sorry I am to disturb you, Miss, but there won't be time to do a proper job of dressing if we don't make a start soon."

Georgiana opened her eyes. The fact that Agatha had lighted the candles in the room told her that it was indeed time to be about her toilette. "Yes, Aggie, thank you. You know which dress."

"Yes, indeed, my Lady. It's the most beautiful one you've ever worn, if I may say so."

The deep-rose silk gown which so perfectly displayed Georgiana's own delicate pink and gold coloring was cut low on her shoulders, with softly puffed sleeves balancing the ornamentation of plush and silk roses and tuberoses arranged in rows around the bottom half of the skirt. And the dressmaker had supplied additional matching flowers which Agatha cleverly arranged in a pyramid behind Georgiana's high golden curls.

Agatha administered the finishing touches by fastening on the opal, pearl, and diamond earrings and necklace that had belonged to Georgiana's grandmother, the fifth Duchess, while Georgiana pulled on her mitts of Brabant lace and picked up her fan.

Apparently the Duchess had been waiting for her daughter's appearance, because as soon as Georgiana entered the Great Drawing Room, with its green silk walls and crystal chandeliers shimmering in candlelight, the Duchess signaled the liveried and powdered footman to begin. The cheerful buzz of conversation from the assembled company quieted as the musicians struck up a merry tune and four footmen entered the room bearing the wassail bowl decorated with standing sprays of evergreens and paraded it around the room so that all could be enticed by its pungent aroma of cinnamon, nutmeg, ginger and cloves.

When the bowl began its second circle around the floor, the Duke took up the musician's tune and burst forth with the traditional Gloucestershire carol in which the entire company immediately joined him:

> Wassail, wassail, all over the town;
> Our bread, it is white and our ale, it is brown.
> Our bowl, it is made of the white maple tree;
> With the Wassailing bowl we will drink unto thee!

Amid laughter and applause, the bowl was set in front of the fireplace to keep it warm, and Dixon served the warm, spicy drink.

"I brought you a cup with bits of apple in it. I hope you like it that way." Georgiana turned to see Granville before her.

For a moment she stared. It had been so long since she had seen him in formal evening attire that she had forgotten how he stood out from all those around him. His perfectly cut black evening clothes and gleaming white pleated shirt with a fluted ruffle between collar and waistcoat were the perfect accompaniment to his military bearing and strong features. "Oh, I'm sorry, I didn't see you approach." Georgiana gathered her wits. "Yes, by all means, we must have bits of roasted apple—that's much the best part of a wassail bowl." She raised her cup to him before she drank, then looked around the room. "Your parents are looking well. I haven't had the pleasure of visiting with them since their arrival."

"It's a pleasure I have indulged in only briefly myself."

His slightest emphasis on the word *pleasure* made Georgiana raise her eyebrows; but the sight of her brother bowing over the Countess Susan's hand and then leading her to the floor with a flourish made her choose another subject. "There is Worcester dancing with your mama. I'm happy to see that he doesn't appear at all blue-deviled over Lady Jane's departure."

"If the truth were told, I should say he looks quite relieved," Granville said. "I only hope poor Freddie Calthorpe doesn't have too ramshackle a time escorting her back to London."

"Oh, is that where Fred is? Dear faithful Calthe. How gallant of him to do escort duty." And then she smiled. "I shouldn't wonder if you were relieved to see the back of him."

"The harm has already been done in that quarter." His dark tone made Georgiana regret having taken that turn in their conversation. "When I have a serious talk with my father, I fear I shall learn the extent of the harm. Ah, but here's old Peacock come to wish us merry, haven't you?"

The tutor gave a slight bow. "Indeed, I have. The very merriest felicitations of the season, Miss Somerset."

"Thank you, Mr. Peacock. But my sister is Miss Somerset, she is the older. Have you been introduced?" Georgiana waved to Charlotte who joined them in a shimmering dress of green and silver shot India gauze, its white mull skirt embroidered in green and silver flowers to match her diamond and emerald jewels.

After a few moments' conversation among the four of them,

Georgiana wasn't quite sure how it happened that she found herself being led to the far end of the room by Mr. Peacock for the purpose of dancing a lively country reel with that stiffly proper young man. But her suspicion that it had come about because Granville had first bowed over Charlotte's outstretched white hand did nothing to put her in humor with the situation.

And, indeed, her unease increased when, at the end of the air, Charlotte and Granville concluded their dance directly beneath the mistletoe center of the kissing bough and Granville did a rather more complete job of the gallantries than tradition required. *Well,* she reminded herself, *you wanted him to be happy.*

"I should like to join my mama now, Sir," she said to her partner, who appeared to be on the brink of requesting another dance.

The Duchess was standing near the fireplace conversing with her brother's wife, Harriet, Lady Granville, who was newly arrived for the festivities, and was saying, "I am indeed relieved, Sister, to see that you have not discontinued dancing and all entertainments, as some who follow your persuasion have."

The Duchess gave her sister-in-law a patient smile. "I'll allow the question did trouble me severely at first, Harriet. As soon as I saw the Light, I introduced family prayers into our home, a valued custom which still continues. I used for that office a handbook edited by Charles Simeon; so when this troubling question arose concerning entertainments, it was natural that I should turn to Mr. Simeon for advice."

"And he no doubt told you to discontinue them at once, for your soul's sake?"

"On the contrary. He did his best to help me see the difference between Christian liberty and Christian duty. He said that although he himself possessed no talent and felt no inclination for worldly pleasures, he realized that the position of Christians in high society is far different."

"My, my. How encouraging to learn that even the holy Simeon is capable of thinking in shades of gray." Light strains of music and the soft swish of dancers' feet accompanied their conversation.

"Pray, do not be hard on him, Sister. He has been of great help to me. He wrote me a most well-reasoned letter to guide me through my dilemma. 'What would be wrong if done from choice, might not be wrong if done for fear of offending others, or of casting a stumbling block before them, or with a view to win them,' he said."

"And so you chose to continue dancing. Very wise of you, Sophia."

"Yes, I did, and I trust it has been a right decision. In things sinful in themselves, such as card parties and races, I requested the Duke to excuse the attendance of myself and our daughters; but as to balls and rout parties, I assured him we were ready to go whenever he wished it. It has been a most happy arrangement."

"Well, I'm glad to hear it." Harriet waved her purple satin fan. "But still, I cannot but think, Sister, that this Evangelical step is a very melancholy one for the maiden Ladies Somerset. Why, only think, the eldest must content themselves with court balls, and the prospects of those remaining in the nursery grow darker still—why, just look at dear Georgie."

"Shocking, isn't it, Auntie?" Georgiana good-humoredly kissed her Aunt Harriet. "Quite upon the shelf, I know. And then there's poor Charlotte, five years older. Why, she's been at her last prayers for ages."

"You may mock me, Miss. But you'll find to your discredit that not every man wants to marry into a family of enthusiasts, no matter of how high a rank. Why, I don't mind telling you that if it hadn't been for the inducement of seeing his dear sister to whom he's devoted, my husband should not have been above half pleased to come here."

At that moment they were joined by Lord Granville, for whom his sisters had each named their second sons, "Now, now, my Pet, that's doing it much too brown. Mustn't be so hard on my sister, although I will say, Sophia, things have much improved here. Why, I remember when we used to occupy ourselves, all of us, the whole evening in playing chess. Our days were all alike—breakfast about twelve, then the post would come in about two, then Harriet and I would read the *Nouveile Heloise* together till time to dress for dinner, after dinner play at chess and go to bed between one and two."

"What a shocking bore, Uncle! How did you ever manage to bear with us?" Georgiana asked, her eyes sparkling in the firelight

"Fond of my sister, my only excuse. But the place was always so full of *children*. Children everywhere, Sophia. Can't imagine what you were thinking of. Much better, now that some of you're grown-up, Puss." And he tweaked Georgiana's cheek. "Do you remember

121

the lessons your Aunt Harriet used to give you and Charlotte upon the harpsichord?"

"Indeed, I do, Uncle. But I fear Charlotte's produced more lasting results than mine. I am a sad duffer at the instrument."

"Your talk of children reminds me of my duty, Brother," the Duchess said. "It is time for the younger ones to bid our guests good-night. Come with me, Georgiana, dear; they'll be none too anxious to leave the party." She gathered the gray and silver skirts of her dress and turned in the glowing light of the festive room.

"Who would ever think you the mother of twelve children? You're quite amazing, Mama. I only hope I shall do as well—unless of course, my aunt's gloomy predictions come true,"

"I have no doubt of your doing far better, my Dear," her mother said, as they walked under one of the dazzling crystal chandeliers.

"Mama, I'm so glad you chose to wear those earrings." Georgiana admired the long pearl and diamond pendants which shone like the chandeliers themselves. She recalled that her mother had worn them at the hunt ball the night Granville returned.

"Yes, my Dear, they are my second best, but quite my favorite. I did want to wear them this one last time."

"Last time?" But Georgiana's question went unanswered as they had reached the side of her little sisters Blanche and Mary Octavia.

"Girls, you must find your sisters—I believe they are playing blindman's bluff in the yellow room—and bid your papa good-night now. We shall be up early to go to church in the morning and I won't have you falling asleep." With only the briefest demur, the girls kissed their mama and went off to do her bidding under the eye of their nurse. "I do wish our dear Granville Charles and Elizabeth Susan could be here too. It has been so long since we were a complete family party." The Duchess thought of her two absent children as she watched Susana, Louisa, and Isabella join their younger sisters in kissing the Duke. "But now, my Dear," she turned to Georgiana, "you have spent enough time doing the polite, so go join the young people. I do hope your brother Worcester isn't taking the departure of Lady Jane too much to heart. Do see if he's in want of cheering up."

Georgiana kissed her mama and joined her brother just in time for them to make up a set in a country dance and then allow him to serve her from the sumptuous supper buffet set up in the dining room.

"Shall we sit in the red room with these?" he asked, doing a valiant job of balancing two plates piled high with cakes, jellies, creams, and fruit.

The warm, red flocked wallpaper, the family portraits brought from Raglan Castle and now draped with Christmas greens, the glowing flames in the marble fireplace that was painted by Angelica Kaufman, all welcomed the brother and sister as they settled in one of the pair of red leather sofas that flanked the fireplace. "Not suffering any ill effects from your dunking in the field yesterday, are you, Georgiana?"

Ignoring the soreness of her throat which refused to go away, Georgiana swallowed a bit of smooth lemon cream. "Not the least, Henry. But, if I may inquire without prying, what about the results of *your* day?"

"You refer, I assume, to the hasty departure of Lady Jane Paget after our public tete-a-tete in the field? What a wetgoose—to think she should demand that I leave the hounds to ride home with her."

"You were lucky to find out then."

"Dashed lucky! Can you imagine being legshackled to such a creature? But Georgiana, it's more than that—if she'd been the hardest goer in the field, I knew it wasn't *right*. Do you know what I'm saying? Marriage is more than catching the prime prize in the marriage mart. . . . "

"Which you are, Henry!"

"Don't I know it—with half the mamas in London throwing their daughters at my head." He shook his head ruefully. "I won't go to Almacks anymore—it's a veritable onrush. But that's by the by—I didn't wish to discuss my own consequence. What I want to say, wanted you to remember, Georgiana—for yourself—is that there will be someone who is *right*. And don't settle for less just because it's convenient."

"Do you—er, have any ideas who might be right for you?"

Worcester laughed, "Not a word of this to any of those prying London mamas—but, yes, I have an idea."

The sound of voices at the door prevented Georgiana from questioning her brother further. Charlotte and Granville appeared in the doorway, then momentarily checked their entrance, somewhat uncomfortably, at the sight of Georgiana and Worcester. "Come, come," Lord Worcester indicated the empty sofa facing them. "Season's felicitations and all that. Join us in celebrating."

"Don't want to interrupt," Granville said.

"Nonsense, we're all family," Worcester insisted.

Georgiana's mind faltered at the words, then reminded herself that he was right, but it was impossible to think of Granville as just a cousin. As he handed Charlotte her plate and attended to her bright chatter, Georgiana wondered how Charlotte regarded their cousin—and more importantly, how he regarded her.

Then Georgiana thought of the Christmas piece she had tucked in one of the drawers of the Florentine cabinet in the Great Drawing Room. Would she find a chance to give it to Granville?

Well, she thought, as she looked across at the couple facing them, *not if he continues to dance attendance on Charlotte the rest of the evening.*

As Charlotte's flow of chatter continued (much to Granville's apparent amusement), Georgiana became convinced that indeed, that was what was going to occur and she mentally assigned her carefully composed note to oblivion.

Then her brother spoke, "Well Char, there's the musicians beginning their racket again. What do you say we take a turn around the floor before toddling off to bed? Mama will have us all up while it's still dark in the morning—must set the right example for the village folk by filling the family box. Thank goodness the rails are high enough no one can see if we fall asleep—especially since the Bishop of Gloucester is to preach. Sorry, Gran, know he's your uncle, but what a man to prose on."

On this note of slander about one who was often declared to be among the best preachers of the day, Lord Worcester swept his sister from the room, leaving Georgiana and Granville facing one another across the expanse of Persian carpet.

As Georgiana watched her brother leave, she mused, "Worcester said the most brotherly things to me. I'm quite amazed."

Granville leaned forward at her soft words. "What did you say?" Then he put a hand to his ear in irritation. "What a blasted nuisance! I hope you do not find it"—he hesitated with a diffidence she had never before seen in him—"annoying."

"O Gran, you silly!" She crossed the room to him, then could say no more as their eyes held.

"Would you care to dance, Georgie-ana?"

Georgiana caught her breath at his purposeful use of her full name and, meeting the serious look in his eye, she took his hand.

At the end of the next tune the company thinned noticeably as their elders took to their beds. Georgiana expected Granville to release her at any moment and bid her good-night; but instead, when the musicians slid easily from one melody into the next with barely a pause, he continued to turn her around the floor without so much as requesting her permission.

At the conclusion of that number, the room was all but deserted and the musicians began folding their music and wearily putting their instruments in their cases. As the steps of the dance had led them to the north end of the room, Georgiana found herself standing directly in front of the Pieturadura cabinet where Aggie had secreted her Christmas greeting for Gran. Georgiana looked up at the stupendous piece of ebony furniture rising almost to the ceiling, knowing that now was the time to make her presentation, if she was ever to do it.

Granville caught the drift of her gaze. "It's a magnificent piece of work, isn't it?"

Georgiana ran her finger over one of the bird and flower designs fashioned from inset marble and semiprecious stones which decorated each drawer. "Yes, the third Duke purchased this on his Grand Tour a hundred years ago. Many of his treasures were lost to Spanish pirates on the way home, but I am glad this one survived."

"Perfect for the display of *objets d'art*, as well as being one itself."

Granville's remark was off-handed, but it gave Georgiana the lead-in she needed to talk about things contained in the chest. "Well, there's *one* thing in it that isn't exactly art," and she pulled open the drawer on the lower right, "but I thought it might interest you."

He peered into the small drawer with a quizzical look and drew out the cylinder of paper. "For me?" She nodded and looked shyly away before he broke the wafer.

He read the small verse three times, each time the look of wonder—and of something else—deepening on his face. At last he folded the crisp parchment and slipped it into his inside coat pocket over his heart.

His hand on Georgiana's shoulder, he drew her wordlessly to the center of the room beneath the kissing bough. The room was deserted now except for a few servants clearing up at the far end of the room; but Georgiana wouldn't have noticed if there had been a roomful of guests, as Granville pulled her into his arms.

125

· *13* ·

THE NEXT MORNING, as the family walked to the chapel well before
the first light of dawn, Georgiana's way was lighted for her not by
the candle she carried but by the glow Granville's kiss had lighted
in her heart. Since the family pew was in a gallery at the back of the
church that was reached from a passage through the library, it
wasn't necessary to go out in the chill morning; but Georgiana knew
that even if it had been, the memory of those moments would have
kept her warm.

As three bells in the tower rang changes, the high wooden pews
running between walls lined with monuments to all the previous
five Dukes of Beaufort filled rapidly with villagers—the church was
both family chapel and parish church. In the back, the families
Somerset and Ryder settled into large leather armchairs beside a
splendid fireplace. The local vicar led their presiding guest, Henry
Ryder, Bishop of Gloucester, to the altar, and those in the gallery
gathered around the large prayer books at the front of the box for
the only time their presence would be visible to those below, and
joined the congregation in the Christmas Day Collect.

"Almighty God, who hast given us Thy only begotten Son to
take our nature upon Him, and as at this time to be born of a pure
virgin. . . ."

Georgiana looked across the bowed heads of her family to Granville. His dark curly hair fell forward on his brow bent over the
prayer book, his face sober, his attention focused on the words he
was saying:

"Grant that we being regenerate, and made Thy children by

adoption and grace, may daily be renewed by Thy Holy Spirit; through the same our Lord Jesus Christ, who liveth and reigneth with Thee and the same Spirit ever, one God, world without end. Amen."

They then sang all nine verses of the Charles Wesley-George Whitefield hymn, "Hark! the Herald Angels Sing," and Georgiana, in her state of euphoria, sang "Glory to the newborn King!" from the depths of her heart. At the conclusion of the song, the men in the gallery resumed their seats rather than sneaking out before the sermon, as her father and brother often did. But then, they didn't often have the opportunity to hear so noted a speaker as the Bishop.

In spite of his eloquence, however, Georgiana had some trouble focusing on his words as her mind and heart kept repeating the words of the carol:

Hail the Heav'n-born Prince of Peace!
Hail the Sun of righteousness!
Light and life to all He brings. . . .

As if he were recalling her prayer for his own peace, Granville smiled at her across the balcony. In an attempt to focus her thoughts on the service, Georgiana looked at the Christmas crib by the altar. Such a scene was common only in Roman Catholic homes, but these china figures of the nativity had been in their family since the time of Charles I when the Somersets were Catholic. This year, however, there seemed to be something new. Georgiana puzzled over it for some time. Perhaps it was just the streaks of light beginning to come through the leaded-glass window behind the altar but there was something shiny in the straw beside the baby.

Georgiana's mind could well have continued to wander throughout the service had she not ventured another glance at her cousin. His obviously intent interest in the sermon finally led her to the Bishop's words.

"We must, then, embrace our own thorough sinfulness and helplessness, and our unqualified need of the atonement of Christ, and the renewing influence of the Holy Spirit . . . "

Apparently, even on Christmas morning, the Bishop was preaching salvation; but then, Georgiana considered, when could it be more appropriate? Especially as the church was filled with those who would only come again next year at Easter and Harvest Home.

"Eternal life, therefore—not only forgiveness, but also acceptance as righteous, not only acquittal from guilt, but also title to a gracious recompense—are to be ascribed to the mercy of God, to the sacrifice and righteousness of Christ, and to faith only as the instrumental cause. . . . "

The light outside the window grew stronger and Georgiana looked again at the crib—it looked for all the world as if someone had scattered diamonds among the figures. . . . But then the Bishop's closing words drew her back:

"Come then, in true repentance and lively faith to the Saviour and receive your portion of His meritorious atonement, prevailing intercession, efficacious grace, and unspotted righteousness, if peradventure you may be converted and saved."

And then in the full glory of a Christmas morning sunrise, they sang the final hymn:

> O Christ, Redeemer of our race . . .
> Thou that art very Light of Light,
> Unfailing Hope in sin's dark night,
> Today, as year by year its light
> Sheds o'er the world a radiance bright,
> One precious truth is echoed on,
> 'Tis Thou hast saved us, Thou alone,
> And gladsome too are we today,
> Redeem'd the newmade song we sing;
> It is the birthday of our King.

As they left the service, they were accompanied by that most English of sounds, the pealing of church bells, which would continue to ring in Christmas throughout the day and on to the New Year. Breakfast followed immediately, where they were served from a sideboard groaning under the weight of its bounty. Beside the more usual breakfast foods were miniature mince pies, a dish that would continue to be served at each breakfast throughout the season. As the little pastry 'coffins' of minced chicken, neats' tongue, mutton, eggs, spices, and raisins were passed around, Georgiana raised hers to Granville, sitting across the table from her. "Eat one on each of the twelve days of Christmas and have twelve happy months ahead," she quoted the traditional proverb.

He smiled at her, but the smile did not reach his somber eyes, and he returned his attention to his father beside him who was saying, "But enough of that today. We shall talk more tomorrow."

"Yes, Sir."

Georgiana hoped that she and Granville might talk more later too, but after breakfast the family gathered around the kissing bough where the Duke mounted a stepladder held by three footmen and cut the presents from their ribbons. The Duchess distributed packages that were received with exclamations of delight.

The Duchess handed Granville a four-inch square package wrapped in white paper and tied with red ribbon. His face registered absolute amazement when he read the attached card and discovered the gift was from his father.

Withdrawing from the jovial group, he was undoing the ribbon when Georgiana joined him. "A present from my father. Can you credit that?"

"Well, pray, hurry up and see what it is!" Georgiana was holding a velvet case containing a string of pearls from her father.

Granville tore the rest of the wrapping off and there, looking like a cockleshell in a nest of white tissue paper was a hearing device like the one Charles Simeon had invented for the Duchess. Still feeling completely thunderstruck, Granville held it out to Georgiana. "My father had this made for me."

"How very thoughtful of him! Mama finds hers a great convenience; I'm sure you shall too."

"Yes, quite," Granville said slowly, and turned to find the Earl.

Lord Harrowby was standing near the fireplace. "Father, I— thank you, Sir. It's very thoughtful of you."

"You're quite welcome, Granville. I thought you might find it useful." That seemed to be all the Earl had to say. Then he added, almost gruffly, "And Happy Christmas."

"And Happy Christmas to you too, Sir." Granville shook hands with his father briefly, then turned to wish his mother a happy holiday and see if she liked the small volume of poems he had given her.

Georgiana was obliged to spend the next few hours conversing with various visiting family members. And so it was midafternoon before she handed her Aunt Susan over to Lady Granville in the library and went in search of her cousin. But when she looked in the Octagon room her progress was halted by her twelve-year-old sister, Blanche. "Georgiana, it's so cold outside, Primrose said we might play shuttlecocks in the Entrance Hall, but we need one more. Will you help us?"

Not wanting to disappoint the youngsters, Georgiana spent the next hour playing with her young sisters in the large Palladian Hall, beneath the magnificent hunting scenes painted by John Wootton in gratitude to the third Duke who had spotted remarkable talent in a servant's child and paid for his art training in Italy. "Louisa, mind the clock!" Georgiana cried as her sister's shot landed on the renaissance clock brought from Raglan Castle.

Georgiana failed to return the next serve and the feathered missile fell unnoticed to the stone-and-slate floor as the sound of carriage wheels on the drive sent them all to the windows to see who their newest arrival was. But before anyone could decipher the crest on the carriage door, Lord Worcester hurried through the Hall and down the steps in time to hand the ladies out of the carriage himself.

"Who is it, Georgie?" Mary Octavia, the youngest of the brood, pushed Georgiana aside for a better view.

"It is Charles Culling-Smith, his wife, Lady Ann Culling-Smith, and his daughter, Emily Frances," she said in as matter-of-fact a voice as she could manage.

"But that's . . . "

"Yes, Dear," Georgiana began herding the children away from the windows. "It is the mother and stepfather of the late Lady Worcester, and her half sister. Now, pray do not be so ragmannered as to stand here gaping at your brother's guests."

Georgiana led the retreat from the room in some confusion. Could this be what Henry had in mind when he said there was someone who would be *right?* If he did, they were sure to be in for some stormy weather—what a duster an attachment to his former sister-in-law would raise. Could such an attachment be *right?* Let's see, the Table of Kindred and Affinity forbade a man's marrying his wife's father's mother. Could he marry his wife's father's daughter? Well, it was too much for her to puzzle out. Worcester must settle his own affairs.

There was, however, no sign of anything but good will and holiday merriment two hours later when all the company gathered in the dining room. In renaissance style that could not have been outdone at Raglan Castle, the boar's head was brought to the table, heralded by trumpets, garlanded with herbs, and borne by two footmen carrying the silver basin between them. The entire company sang the traditional song.

> The boar's head, as I understand,
> is the rarest dish in all this land,
> which thus bedeck'd with a gay garland,
> let us *servire cantico*.

> Our steward hath provided this,
> in honor of the King of bliss;
> which on this day to be served is,
> *In Reginensi atrio*

The dish was set before the Duke who, to the applause of the guests, removed the orange from the boar's mouth and presented it to Dixon who in his once-a-year unbending, had led the singers. The Duke then proceeded to present sprigs of bay and rosemary from the dish to the principal guests, which he diplomatically chose to bestow upon the head of each household represented. The last one, again to the approval of the company, he presented to his wife. "Happy Christmas, my Dear."

The Duchess thanked him prettily and signaled Dixon that he could begin serving the family-stirred plum porridge.

Eating her porridge, Georgiana was reminded of the wish she had made the day before and smiled at the delightful circumstances that had seated her next to the very person she had been longing to talk to all day. "I have been singing that carol since I was out of leading strings, but I must confess I have never understood why we sing part of it in Latin."

Granville returned her smile. "The tradition is sacred—from the hallowed halls of Oxford where it all began."

"Yes, but *why?*"

"Because a scholar at Queen's in the murky days of the fourteenth century was walking unarmed in the forest with only a Latin text of Aristotle when he was attacked by a wild boar. The nacky student thrust the volume down the boar's throat, crying, "Swallow that if you can," to which the boar replied "*Graecum est*" and died.

"And Latin students have continued disrespectful of the subject to this day, right, Peacock?"

"I believe there are many who contend that boar hunting is the only proper use for a Latin text," the tutor replied.

"But I hope, Sir, that my son is not among them," the Earl said drily.

Fortunately, further discussion was interrupted by footmen serving the next course. A train of servants circled the table presenting roast goose, Westphalian ham, turkey garlanded with sausages, stuffed pike and oysters, fricassee of turnips, vegetable pie, boiled beetroot, carrots, and roast potatoes. The lack of variety in dishes testifying to the fact that at the Christmas feast the emphasis was on the quantity consumed, rather than on the diversity of menu.

Georgiana followed the footman's progress to the end of the table where the Duchess accepted a slice of ham. The topaz and filagree jewels she was wearing with her brocaded gown surprised her daughter. Since Bishop Ryder, seated on the Duchess' right, was sufficiently caught up in the informality of the occasion to converse with his sister, the Countess, who was sitting across from him, Georgiana took the opportunity to comment, "You look perfectly beautiful, Mama, but you always used to wear your pearl and diamond drops with that gown. I wonder that you changed."

"My Dear, I haven't had a chance to tell you my news. Did you notice anything unusual in church this morning?"

"Apart from the fact that all the men stayed through the service?" she asked flippantly. Then she remembered, "Yes, I did. It looked like diamonds in the crib—but what . . . ?"

The Duchess laughed, "A very, silly piece of sentiment, I fear, but since it was Christmas and all . . . I am selling them to build my chapel in Wales."

"But, Mama, they were your second-best pair."

The Duchess sighed. "Yes, and my favorite, I fear. I would much rather have sold my best, those odious blue diamonds that are so large they give one a headache; they would have fetched at least two hundred pounds more. But they belonged to Mary, the first Duchess, so parting with them was unthinkable."

"Have you told Papa? What will he say?"

"I daresay, so long as no one asks him to contribute his second-best hunter, he will be quite content."

The conversation next to her concluded so Georgiana turned to the Bishop and commented on what a fine sermon he had preached.

"Thank you, my Dear." he smiled kindly at her. "It gives me great pleasure to hear one of your tender years say that. We must reach our young people." And then, in his humble way, he inquired earnestly, "But did I speak too harshly?"

"No, indeed, my Lord Bishop. Your tone was just right. It is easy to see how you have accomplished so much in your ministry."

"Any little good I may have done, my Dear, has been entirely owing, under God, to my preaching the fundamental doctrine of the Gospel—Jesus Christ and Him Crucified."

From the other side of Georgiana, Granville joined the conversation, giving Georgiana a chance to savor a tender morsel of braised turkey. "Your sermon was excellent, Uncle, but what of the good works without which we are told faith is dead?"

"Indeed, Gravnille. Much good is accomplished by works. Just thinking of the compassionate work represented by those sitting around this table quite overpowers one; but good works cannot be the instrument of justification. They are, rather, necessary accompanying fruits or evidence, and that is the point so often missed by some of my High Church brethren."

"Yes, yes, Uncle, to be sure. But that some in high office, who have neither justification nor good works on their plates, should oppose your elevation is past enduring." Granville brought his fork down with a far louder crash than he could have intended, and then looked at his plate to be sure the china wasn't chipped.

"I agree," Georgiana said more quietly, but with equal depth of feeling. "It seems quite wicked in them."

"No, no, my Children," the Bishop said in his gentle voice. "These men *do* intend to act for the good of their country. Being in opposition brings out, in a peculiar way, the worst feeling of human nature. We must watch and pray against all that tends to an uncharitable view of the action of public men.

"You must not only abstain from evil speaking, but also refuse to entertain evil thoughts of others. Keep looking forward that increased means of good may be abundantly blessed and may bring forth fruit to God's glory."

"I'm sure you are right, Sir. But to my mind, one way to bring fruit to God's glory will be in your translation to a wider field of influence," Georgiana insisted.

"Thank you most kindly, my Dear."

"And I cannot for the life of me think it right that such a thing should be held back by Parliament—as if you were a piece of legislation!" she continued.

133

"Persevere in your prayers for me that I may ever have inward peace—peace by the blood of the cross, applied by the power of the Holy Spirit. I shall treasure your remembrance."

Granville then inquired about the Bishop's young son, Charles Dudley, who was serving as midshipman in *HMS Naiad*, and the conversation moved on as the footmen passed everything on the sideboard around a second time, as at least two servings of each dish were considered minimal at the Christmas feast.

At the head of the table, Georgiana's father was discussing his new interest in his role as Hereditary Keeper of Raglan Castle. "It's a beautiful old place and should be open to the public. My father had all entrances to the place blocked up and he ordered that not a stone should be touched. Utter nonsense! The place was becoming nothing but a heap of old stone, so covered with ivy you couldn't distinguish it from the rest of the countryside. I've ordered the rubbish taken away, the briars and thorns cut from the bulwarks, and I hired a resident warden. . . . Don't suppose they're making much headway this winter—bitterly cold in Wales this time of year—but next spring I shall go see their progress."

"Amazing fellow, the first Marquess," Lord Worcester said, referring to the first bearer of the title he now held. "He was eighty-five when he defended Raglan for the crown against Cromwell's men. Almost beat them too. He held out eleven weeks with the enemy chipping away at the tower with pickaxes. But their guns finally breached the eastern wall, so he consented to treat."

"What a marvelous heritage—you must be very proud. I think opening Raglan Castle to the public is a splendid idea, Your Grace," Emily Culling-Smith addressed first Worcester and then his father, leaving them both beaming at her.

The Duke then turned the conversation from his interests to those of his brother-in-law. "And what news do you bring of our friend Wilberforce?" he asked the Earl.

"Most unfortunately, Wilberforce has been very unwell and unable to attend regular sessions in the commons; but I presented a petition in the House of Lords on behalf of the Free People of Color in Jamaica—a large, wealthy, loyal class of people of good conduct, themselves landowners—in possession of the whole of the pimento plantations—who desire simply the possibility of attaining that degree of consideration to which wealth and talents are in other parts of the world entitled."

"Such as, Sir?" Granville was following his father's speech with open interest.

"Such as eligibility to serve in parish vestries or in the General Assembly, or to serve in any public office of trust; to hold commission in the regiments; to serve as jurors; and to have free admission to schools for their children." The Earl's voice took on a ring that suggested that the present company was hearing the facts much as Parliament had heard them, when he first gave the speech.

"But for what purpose did you bring the petition forth?" the Bishop asked.

"At that period of the session it was, of course, impossible to introduce a measure. Because of the extreme difficulty and complicated nature of the subject, I wished it to be understood that if ever it should be taken up by Parliament with a view to a measure of relief, its introduction must be committed to the hands of an individual of far more ability than I can pretend to."

"Wilberforce, do you mean?" Worcester asked, waving away the footman offering a third round of roast goose.

"Quite likely, I should think—if only his health will permit." The Earl also refused a third portion of food. "I am satisfied, from the respectful nature and moderate terms of the petition, that its prayer must, one time or another, be granted."

Worcester threw down his napkin with some asperity. "Moderate terms! That's precisely the problem—and with Canning doing his possible to block the Amelioration measures we are to consider this session, all we've gained so far might yet be lost. What is needed is for more sweeping measures. Wilberforce himself will be the first to tell you so."

"Emancipation, you mean?"

"Indeed, I do."

"Yes, certainly. In due time. But for the moment, it was something for the petitioners to know that the individuals of that unfortunate and degraded race are considered by the peers of Great Britain as their brethren. I agree with Wilberforce that it is essential to keep hope alive in these downtrodden peoples. If they feel forced to take up desperate measures, it could prove fatal to their cause."

Then the topic of conversation shifted as Worcester remarked, "I say, Father, I think I failed to mention that I received a letter from Fitz yesterday." Lord Fitzroy Somerset was one of the most noted members of their family. The youngest son of the fifth Duke of Beaufort, Lord Fitzroy had gone to Portugal with Wellington, where he served as aide-de-camp throughout the peninsular war, and then married a niece of the Iron Duke shortly before Waterloo.

Peacock, sitting next to Georgiana, asked "Fitzroy Somerset? Isn't he Wellington's secretary who lost an arm at Waterloo?"

Georgiana wiped her mouth with her napkin, then answered, "Yes. It was near the close of the day and he was standing beside Wellington when his right elbow was struck. It's one of our favorite family stories that he bore the operation without a word, but when it was ended, called to the orderly, 'Hallo! Don't carry away that arm till I have taken off my ring.' It was one his wife had given him. She is a niece of Wellington, you know." She looked across the table at Emily Culling-Smith. "I believe my aunt, Lady Emily Harriet Somerset, Lord Fitzroy's wife, is a relation of yours also, is she not?"

Emily bobbed her soft brown curls and gave a nervous smile, "I daresay she is, but the connection is far too convoluted to untangle." Her final words were almost strangled by a rising blush.

"Well, Henry, what of my nephew?" The Duke brought the conversation back to the topic that had begun this digression.

"He reports that he has returned from his mission to Spain, as Wellington's envoy. He says Wellington's views upon the constitutional crisis in that country were well received and he has every hope that French intervention on the peninsula may have been averted."

Conversation then turned to the claims of Don Carlos to the throne of Spain, but Georgiana was puzzling why her mention of Miss Culling-Smith's connection to the Duke of Wellington should have embarrassed their guest. It was certainly the last thing Georgiana had intended, as she was quickly becoming fond of her brother's gentle friend. Then Georgiana realized—Worcester's first wife had also been a niece of Wellington, and that possibly stood in the way of an attachment between Emily and Henry.

Horrified at her want of tact, Georgiana turned to say something that would be soothing to Emily's feelings, but found another had accomplished the task for her. Granville was entertaining Miss Culling-Smith by showing her his new miniature hearing device. When Emily held the tiny cockleshell to her ear and gave a light trill of laughter, Georgiana knew that any earlier embarrassment had vanished. How like Gran to expose his own vulnerability to achieve another's comfort. It was as if his having been hurt in the past made him more atune to the needs of others.

The company ate but sparingly of the selection of milk and fruit puddings, cheesecakes, and currant cakes with Cumberland sauce. And Georgiana, who was feeling a little sick to her stomach, declined even a small serving. Then, because of the family nature of the festivities, the men didn't linger in the dining room over the Duke's fine old brandy, but instead all returned to the Great Drawing Room to be served from the tea tray and witness the burning of the Ashen Fagot.

Dixon oversaw the bringing in of the fagot, a large bundle of green ash sticks, very thick in the middle, and bound together with bands of ash and hazel saplings. "This band is mine," Charlotte cried, touching a slim shoot wrapping the end of the bundle. "You must each choose one—Emily, Mr. Peacock, everyone. If yours is the first to break in the fire, you will be the first to marry."

Each of the unmarried people named a band for themselves and the bundle was set ablaze on the wide, deep hearth. The green branches snapped and crackled in the heat of the blaze, sending a shower of sparks up the chimney; but the bands held.

"I declare," Charlotte cried, "We shall all be left upon the shelf! Can you credit it?"

No sooner had she spoken than, with a small snapping sound, the first band gave way and fell into the flames. "Well, that settles it—it's yours, Char." Granville said.

"Shall we wish you happy?" her brother teased.

"Perhaps not quite yet," Charlotte replied, but Georgiana distrusted the smug gleam in her eye.

"Oh, listen—how charming!" Emily held up a quieting hand to the company. As the chatter ceased, the high, sweet sound of carols sung on the cold, clear air came into the room.

"It's the waits." The Duchess rose and set her cup aside. "Shall we go into the Hall so we can hear them better?"

> Good Christian men, rejoice,
> With heart, and soul and voice,
> Give ye heed to what we say:
> Jesus Christ is born today. . . .

The rustic serenaders accompanied themselves on handbells, as with voice and instrument they pealed forth the Good News.

Only Georgiana and Granville remained by the fire. "I have hoped for a few moments with you all day," she said softly.

"And I with you—to thank you for your Christmas piece."

"You did that very adequately last night." She smiled at him in the glow of the fire.

> Love and joy come to you,
> And to your wassail too,
> And God bless you,
> And send you a Happy New Year,

The carolers provided a private serenade for the pair sitting in the great empty room. "And God send *you* a happy new year."

"He's going to, you know," Georgiana said softly.

"Yes. I'm determined," Granville's words carried a quiet emphasis. "When I heard them discussing matters of such import tonight after dinner, I decided I've wasted far too much time. I shall join Lincoln's Inn and become a solicitor as soon as possible, then stand for a seat in Parliament. When Emancipation is voted on, I want to have a part in it. Sandon shall soon want bigger fish than the family borough and then I shall hope to represent Tiverton."

He paused to regard her intently, "And when I do, Georgiana—" He seized her hands, then dropped them in alarm, "Georgie! You're burning up!"

He crossed to the bellpull in two strides and yanked it vehemently. "Send for the doctor!" he barked at the footman as only an officer of His Majesty's Navy could.

When he returned to Georgiana she was shivering. The waits were singing an old Sussex carol—"When sin departs before His grace, then life and health come in its place"—but Granville didn't hear them as he cradled his trembling love in his arms.

· *14* ·

BOXING DAY BROUGHT ANOTHER ROUND OF ACTIVITIES. Her Grace gave gifts to all the servants, and assisted as the vicar opened the almsbox in the church and distributed its contents to the poor. A steady stream of dustmen, postmen, lamplighters, turncocks, and errand boys came round for their Christmas boxes. Then the children gathered in the Hall for the Punch and Judy show, and Worcester got a party up to go into Gloucester to see a monkey and bear troupe.

But two people were absent from all the festivities—Georgiana who was confined to her room under strict orders from Dr. Milkwood, and Granville, who had received a summons from his father to meet him in the Duke's study after luncheon and was left to cool his heels with nothing to do but worry about Georgiana until time for the interview.

He sat staring at an open book before he closed it in irritation and strode across the room to give two abrupt jerks to the bellpull. "Send Agatha to me," he ordered the junior underfootman who appeared in the doorway. "No, wait. Don't interrupt her. Just bring me word of Miss Georgiana's health. That sawbones has been with her above an hour. What can he be about so long? If he doesn't know his business, I shall ride to Harley Street for Dr. Knighton. Well, what are you standing about gawking for? Bring me word!"

The servant departed and Granville paced the length of the room, alternately running his fingers through his hair and making a shambles of his formerly crisp white neckcloth. "Well?" he demanded of the harried servant before the young man was across the threshold.

"The doctor has just left, Sir. He says the case is serious, but not dangerous. Her Grace asked me to say that she will bring you a full report soon." The footman bowed and departed, leaving Granville to continue his pacing. He felt he had been waiting an eternity when the wheels of the physician's departing carriage sounded on the gravel and Granville heard the Duchess' footsteps as she crossed the room to him.

In spite of having been up with her daughter most of the night, she still exhibited that hopeful disposition and fresh enthusiasm which rendered so much of her special charm. "Granville, I am sorry to keep you in suspense so long, but I simply couldn't leave until Dr. Milkwood was quite finished with his examination."

"No, most assuredly not, Ma'am. I thank you for coming now. How is she?"

"She is resting quite easy with a kettle of water boiling on the hearth, and Aggie is to administer two grains of tartar of emetic in water every two hours until the fever passes. Dr. Milkwood feels we have every right to hope that it may not develop into pneumonia."

"Pneumonia!" Granville's ashen face clearly showed the terror the word carried with it. "But how is that possible? She seemed quite recovered from her chill."

"I fear she was not so fully recovered as she led us to believe."

Granville turned his back to the Duchess and, his arms braced against the mantlepiece, lowered his head, "It's my fault. I was with her when it happened. . . . I should have prevented it. . . . I should have insisted she go to the inn rather than ride home. . . . I should have—"

"Nonsense!" The Duchess cut through his self-incrimination. "That ditch bank is notoriously dangerous. She has hunted that field since she was a child and should have known better. If anyone is at fault, it is I. As her mother I should have been more attentive."

"But you don't know the worst—I had behaved abominably—she had just learned of it and was angry and upset—she was racing to escape me—"

"Now, no more of your fustian." The Duchess spoke with the energy and firmness for which she was famous. "We must place her in the hands of our dear Heavenly Father and trust in His mercy." Then she lay her hand on his and spoke more quietly, "Granville,

140

you are very special to us." And with a soft swish of her cambric skirt she was gone and he was alone.

Alone with his self-accusations. It was easy enough for the Duchess to tell him not to blame himself, but it was quite impossible for him to follow her instructions. Would God punish him for his transgressions by taking away the dearest thing in his life? He resumed his pacing, but after one turn around the room, he stopped again before the fireplace. Moments of agonized turmoil passed, then he struck his fist against the cold, hard marble. *All right, God. Let Georgiana recover and I'll make myself worthy of Your grace.*

He stood there for some time sunk in a brown study until the entrance of his tutor obliged him to look up. "Hullo, Peacock," his voice was grim.

"I have just come from an interview with your father."

"The devil," Granville muttered.

"Oh, he's not *that* bad."

"Confounded time for you to develop a sense of humor," Granville growled. "What did my father want of you?"

"He wanted to know my duties to the university—regarding my position as a tutor."

"And you told him—?"

"I informed his lordship that the requirement for your degree was that you explain the ground of your claim to a degree by a writing to which I subscribe and then send to the Master of Trinity. I explained that in the obligatory paper you will set out your pedigree in full, and I am required to shoulder the responsibility of its accuracy."

"Senseless procedure, conferring academic degrees because of who one's father is—with no requirement of earning it. And was he satisfied with your answer?"

Peacock raised his thin eyebrows, "How could he be otherwise? The answer was quite precise."

"But did he quiz you on my attendance at chapel and lectures, upon my reading habits and—er, pastimes?"

"I told him there were no requirements for you to attend to a daily schedule and that you did more reading than most of your rank. I have no personal knowledge of your other activities."

"Quite so. And he informed you, I have no doubt, that my brother, who is naturally of higher rank than I, applied himself so studiously as to obtain a double first at Oxford. And that while

141

serving in Parliament, he continues his literary and scientific pursuits as well as being on his way to becoming an accomplished French and Italian scholar. And that this paragon has married the daughter of the first Marquess of Bute, a lady of great beauty and character."

Peacock paused, apparently considering how to choose his words wisely. "He mentioned that Lord Sandon is spending the holidays in Switzerland with the Marquess' family."

"Don't spare my feelings, 'Cock. I can well imagine the homily he treated you to. Don't mistake me. Sandon is a fine fellow, much deserving our father's approbation. I like him myself, in spite of having had him thrown at my head since I was in short pants. I just can't live up to his pattern card."

"No need you should, you know."

Granville snorted, "Tell that to my honorable father!"

"You'd best tell him yourself. He said I was to send you to him."

Granville strode through the Red Room and entered the East Room which the Duke used as his private study. The room was so roundly hung with family portraits that Granville felt as if he were on public trial; but he stifled the thought, knowing that a public trial could be far preferable to a private interview with Lord Harrowby.

"I wish to inform you first, Granville, that I have discharged your debt to Lord Calthorpe."

"Confound it, Father! I pay my own debts!"

"Not when they are contracted with my friends under dishonorable circumstances. Sit down, Granville."

In an attempt to conciliate his father, Granville sat. "I wish you to understand, Father, that the circumstances were the height of folly, of which I am profoundly ashamed, but they were not dishonorable."

"Indeed. It strikes me that you have a remarkable sense of honor. To spend the night in the company of what is generally known, I believe, as a Bird of Paradise is sufficiently debased in itself, but then not to be able to settle your account. . . . "

"That is not how it was, Father. But if you wish to take Lord Calthorpe's word over mine, there is nothing I can say to it. I shall send you a draught to repay your outlay on my behalf.'

"That will not be necessary. We shall consider the matter closed between us. What concerns me far more is the behavior of which this is only an example. How a son of mine—a *Ryder*—could be such a wastrel, so prodigal of the talents with which the Lord has endowed him . . . "

"Are you quite sure He has endowed me with any, Father?"

"Nonsense, Granville. All that is required is to cease these coltish indulgences and set yourself a worthwhile course."

Here was more than Granville had hoped for in this interview: a chance to at least mollify, if not actually satisfy, his father. "I have, Father. I am determined to serve in Parliament."

But this announcement did not draw the hoped for response from the Earl. "Poppycock! You young cub, do you propose to prepare yourself to serve God and country in that high position by playing at cards, drinking to excess, and attending horseraces with fashionable impures?"

Granville stiffened, his hand tightening on the arm of his chair so that his knuckles whitened. For a moment his eyes blazed; then, with barely controlled effort, he lowered his gaze and unclenched his fingers. "You quite mistake the matter, Sir."

Lord Harrowby rubbed his forehead with the knuckles of his left hand, closing his eyes briefly. "I spoke too harshly. It is a failing of mine."

Shocked at what almost amounted to an apology, Granville remained silent as his father massaged his head again.

"If you think to fill Sandon's shoes, you must depress your animal spirits, attend to your studies—no matter how little the University requires of you, cease your indulgence in worldly amusements, and fraternize with friends of higher mind."

Granville jumped to his feet, barely able to keep his clenched fists stiffly at his side. "I have no desire to fill Sandon's shoes. It is my own I wish to fill."

"I can see that I have angered you, and that was not my intention. But there is one more matter I must speak to you on—of more import than all others. I would be unfit to call myself a father if I did not adjure you to look to your soul. If you are thinking of being worthy of public service, as indeed I hope you are, I should remind you of what Wilberforce has said, 'Submission to Christ is a man's most important political as well as religious decision.' "

"Thank you, Father. I am not likely to forget it." Still white around the mouth, Granville bowed and left the room.

His tutor was waiting in the library. "How soon can you be

packed, Peacock? I would like to leave within the hour."

In less than sixty minutes, after giving a brief but unfeigned expression of appreciation to his hostess, penning a short farewell to Georgiana, and taking affectionate leave of his mother, Granville tossed his luggage into his phaeton and sprung his pair in the direction of the gatehouse. Only once did he pause, to look up at Georgiana's rooms where the half-lowered curtains looked back at him ominously.

He clutched the reins, recalling the times in recent days when he longed to take Georgiana into his arms and tell her all he felt. Even now, he yearned to turn his team and go to her. And yet he knew he must restrain himself. He had no assurance that her feelings toward him exceeded the cousinly. And even if he could be sure she would welcome such overtures from him, he wasn't ready to receive her affection. Until he could be assured of God's acceptance, he could seek no other.

Behind her half-curtained windows, Georgiana sat propped up in bed, still holding Granville's farewell note, and looking out the window at the driver below, wishing she could read his thoughts. She followed him down the lane with her eyes; then, as he turned through the gate, she followed him with her heart. She loved him so much—if he could just quit struggling.

Now it was time for her to apply some of that faith her mother said had always come to her so naturally. Apply it for herself, for Gran, and—hardest of all—for them.

Yes, Lord, I do believe that Thou art above all; that Thou wilt make everything turn out right. Only help me to do what gratifies Thee. Please.

· *15* ·

THE SKIFF OF SNOW on the frozen quad of Trinity college and the barren branches of the trees on the backs matched Granville's icy determination as he crossed the path to attend his maths lecture. The fact that a solid classical education had produced England's greatest lawyers spurred him on. He had declared himself to his father and had bargained with God for Georgiana's health—two circumstances that precluded any possibility of his going back to his former, easy lifestyle, no matter how daunting the task ahead of him.

"Gran!" Freddie Perkins' jovial voice rang on the frosty air. "Missed you at Combi. Strange notion you've taken—all this studying. Club at Merry's tonight."

The thought was tempting. Granville hesitated, "Sorry. Need to read."

"Peacock on his high ropes again? Shouldn't let him bear-lead you, Gran."

"No, it's not my crammie. I—er, promised someone else."

"Rich aunt threatened to cut the purse strings?"

Granville shook his head. "You're out there, Freddie, but I can't explain now." He strode on with the chill wind whipping his black academical about his knees, leaving Freddie looking after him much perplexed. Several weeks into term now and he had not missed a lecture nor a chapel service. Nor had he found peace or contentment in his new regimen.

So why not just one night with his friends? Surely God didn't require that he become a hermit—a recluse with no friends or pleasures? It often occurred to him lately that perhaps the fault was not with himself but with God—the divine requirements were simply unreasonable. Depressing thought, because logic dictated that if unreasonable, then unreachable.

But later that night, when he finally surrendered to Freddie's urgings and went to Merry's, he found that the scene, so like that of the numerous nights he had spent in the preceding terms, offered little satisfaction. "What you need, Gran, is more port. Loosen you up. Relax you," Freddie said.

"Gloucestershire must be excessively cold country, Granville. You haven't thawed out since you came back from hols." Merry sloshed a bit over the brim as he refilled Granville's glass.

"Want to play for pound points?" Lord Hervey called them back to the whist game.

Badly dipped from unlucky punting, as the cards never did fall out for him, and with an aching head from the unaccustomed amount of strong port he had consumed, Granville sat in morose depression in chapel the next morning. The fact that the sermon was to be preached by his old acquaintance, Charles Simeon, was Granville's only inducement for making the effort to stay awake. Furthermore, Simeon's announced title, "Despondency Reproved," had a certain autobiographical appeal to Granville.

"Nothing is more common for men than to cast reflection upon God when the fault is wholly in themselves. The ungodly world, when urged to devote themselves to God, will allege that those commands are themselves unreasonable because it is not in their power to obey them. Thus they cast the blame not on themselves, for the inveteracy of their evil habits and the alienation of their hearts from God, but upon God Himself, as requiring too much at their hands."

Granville sat forward. Not twenty-four hours ago those very thoughts had entered his mind.

"We withdraw from a belief in God for fear that our sins will be exposed. Doubt becomes the defense of a guilty, nontrusting soul."

Yes, Granville thought, *that is what I have been doing—doubting God's willingness or ability to perform His good pleasure. I don't trust in myself or my friends, or God.* Did Simeon have an answer? But then Granville's shoulders slumped. If the answer was that he must work harder, he was beaten already. It was impossible. He could toe the line no closer than he had the past weeks. As if the speaker had read his mind, Simeon continued:

"There is no condition that can justify a despondent inactivity. The Word of God is full of exceeding great and precious promises, which shall all be fulfilled in their season to those who rely upon God. These we should contemplate; we should treasure them up in our minds; we should plead them before God in prayer; we should expect abundantly the fulfillment of them. However long or dark our night may be, we should look with confidence for the returning light of day. We should know that the goings-forth of Jehovah for the Salvation of His people are prepared as the morning, and that He will appear at the appointed hour."

Granville listened solemnly, neither rejecting the words nor accepting them without thought, but taking them to his heart for consideration.

Simeon reached out to his listeners, then folded his hands as for prayer, a characteristic gesture of his.

"However frequently vanquished by our spiritual foes, we should return to the charge, 'Strong in the Lord, and in the power of His might.' We should never for a moment suffer the thought of our weakness to discourage us. We should rather make it a reason for exertion in the full confidence that, 'When we are weak we are strong,' and that God will perfect His strength in our weakness. 'It is God that worketh in you both to will and to do His good pleasure.'

"We should expect everything from God, as if there were no need of personal exertion and then go forth to do His will in His strength."

His mind on the speaker's words, Granville was leaving the chapel when Simeon approached him. "I have received a letter from your father and my friend, the Earl of Harrowby. He is much concerned for you."

"A letter from my father, Sir?" Granville was astounded. With all the activities of a newly convened Parliament and the pressures of his office as Lord President of the Council, Lord Harrowby had taken time to write to Charles Simeon concerning his younger son?

"Yes, arrived not above five days ago. I have been hoping to see you. Please call on me in my rooms at any time if I may be of service."

The men bowed to each other and Granville returned to his rooms, determined to struggle on in his resolve. But now he had a new impetus to fire his resolution. As he looked at the small hearing aid on the table beside his books, Granville smiled. Two times in as many months his father had shown thought and caring for him. Was it possible that he could have misunderstood his father's feelings in the past?

Putting the question aside for more pressing concerns, Granville called to Creighton to bring coffee and another log for the fire and then settled down to read.

But the Latin ode was quickly dropped when the coffee Creighton brought was accompanied by the post—a letter franked by the Duke of Beaufort, but unmistakably written in his daughter's hand:

January

My Dear Cousin:

 This is only the second time that I have taken up my pen and I am sure I cannot make a better use of it than in thanking you for your many kind inquiries about me and in assuring you I have now no remains of pain or illness left and am eating and exercising at such a rate that I astonish our little family circle who did not expect such a rapid improvement.

 The hard frost we have had lately has delighted my papa, as it enabled him to have his ice house filled. I was allowed a little airing in the carriage and went to the bottom of the park to see the ice house filling and thought it very curious. It contains fifteen feet deep of ice and requires some time and trouble to beat all that quantity into small pieces. The ice house called to mind our riding around it when first you returned from the sea. May I flatter myself that you remember it too?

 Our Worcester has refused to return to London and is quite sunk in the mopes because he is certain that Mr. Culling-Smith is trying to keep Emily away from him. There is great concern over the question of whether an attachment between them would be within the proscribed degree of affinity. Poor Henry, I am persuaded that he is quite in love with the lady and am certain they should suit. If only it can be brought about. Henry has applied to his friend Lord Lauderdale for advice. This must be a very trying time for Emily too, as my Aunt Harriet saw her in London and said her appearance was most touching—she looked careworn and her eyes sad.

But enough of my tittletattle. My mama desires my pen to send you a few lines herself, so I shall yield.

Adieu, dear Gran. I could willingly chatter a few pages more with you, but my foolish head will not let me.

I am Yrs ever,
GS

Granville sat perfectly still and read the letter through again, his impassive face giving no clue to the tumult the words stirred inside him: The immeasurable relief he felt at Georgiana's own account of her recovery fought for supremacy of feeling over his unbounded joy at the tenderness hinted in her closing. It was enough to give him hope. He could ask for nothing more.

After his second reading he turned the letter sideways and read the brief note penned by the Duchess:

Dear Granville,

After the very deep concern you expressed for our dear Georgiana's health, I think myself indebted to scribble a few lines to tell you that nothing can equal my joy at seeing her look so well. Really, miracles are growing common again.

C.S.S.

The Duchess' light words brought Granville bolt upright. If there had been any question of his going back on his resolve, now there could be none. He had offered God his service in return for Georgiana's recovery. He now had a debt of honor to fulfill. He regretted more than ever his lapse of the night before, but it would not happen again.

And it did not. No one could have been happier with the Hon. G. Ryder's academic excellence than Mr. Peacock, who suddenly found himself that most fortunate of crammies—tutor to a nobleman who chose to study.

And sharing that joy were Granville's spiritual supporters, and fellow stairmates, Andrew Anderson and John Henry Rennard, who gave satisfied smiles and never failed to give thanks that their prayers had been answered each time they saw Granville sitting stiffly upright in chapel.

But if his reformed lifestyle brought joy to his associates, it brought none to Granville. He thought often of his greatest treasure, Georgiana's Christmas prayer for him, and often unfolded and reread it, not because he didn't remember the words, but because seeing them in her handwriting so vividly brought back the moment she gave it to him:

A Christmas prayer I wish for you,
Of peace and joy the whole year through;
Of laughter, love, and much content,
That all may be from Heaven sent.

The memory of Georgiana warmed him, but the words mocked him. Peace, joy, laughter, love, contentment—all were conspiciously missing in the cold, dark barrenness of his rigid days.

And counterbalancing, sometimes even blotting out, the endearing image of his beloved, was the vision of his scowling father, impatient over his lack of progress. The vision bore even more weight now that the Earl had written to Charles Simeon. As Lord Harrowby loomed before him in memory, Granville recalled the words of the clergyman inviting him to visit. Yes, perhaps he would do that someday. But for now he must read until time for Hall.

And the daily grind continued. The snow melted from the quad, to be replaced by a wind that drove the sleeting rain mercilessly. If Granville had not felt that his obligation to God was one no gentleman could turn his back on, he would have abandoned it many times over. After all, one had as well be miserable from an excess of revelry as from an excess of piety.

On the last Friday of February, Anderson was awaiting Granville's exit from Hall to inquire if he was going to the conversation party that night. Granville started to decline, but then was struck with a desire to see the kindly counselor who exuded such joy with his religion. "Crammie's coming over tonight, but tell Mr. Simeon I shall accept his invitation to call on him. Tomorrow afternoon, if it's convenient for him."

Simeon returned a note with Andy, saying that he would be most delighted to receive Mr. Ryder the following afternoon any time between two and three o'clock.

And so, at two-fifteen the next day, Granville donned his fur-lined Polish coat, wrapped a muffler around his neck up to his nose, and made his way down King's Parade to the Gibbs Building and up the four flights of stairs to the door on the right.

"Ah, my young Friend, how I have longed for a visit with you. Come, sit by the fire," Simeon greeted him.

The servant poured tea from Simeon's much-used black Wedgwood teapot, then departed. And a few moments later, Granville was disclosing his story to his venerable host who seemed to become increasingly disturbed by the moment. "A bargain with God! *Earn* grace? Sir, that is an oxymoron, a contradiction of terms, a thing impossible. . . . A debt of honor, you say? Consider it paid! Eighteen hundred years ago by Christ upon the cross—paid in full. Yours is but to be grateful and say, 'Thank You, Lord. I accept.' "

Granville, who had expected a strict lecture on the things he must do and refrain from doing if he hoped to reach his goal, sat speechless before his host.

"I see that my words confound you. But only consider how great a sinner each of us is, how bent to worldliness and selfishness. Is it conceivable that any of us should make ourselves righteous? No, no. See here, let me show you the words of another." He turned to a low bookshelf and drew out a small leather volume that Granville recognized instantly as *Acquaintances With God*, a twin of the one he had read in the library last fall; but this one, he saw, was inscribed and underlined in Simeon's own hand. Opening it to a page past the middle, Simeon said, "Ah, here is the part I find so heartwarming. Allow me to read it out to you."

"If we grow acquainted with God, we make sure of a constant, loving Friend, as able as willing to direct and succour us in every difficulty of life.

"He admits, nay, invites the worst of men to His fellowship, even publicans and sinners of the greatest size. This is a vast encouragement to all, to any, even to the vilest, to seek after Him. However miserable they have made themselves in this world, or unworthy of a better, yet He calls and encourages them, though they so long despised and provoked Him. Marvelous Condescension! Boundless Love and Compassion! Press on into His presence."

Simeon closed the volume and wiped his brow which was shining from the fervor with which he had read the final passage.

"If you have not found joy in your heavenly friendship, you have not found your heavenly Friend, my Son.

"If you, like Bunyan's Mr. Fearing, are always afraid you shall come short of whither you desire to go, if you carry a slough of despond in your mind, you need to hear the words of the Master, 'Come in, for thou art blessed.'

"You feel you are not good enough to approach a Holy God? You are a sinner—how can you approach a Holy God who hates sin and punishes sinners? you ask.

"By coming before Him as a sinner—coming to Jesus Christ who is intent on loving sinners, who offers you a love which asks no questions about worthiness.

"*Your* answer was to become a perfect person by your own will. *God's* answer is Jesus Christ who *is* perfect and shares His robe of righteousness with us—to drape our shoulders with His garment of grace so that we can walk into the presence of God. We are then treated like a perfect person even though we aren't, for the righteousness of Christ is credited to us. We are accepted as members of God's family.

"Our hope is not perfection, but reconciliation."

Granville's mind was so taken with these revolutionary statements that he had no reply. The preacher was on his feet. "But come back, come back any time. I flatter myself to be counted among your earthly friends. Do not stay away long." When Granville left the Gibbs building, the wind still whipped across the courtyard, blowing damp and chill from the river. But in a protected, sunny corner, he saw that a bright yellow crocus was blooming.

At Badminton, where Georgiana sat at her writing desk, she could look out the window toward the park and see masses of yellow and purple crocus. She held her pen above the inkwell, daydreaming of riding in the park with Gran. Then her thoughts moved on to their riding together at the hunt and to her own foolishness which led to her accident and illness.

She smiled as she recalled his careful concern for her. Even if sometimes accompanied by curt words to compel her to obey, his actions were all gentleness as he helped her with her waterlogged clothing and wrapped her in his own coat. Such infinite kindness was born of qualities one could build a lifetime together on—no matter what the years would hold. She smiled and amended her thought: that is, *two* could build a lifetime on. She wanted nothing more than to go through life the recipient of Granville's courtesy and love.

With another smile, she dipped her pen.

By the following week, when Georgiana's letter arrived, the Backs were also carpeted with the early yellow and lavender flowers. But Granville, cloistered in his room inside Great Court, had not seen them yet. And if Creighton had not taken it upon himself to draw back the dark red moreen curtains when he brought in the post, Granville would have read his cousin's letter with the aid of only a candle, rather than accompanied by the soft spring sun touching the windowsill.

                                                        February
Dear Coz,

My mama desires me to begin by making her apology for not writing to you, and to assure you that she had promised herself to write to you today to give you a long account of all our transactions. I assured her, however, that I would be most happy to undertake to do that for her; and although I know you will be downcast to find that you must read a missive from my pen rather than hers, I beg you to bear it in the best of heart.

First, let me take the pleasure of informing you that I have had the happiness of riding twice in the past week and have felt not the least bit the worse for it. Further, I have aired in the carriage several times on purpose to accustom myself to the motion, as a kind of preparation for our great removal to London, although I do not know when we shall set out. I should like to inquire if we shall have the pleasure of seeing you there when we arrive; but as I am unsure of the date of our arrival, the question would not signify. But your father assures Papa that Mr. Wilberforce will present a measure in Parliament in March and Papa is determined to be there for the occasion before we journey to Wales for Easter. Such rackety gadabouts you must think us!

What charming delightful weather we have had for these few days past, such bright sunshine with a pleasant bracing air; we have all enjoyed it to the utmost degree. I have basked on the south side of the house with as much pleasure as if I were a newborn butterfly laid on the sweetest flowers, but the utmost extent of my excursions has been four times back and forth along the length of the house. Although I am persuaded I am capable of doing far more, Aggie *will* cosset me.

Then yesterday the rains returned to dash all our spirits. The infants were so moped at being required to stay indoors after their days of sunnier frolics that I joined them in the Entrance Hall to watch them play shuttlecocks and battledores. We increased the skill required for the game by stringing a rope across from the fireplace to the door for the shuttlecocks to fly over. Our games-mad friend John Baldwin was visiting us from Oxford, and he wrote down all our rules and even directed the servants to measure the hall for what he called "the precise size of the court." We were all so delighted with our sport that we have decided to name it Badminton.

I long to see you again—do not think me a sad baggage for saying so.

Yr ever affectionate Cousin,
Georgiana Somerset

The teasing tone of his cousin's charming letter delighted and stung Granville at the same time. His feelings for her were deep and confused. They shared so many childhood memories, so many family experiences—but the memories he wanted to make with her, the experiences he now wanted to share, were of an entirely different variety.

An insistent knocking at the oak prevented Granville from re-reading the letter for the present, but he was not displeased to see Freddie. "Windmills in your head, must have. Only a gudgeon would stay indoors on a day like this."

Granville smiled, "Just give me time to pull on my boots, Freddie. What do you say to a walk to the three-mile stone? I have heard it is much in want of care."

"You foxed? Ain't seen you smile this term. Tell you what, Gran, you worry too much. Ain't healthy. Make an old woman of you. Becoming prim and prosey, that's what."

"No. You slander me, Freddie." Granville led the way out the door. "I've had a lot on my mind lately, that's all. And no, I'm not foxed; I haven't had anything stronger than coffee."

But that night, in spite of the salubrious effect of the walk and

154

Freddie's company on his spirits, Granville found himself much out of sorts at the conclusion of a session of Bible reading in Rennard's rooms. "You need to apply yourself more rigorously, Ryder," the elder man said. "Have you yet undertaken a schedule of visiting the gaol or the sick?"

Granville blanched at the suggestion, but remained quiet.

"I myself am going to the Spinning House and to Addenbrooke's Hospital tomorrow morning. Shall you accompany me?"

"I'll let you know." Granville took his leave quickly.

Was Simeon right? Or was Rennard right? Their approach to "true religion" seemed miles apart. Things had improved somewhat since Granville's visit to Simeon. If he hadn't exactly found peace and joy, there had been pleasure——pleasure in Georgiana's letter and in Freddie's company. But the promised joy and pleasure in heavenly conversation still eluded him.

He shivered at the thought of undertaking a round of visits with Rennard. He would rather trust Simeon's counsel. . . .

Granville hesitated to knock on the preacher's door at such an early hour, and yet he had been awake since before dawn and felt he could wait no longer. Simeon opened the door himself and Granville breathed a sigh of relief to see that his host was dressed and not averse to receiving an early morning caller. "Come in, come in. You have arrived at precisely the appointed hour—in the fulness of time, eh? It is my custom to spend some time in meditation each morning upon the roof and you must accompany me."

Somewhat shocked at so singular an invitation, Granville followed the portly man through his sitting room, up a flight of stairs, through the servant's room containing the small rose window which ornamented the central pediment in the roofline, then on up a tiny, winding staircase and out a small window which, indeed, opened onto the roof of the Gibbs Building.

Although only a breeze in the courtyard, the wind here was strong, bringing with it sounds of the splashing fountain and light strains of organ music from the chapel. The sun was bright and clear in the blue sky. Behind them the chimney-lined roof rose steeply, and two feet in front of them the stone balustrade ran along the edge of the building. Simeon opened a small hatch and pulled out two folding stools.

"I always feel this is as close to heaven as I shall get in this life."

Simeon gazed upward at the uncluttered expanse between them and the firmament.

Finding the noises being blown up to them a little distracting, Granville took his reverberator from his pocket and held it to his ear. "Ah," Simeon cried, "I am delighted to see you are using my little deaf aid. Do you find it helpful?"

Granville assured him he did.

"Yes, I was certain you would. Nice that you carry it in the palm of your hand without its being seen, eh? I do enjoy my little experiments. I have very nearly perfected a cure for smoking fireplaces, also. Thought I had done it, but applied the process at a friend's house the other day, and I blush to admit that the room was worse after my efforts than before." Simeon shook his head and clucked his tongue.

Granville smiled at his friend's account, and then Simeon changed the subject. "But what of your spiritual journey, my Son?"

Granville gave a rueful smile, "I'm afraid I've come to you as sanctuary from being pressed into visiting the sick and imprisoned."

Simeon nodded, a twinkle in his bright eyes, "Ah, yes. Noble work for those called to it. But perhaps not your calling?"

Granville smiled his agreement.

"Piety, you will discover, is not always accompanied by discretion, and you may be sometimes urged to things which, though desirable in themselves, are not expedient. And people may constrain you to seek your comfort in the testimony of your own conscience rather than in the approbation of God."

"My friends assure me my soul-searching is superfluous."

Simeon nodded. "Indeed. You see yourself guilty of sins which preclude hope of forgiveness. Your friends have endeavored to show you that you judge yourself too harshly. Be glad they have erred, for if they had succeeded, they would have given you a peace founded on your own worthiness, a peace that would last no longer than the next temptation."

Granville's penitent expression gave silent witness to the truth of the speaker's words.

"Since they have not succeeded, they have only confirmed you in your views. I say to you the very reverse. Your views of yourself and your own sinfulness, though they may be erroneous, are not one atom too strong. Your sinfulness far exceeds all that you have

156

stated, or have any conception of."

At these alarming words, to which Granville readily subscribed, he dropped his head in his hands.

"Your heart is 'deceitful above all things, and desperately wicked: who can know it?' " Simeon quoted in the tones of an Old Testament prophet. Then his face was transformed with a smile of true radiance. "But I have an effectual remedy for them all, the blood of Jesus Christ which cleanses from *all* sin. I grant that you are lost and utterly undone. So are all men, some for gross sins, some for impenitence, some for other faults. You are lost for the very sins you mention: hardness of heart, indifference, over-indulgence. . . .

"Do this, then. Take a book as large as any that is in the Bank of England. Put down all the sins of which either conscience or a morbid imagination can accuse you. Fear not to add to their number all that Satan himself can suggest.

"And this I will do. I will put on the creditor side, 'The unsearchable riches of Christ, and will leave you to draw the balance."

His head still down, his words bearly audible, Granville said, "It is so beautiful, so glorious. But I am not worthy—"

"Worthy!" Simeon struck the balustrade with his open hand. "Haven't you heard a word I've said? Of course, you're not worthy! None of us is. But 'Worthy is the Lamb that was slain, and hath redeemed us to God by His blood.' " The words, spoken with vibrance of faith, were accompanied by strains from the chapel organ.

"In the light of God's love, the concept of worthiness loses its significance—the whole idea becomes almost laughable—since no one could ever, by himself, be worthy to be loved by such Love. Until this understanding is brought to light by Divine mercy, man is imprisoned in hopelessness.

"The root of Christian love is not the will to love, but the faith that one is loved—the faith that one is loved by God."

Granville raised his head. Now he understood, and it was wonderful. "It was there all along, wasn't it? But I didn't see it—my eyes were too much on my weakness and unworthiness to see His strength and sufficiency."

"Your error was in keeping control of your own life—in not turning it, with all its problems, over to God. Thereby, peace with God and a sense of self-worth evaded you. The level of the

Lordship of Christ in a life can be measured by the level of self-worth, because it is He who gives it to us; all else is vanity."

"I see it now. I must have heard similar words dozens of times—certainly every time I heard you preach, and from my Uncle Henry, why, even my father—" At those words he stopped. In his mind, his father was before him, exasperated at the son's failings, stifling his newfound joy.

Simeon nodded, "Yes, I believe I see what I suspected all along, but I hestitated to advise a son concerning a father of such distinction. . . . "

"Please go on, Sir."

"Estrangement from your earthly father has kept you from accepting reconciliation with your Heavenly Father. Because you felt your father judged you harshly, you believed God also judged you harshly. Because of your lifelong need to earn esteem before the Earl, you tried to earn esteem before Christ. Salvation, like your advancement in the Navy and your academic degree, is conferred on you because of who your father is—but in this case, it is the person of your Heavenly Father."

"Yes. I see that now."

"Through our relations to the Heavenly Father, our humility is assured even while our honor is established. If your worth as a person is rooted in your relationship as a son of the Almighty, then a high sense of self-worth based on the fatherhood of God gives you the deep foundation for a faith that can build hope for human dignity."

Granville nodded as his mind kept pace with Simeon's words. Only reconciliation with his Heavenly Father could teach him his worth—and now he was free to seek reconciliation with his earthly father. This new comprehension and acceptance of God's grace was wonderful, but he could not relax in the freedom of his newfound insight. He must be reconciled to his earthly father before experiencing fulness of joy in his reconciliation to his Heavenly Father. But not as a matter of salvation. Now he understood the difference.

And he understood, as Simeon explained to him, "We are not to imagine salvation is either the reward of our merits or the effect of our unassisted exertion. We do not save ourselves by our hard work or by our good deeds. Nevertheless, we have a work to do, a work of infinite importance, in the performing of which we are not mere machines but voluntary agents."

Now he was free—free of the burden of feeling rejected by his father and rejecting his father in return; free of having to measure every action by his father's yardstick. Free to set his own goals. His first task would be to bridge the gap between his father and himself.

With a rush of excitement, Granville realized that all the energy he had formerly put into worry and guilt he could now put into creative energy to reach his goals—because he truly wanted to reach them, not because they were expected of him or because he needed to prove something.

And best of all, he could love and serve God freely. Now that the barriers he had erected in the names of remorse and unworthiness had crumbled, he could be the man he had always wanted to be.

But before Granville saw his father again, there was another reconciliation that needed to take place. Granville considered writing to his brother who was now in London, recently returned from vacationing on the Continent, to resume his Parliamentary duties. But each attempted letter sounded either stilted or maudlin. So Granville gave up in disgust, determining to wait until he should see Sandon in person.

That opportunity came far sooner than he could have imagined, as two days later, Granville returned from a lecture to find his brother awaiting him in his rooms. "Sandon! What a surprise! Been thinking of you." he grasped the Viscount's hand warmly. "What brings you to Cambridge?" Then a look of alarm crossed his face, "Our parents—?"

"No, no. Everyone's fine. Nothing like that. Fact is, might as well come straight to the point—I'm a bit dipped; thought you might be able to help."

Granville was flabbergasted. *Sandon* needed help? *His* help? "What! You in dun territory?" He put his hand to his ear—"Or did I hear you wrong?"

Sandon ran his fingers through hair a shade lighter than Granville's. "No, little Brother, although I could wish you had. Expenses ran higher on the Continent than I expected. Couldn't expect Frances to go to Paris without ordering new gowns—not that she's really extravagant—but there it is. I didn't like to appeal to our father."

"No! I should think not. How much do you need? Glad to let you have what I can." Granville was thankful he had stayed away from card tables and racetracks recently and so was not faced with any shortages himself. He turned to his desk and wrote a draft on his bank.

"Dashed glad to see you," Granville said, when the monetary matter had been settled. "Been trying to write, but some things look so awkward on paper."

"Write to me? I should be very glad to receive a letter from you, but is something amiss?"

"Truth is, I need to beg your pardon—always resented you. It really won't do—can't have such feelings between brothers—" It came out in jerks, but it was said.

Sandon's mouth fell open in surprise. "What! You astound me! No need to beg my pardon—it's I who should beg yours. Can't fathom why you should have resented me, since the shoe was rather on the other foot." And he paused to give a forced laugh. 'Afraid I couldn't accept the fact that my little brother was better looking and that Father preferred you."

Now it was Granville's turn to gasp in amazement, "What a hoax!"

"It's the truth. Don't wonder that he never let you know, but it was always, 'Granville this' and 'Granville that'—so proud of your accomplishments in the Navy—always said you were the best of the lot. But I'll admit it provided me a healthy spur to work harder."

Granville opened his mouth to reply, but no words would come out—only the laughter that was building inside him. The two brothers clasped hands, beat one another upon the back, and laughed until tears ran down their faces.

At Granville's order, Creighton brought coffee and cold meats. After a further hour spent sharing childhood memories and plans for the future, Sandon departed for London, assuring Granville he would repay him when they met again in London, but Granville knew that his brother could never give him more than the lightness of heart he felt.

· 16 ·

Leaving Cambridge and the end of Hilary term behind him, Granville joined his family in London where his first step in reaching his new goals was to present himself in chambers at Lincoln's Inn, an exclusive society through which he would gain admission to the practice of law. Following a closed meeting by that body, his sponsor was able to inform him that he had been elected to membership. He could now pursue his legal training along with his academic education.

Elation accompanied his success on this first step toward his career goal and served as an impetus to attempt that hardest-of-all step toward bridging the gap between himself and his father. But opportunity for taking that stride was difficult to find.

Granville had attempted only once to obtain an interview with the Earl. But as Parliament was sitting late almost every night and it was after midnight when Lord Harrowby returned, clearly exhibiting the strain of great weariness and an abominably aching head, Granville merely informed his father of his acceptance at the Inn of Court and retired.

The next morning, the inhabitants of Harrowby House in Grosvenor Square received news that the Duke of Beaufort and his family were in residence across the Square and would be among the party attending the Parlimentary debate that day. So it was that the first time Granville saw Georgiana since Christmas was in the long, tone-vaulted St. Stephen's Chapel of Westminster Palace as they made their way into one of the pillar-supported galleries added by Christoper Wren to provide additional seating in the narrow room.

161

Hearing a peal of familiar laughter behind him, Granville turned and offered his hand to help Georgiana accomplish the last of the steep stairs.

In her crepe hat banded in lilac satin folds with blond curls peeking from under the brim, and her slim person clad in a lilac redingote of *gros de Naples* trimmed with braided satin, Georgiana was a sight to turn every head in the room. But she almost demurely withdrew her hand from Granville and passed on into the gallery to allow him to hand Charlotte and their mama into the balcony. And so she passed before him with no more than an exchange of murmured greetings and he took his seat next to Charlotte, the curly ostrich feathers on her wide-brimmed yellow straw hat with grayish-green ribbons blocking Georgiana from his view.

But then every attention was focused on the event unfolding on the floor below. Mr. Secretary Canning rose to address the House of Commons on the substitute measure that Canning's forces hoped would delay Wilberforce's Amelioration Bill for bettering the condition of the slave population in the West Indies. There was much personal drama in the fact that it was Canning who led the forces in favor of the measure so opposed by Wilberforce and those working ultimately for abolition. Canning had long been one of Wilberforce's closest personal friends; but recently, in division over the slavery question, he had turned against Wilberforce politically. It was with a great sense of personal loss that Wilberforce had remarked to Lord Harrowby only the day before that he feared George Canning was becoming more their enemy every day.

Granville, listening from the gallery, rejected the Canning arguments that the cause of the slaves could best be served by allowing colonial governments—rather than Parliament—to alleviate slavery. And he winced as the Secretary adjured Parliament not to let their judgment be misled by passions of anger and fear, calculated by Mr. Wilberforce to lead them to less temperate action "through the indulgence by my right honorable friend in the brilliance of his talents, and the exuberance of his fancy. I tell you, my Friends, if we act precipitiously on this, we may kindle a flame that is only to be quenched in blood."

Then it was Wilberforce's turn to reply. Sunlight shone through the jewel tones of the arched stained-glass windows lining the room and warmed the Wren oak paneling and green-cushioned seats of the benches. Everyone in the room seemed to hold their breath as the little giant, who for almost twenty years had borne the title "The Arbiter of England," stood to his feet. There was not a person in the house who did not know that throughout the past winter Wilberforce had suffered severely from chest colds and that overtaxing his strength could easily bring on the much-feared pneumonia. The House leaned forward to hear what might well be Wilberforce's last speech:

"Gentlemen, if I had come into this House for the first time and heard the beautiful and flowing language of my right honorable friend, Mr. Canning, I should no doubt have rejoiced. I would have rejoiced that through my right honorable friend's plan, the blessings he outlines are about to be extended to so large a portion of the human race. But, Gentlemen, I did not just come into this House for the first time, and any feelings I have to rejoice are overborne by the knowledge that the measure passed by this House in the last session has not been carried into effect. In the light of this consideration, I am determined that a much stronger action is needed."

Even from the gallery, Granville could see the piercing blue eyes and the high wrinkling forehead of the man God had called to stand against the entrenched evils of his day, the man who had so lived his conviction that true Christianity must not only save, but also serve, that all England now honored him.

"After the long experience which I have had of colonial assemblies, it would be criminal on my part to deceive either myself or the House with any idle hopes that humane measures will emanate from those local bodies.

"The question we face is of awful magnitude, for it is not the limited interest of a few individuals that we must consider. The question concerns the temporal and eternal happiness of hundreds of thousands of immortal beings like ourselves.

"We stand now on a precipice, and if we do not take great care, we shall find that the more we pause—the less energetic we are in the pursuit of right—the greater is the danger likely to become."

The famous voice, undimmed by age and illness, reached every corner of the room, and the walls of the chamber rang in response, "Hear, hear." Granville, stirred to pledge again his commitment to such service, cried with them.

Wilberforce then called his listeners to consider the harm that should be done if they were to draw back now, after having held out the promise of amelioration a year ago:

163

"Let the House only consider what a terrible thing it would be for men who have long lived in the state of darkness, and just when the bright beams of day begin to break in upon the gloom of their situation, to have the boon suddenly withdrawn, and to be afresh consigned to darkness, to uncertainty—nay, to absolute despair!

"Let every man present appeal to his own feelings for the truth of the position. Does not every one of you know that an evil is much more easily borne before temporary hope has been excited in the breast of the sufferer? If an effort to alleviate the suffering proves unsuccessful, is not your anguish redoubled? Is not your misery rendered nearly insupportable? When hope has been once suffered to beam upon the heart, does it not set the whole man in a fever? And when that hope is destroyed, does not desperation result?"

Granville noted the Earl of Harrowby on the first row and Sandon farther back, both following the speech intently. The thought that, in a few years he too might sit in that august house and work with his father and brother, exhilirated him.

And then, because he was leaning forward, and by the slight turning of his head was now able to see the object of his dearest hopes, the one he wanted by his side when he undertook such service as he was now determined on, Wilberforce's graphic picture of ruined hopes brought forcibly to him the desperation he should experience if his hopes of winning Georgiana were to be dashed from him.

His attention returned to the floor where it seemed that the hopes of the antislavery leaders were to be quenched; for the House voted to postpone further consideration of the measure until another day, simply directing the Chairman to report progress.

And a short time later, Granville was not even able to so much as report progress on his desires, as his invitation to the Somerset ladies to attend a concert with him that evening was rejected.

"I am sorry, Gran, but we are already engaged to make up another party." Georgiana's sweet smile was his only reward.

"And are you engaged for a drive in the park tomorrow morning?"

"I sadly fear, Sir—" Georgiana did her best to look crestfallen, but her eyes twinkled—"that my sister is indeed engaged. Would you be too cast down if I alone were to accept your kind offer?"

"I should contrive to make do with so sadly diminished a company," He bowed over her hand. But the smile left his face as he saw the carriage of Mr. Agar-Ellis waiting for her beyond the gardens of the Palace of Westminster. He knew whose party Georgiana would be attending that night.

The next morning, however, the carriage of Mr. Granville Ryder was graced by the charming presence of Miss Georgiana Somerset who was wearing a blue satin hat with clusters of white silk mignonette, ribbon bowknots, and floating ribbon streamers. Granville's chestnut pair stepped smartly over the golden sand of Rotten Row; the trees overhead showed just an etching of the green leaves they would soon unfurl, and the sunshine sparkled on the blue waters of the Serpentine beyond.

Their progress was slow because the Row was jammed with elegant carriages at that fashionable hour, and conversation was difficult due to the number of acquaintances who needed to be greeted. It seemed that every carriage contained at least one passenger who was a friend or connection of one of their families and it would not do to offer anyone the cut direct.

For a time, however, Granville found it pleasure enough simply being in his lady's company and chatting briefly, "And are you truly recovered, Georgie?"

"In absolutely fine feather, quite the top-of-the-trees, I assure you."

"I cannot tell you how I condemned myself for allowing you to expose yourself to such danger."

"Fustian! How could you possibly be to blame because I was such a cawker as to cram my horse at a jump—as you told me at the time."

He wished to say more, but a carriage driven by Worcester's friend Lord Lauderdale pulled alongside and Georgiana exchanged a few words with the driver. "Is your brother in town?" Lauderdale inquired.

"I believe he arrives tomorrow."

"Fine. Tell him I expect to have some good news for him."

Georgiana sighed. "I do hope so; my poor brother has broken his heart quite long enough over this matter."

Lauderdale's carriage pulled ahead and Georgiana explained to Granville that Worcester had applied to Lauderdale to find a solution that would make it possible for him to marry Emily.

At the end of the Row, Granville turned into the less fashionable and less crowded carriage drive which would take them toward

Nash's newly erected Marble Arch, and he lowered his hands to allow his horses to walk at a more leisurely pace.

Georgiana leaned back against the cushions of the phaeton. "And what of your affairs, Granville? You are scandalously uncommunicative. After the lovely letters I put myself forth to write to you, all I receive are a few scribbled notes. You are fortunate, Sir, that I am of a such sweet and forgiving nature to even talk to you."

He opened his mouth to protest, but his companion, much flown with her flummery, continued, "But then, if you prefer your musty Latin and maths to communicating with me, I shall endeavor to bear up under it."

"Now that is doing it too brown," he protested.

But then she turned suddenly serious. "O Gran, I have heard that you are making remarkable progress at your studies, and Mr. Simeon wrote Mama a most charming letter about your advancement. May I hope that it is not presumptuous in me to think that my Christmas wish for you may be coming true?"

"There was a considerable time when I doubted it, but I'm beginning to think . . . Georgiana . . . " Thoughts of George Agar-Ellis came to him and fear made him pause. Now that he was free before God—now that he could speak—what if he were too late?

Georgiana turned to him with a look of solemn intensity in her clear blue eyes that required him to swallow very hard. But before he could continue his speech, the sound of a rapidly approaching carriage took their attention. Granville inclined his head stiffly and muttered under his breath when he saw that the other driver was no other than Agar-Ellis.

After the prescribed exchange of pleasantries, Granville sincerely wished the driver to move on, but George seemed fully determined to divulge all of the news which brought him out at such a puffed pace. "Have you seen *The Times* this morning? I always peruse it with my morning coffee—my man has strictest orders that it is to be brought to me the moment it arrives. It doesn't do to go about uninformed, you know."

"Then, pray, hasten to inform us, Sir, that we may be redeemed from our ignorant state," Georgiana said with a perfectly straight face.

"The King has finally taken a hand in the bumblebroth over the elevation of that religious enthusiast. . . . Oh, I say, Ryder, I beg your pardon, he's some connection of yours, isn't he? Afraid I

166

wasn't thinking."

"That's quite all right, I'm most interested to hear the latest word of my uncle."

"Yes, well," Mr. Agar-Ellis quickly regained any composure he might have lost, or feigned losing, over his faux pas. "It seems His Majesty has consented, although with quite understandable reluctance—forgive me, Ryder."

"Speak your mind. Take no notice of me," Granville waved the matter away, fervently wishing the speaker in Jericho.

"By your leave, I will then. Mr. Walpole knew him as a young man, and you know, *his* insight was always remarkably reliable, and *he* found Henry Ryder shockingly without parts or knowledge. He declared him to be with no characteristics but a sonorous delivery and an assiduity of backstairs influence."

He turned sharply to Granville as if the thought just struck him, "I say, Ryder, you don't suppose you might just drop a hint, being family and all. This religious enthusiasm really doesn't do. What does a bishop want with being religious? And a friend of that dowdy Hannah More—perhaps he could urge her to temper her pen. . . . "

"You do me too much honor," Granville said tightly. "I am not in a position of so great an influence with my uncle, nor would I presume to remark on his choice of friends any more than he would on mine, although *he* possesses the right to do so without gross impropriety."

"Yes, yes, I quite take your point. Indelicate of me to suggest it. I just thought, though—well, one's family connection can be a bit of an embarrassment. . . . "

"I have never found it so. It has always been my concern that they not be embarrassed in me."

"I daresay. Quite so." And Mr. Agar-Ellis took his leave with a tip of his curly beaver to Lady Georgiana.

"Oh, well done, Granville! I never knew you to such an admirable fencer. You had him at *point non plus*." Georgiana giggled and then asked, "But has the King really consented? That's famous! Everyone will be so happy."

"This was the first I'd heard of it—shockingly ill-informed, you know. Shall we go see if my father's papers have arrived?"

Granville and Georgiana found the family in the breakfast room at Harrowby House. The Countess Susan was presiding over the table in her open, natural love of conversation and delightful society. "Oh, I am so happy for it. If the Church doesn't appoint more men of true religion, a very few years will elapse before the Church will really be in danger. People will grow tired of paying so dearly for so bad an article as they have been used to." As she addressed her husband, she tucked a stray brown curl back into a very fetching lace cap with ribbons just brushing the lace mantel of her printed morning dress.

"Quite right. It's about time King George took the matter in hand. Ridiculous to make such a mull of what should have been handled in a routine manner. Can't abide such dilly-dallying. Ah, Granville, here it is, 'King Confirms Ryder,' " and the Earl held out *The Times* to his son who was helping Georgiana with her chair.

Granville took the paper, "Thank you, Father. We were just told of this in the park."

"Read it out, Gran. What did His Majesty say?" Georgiana turned to the footman at her elbow. "Just some toast and an egg, please."

Granville seated himself next to Georgiana, opened the paper, and read, " 'The King consents, though reluctantly, to the offer being made to the Bishop of Gloucester for his translation to Lichfield and Coventry. The Bishop of Gloucester is no doubt a pious and good man and the King is acquainted with many acts of his life which bespeak it.' "

"And I should like to ask His Highness to his face why his consent was given reluctantly, if he is so well acquainted with my brother-in-law's worth," the Countess said warmly.

"Well, that settles it most satisfactorily," Granville said. "We must congratulate my uncle."

"Yes, indeed. I shall send out cards today to a rout in his honor. A week from Wednesday would be convenient, don't you think, Dear, so that it might be done before Holy Week? This Friday we are to have that Cabinet dinner."

"Whatever you think best."

"Well, it certainly couldn't be any sooner—you know how volatile Jean-Luc is. I wouldn't for the world dream of suggesting a change in kitchen plans until after the Cabinet dinner is over."

"Why do you put up with such a tyrant?" the Earl snapped. "To have one's social schedule dictated by the cook is the outside of enough."

"Hush, Sir. You mustn't let Jean-Luc hear that you have so referred to him—*he* is a chef."

"Hmph, and a pretty price I pay for his fancy title."

"Yes, Dear, but you must allow he does produce the most elegant food. And when one is to entertain the Prime Minister and the entire Cabinet—"

"Yes, quite. By the by, most singular event occurred yesterday. I was riding in the park when a man came up to me and asked, 'Are you one of the ministers?' I replied that I was. 'Are you Lord Castlereagh?' he asked. When I denied the honor, he held out a sealed paper and asked, 'Can you give this letter to him? It conveys information of a dreadful conspiracy.' "

"Oh, my Dear, what did you do?" The Countess held her hand to her throat.

"I took the letter and proceeded on to Carlton House, but thought so little of it that no one bothered opening it until Lord Castlereagh arrived from St. James Square."

"And what was in the letter? Can you disclose it?" his wife asked, while all at the table ceased eating to hear the answer.

But the reply was anticlimatic. "Oh, some confused bumblebroth agitated by malcontents, I daresay. Shouldn't have mentioned it."

"But, as you say, a most singular event. Did you recognize the man who gave you the letter?" the Countess persisted.

"I have a notion I might have. Think it was that fellow who brings the milk around—or someone who looks very like him."

But Granville had another topic he wished to discuss. "What is to become of the Amelioration Bill, Father? Can something be done to bring the parties together?"

The Earl pressed a finger against his temple and moved it in a circular motion. "I'm sure I can't. I'm the worst person in the world to conciliate and do the civil—especially on a matter of such clear-cut right and wrong. Wilberforce has every right to feel sadly betrayed by his old friend Canning. Yet I hope the Bill may pass unamended in a few days' time." The Earl pushed his chair away from the table and stood so rapidly that the footman standing in attendance was unable to draw the chair for him.

"My laudanum drops," he ordered the servant.

"Is it very severe, Dear?" His wife held a glass of water out to the Earl.

"Headaches so as to make me unable to see my paper or guide

my pen. Would to God they were over or I out!" He placed the drops on his tongue, then swallowed the water. "At least this dose Wilberforce recommended gives some relief."

"Are you going to Westminster now, Dear?" the Countess asked. "I wonder if you might just take a note to Sandon for me?"

"Send a servant with it—I haven't time," and Harrowby left the room.

The Countess smiled pensively. "If he had not had a headache, he would have carried my note. My poor dear, what he says about his pacificatory powers is quite true, but he has the highest reputation and his opinion is of immense value. If only he had not taken that fall—he was of much more amiable temper before that."

"Fall?" Granville and Georgiana said together.

"Yes, my Dears. You were both in leading strings then, and he doesn't like to have it talked of, so I dare say you may not know the story. . . ."

The blank looks on their faces gave her their answer.

"He had just become foreign secretary under Pitt and we were so rejoiced at the good he should be able to accomplish. But then he was helping old Lord Eccles down the stairway at the Foreign Office—such dreadfully slick marble there. Lord Eccles lost his footing and your father succeeded in righting him, but tumbled on his head himself.

"I despaired of losing him; he was required to leave office for almost a year. But the prayers of faithful friends and a stay in Bath restored him."

Granville said quietly, "I never knew."

"No, my Dear, I don't suppose you did. It is a melancholy story, isn't it? I'm sure that's why I never recounted it. He doesn't like to have his infirmity made much of, and he always works so hard; but many nights he returns from Westminster half dead with headache and terribly irritable.

"I suppose I should have mentioned it sooner, to help you understand his snappish ways. When he is curt with the younger children, I often recall how it was when you were little. But I hope you know your father has always loved you dearly and has been very proud of you. If he has been overly harsh, it is only his extreme concern for your welfare, and his anxiety for your success."

"Yes, Mother. I have only recently come to realize. . . . I do know he cares."

"Your father's greatest guilt is likely to be that he cares too much—and then expresses his concern sharply. But his heart is all goodness.

"And now I must go see Jean-Luc about the fish for the Cabinet dinner." She raised her hand in signal for the footman to hold her chair. "Your father is quite right, you know. Jean-Luc is frightfully overpaid, but what am I to do? I cannot have it said that the Countess of Harrowby keeps a poor table. How would it look if the Cabinet refused my invitation to dine?"

Granville stood till his mother left the room, then resumed his seat. Georgiana requested a fresh cup of coffee, as hers had grown quite cold while listening to the Countess, and Granville sat quietly, considering his mother's disclosures. It certainly made it easier to understand his father—feeling headachy and out of sorts, and having constantly to battle valiantly against ill health could make anyone snappish and impatient.

Just as his Heavenly Father had freely forgiven him, so Granville must freely forgive his earthly father. But Granville's feeling that he must forgive his father left him with the uncomfortable conclusion that he could therefore no longer blame his parent for the lack of understanding between them.

Putting that aside for the moment, he turned to Georgiana. "Will you be attending Lady York's ball on Friday?"

"Assuredly. I have ordered a new gown for the occasion since we are to go early to dine. I am relying on Worcester to escort us, as Papa is suffering from the family enemy."

"Oh, has he the gout again?"

"Yes, and he simply must be recovered before we remove to Troy House, as we always do so much tramping about there in the beautiful Welsh countryside." She then recounted her week of at-homes, concerts, and dinners, as well as attending meetings of two compassionate societies with her mother. Granville could see such a schedule would leave little time for her to spend with him, and he would not be satisfied with a few moments squeezed between appointments. The things he wanted to discuss with Georgiana would require her undivided attention. He would wait.

"Then I shall look forward with greatest pleasure to seeing you at Lady York's. It is the night of the Cabinet dinner, so I shall remove myself from Harrowby House with alacrity." Their breakfast over, he escorted her around the Square to the Duke's house.

On Thursday Granville again took a seat in the House gallery to hear the third reading of the Amelioration Bill, an event which was diminished by the absence of the man who had labored the hardest to bring it about. True to the fears of many of his friends, Wilberforce had overtaxed his strength and suffered a physical collapse. Mr. Secretary Canning, carrying out the wishes of his party, now that his attempts to delay the measure had failed, took the floor to move the third reading of Wilberforce's bill and presented a message from the valiant fighter. "My honorable friend, the member for Bramber, Mr. Wilberforce, is prevented from attending this august body due to an indisposition he has suffered. He asked me to state, however, how much he regretted that he could not be present on this occasion to express his joy at what he considers a major step toward the accomplishment of the great object for which he so long has labored. His presence shall be sadly missed today."

The chamber rang with hearty cries of, "Hear, hear!" In the mood of conciliation that now filled both sides of the House, a member rose and, rightly forecasting the outcome of the vote, said he could not let the present opportunity pass without congratulating the House and the friends of abolition on the success which now attended a measure which he had seen so long opposed. "Looking back at the difficulties with which its friends have had to contend, I could not at one time have thought it possible that they could have been overcome in such a comparatively short space.

"It is also a source of great satisfaction to me to perceive, that by the treaty about to be finally concluded between the two British nations, on both sides of the Atlantic, we shall shortly enter into such arrangements as will shame mankind out of this horrid traffic. It is satisfactory to perceive that while the Americans are emulating the maritime glory of their ancestors, they are not less—"

The speaker yielded to Secretary Canning's gavel. "I beg to remind my learned and honorable friend that the other chamber is waiting to have this Bill sent up to them."

"Thank you, Mr. Secretary. In that case I will not delay the House any longer." He sat down.

The bill was then read a third time, and to a resounding acclamation of "Aye!" the measure for the amelioration of slave conditions in the West Indies was passed.

The House then turned to consideration of the treaty with the United States for both countries to work for the enforcement of the abolition of slave trade on the open seas. The Earl of Harrowby rose, and in the fluid voice that had earned him so much success as a public speaker, he introduced the measure to which the earlier speaker had referred. "My most honorable friends, it gives me great pleasure to inform this House that the American Congress has ratified the treaty proposed by this kingdom to enforce the abolishment of the slave trade."

Shouts of "Hear!" interrupted the speaker.

"And that country has taken independent measures to ensure that the slave trade will be dealt with as piracy, according to the laws of both countries. Further, there is in the treaty a stipulation by which the United States and Great Britain pledge themselves to invite other powers to accede to the same measure. Gentlemen, I urge our ratification of this treaty."

"Hear, hear!" Again the chamber rang. The bill was read a third time and passed. It had been a great day of victory for the forces of abolition in the "two British nations on both sides of the Atlantic."

And it was a major personal victory for William Wilberforce who for fifty years had led the antislavery movement without faltering. There remained but one last step—abolition. *And I will be here to work for it*, Granville vowed.

Leaving Westminster, Granville turned his steps toward Travellers, the Ryder family's club, thinking that perhaps Sandon would be there. It would be pleasant to discuss politics with his brother. But as soon as he got to St. James Street, he was hailed by a familiar voice. "Gran! Fancy finding you running tame around Town."

"Freddie, I didn't know you were coming to London." He offered his hand to his friend.

"Lot you don't know. Remember Fifi at Newmarket?"

Granville's eyes narrowed, "Indeed I do."

"Rum thing. Saw your watch in a pawnbroker window—least, thought it was. Went in to check. That man was there—one that hung around them. Wouldn't have recognized him, but he had on that awful suit—he or his tailor should be arrested for bad taste. At any rate, told him what I thought of his piece of work—couldn't prove it against him, of course, but I put a flea in his ear. Told him he was a rum cove to use females to run his rigs. Told me he wouldn't use Fifi anymore—in St. Bart's Hospital with consumption."

"What? Is it possible?" Freddie's story quite confounded

Granville.

" 's fact," Freddie declared, then, apparently exhausted from the effort of making such a lengthy speech, walked quietly for several moments.

"Oh, almost forgot." He put his hand in his pocket. "Here's your watch."

"Thank you, Freddie." Granville was highly pleased to have his watch returned—and relieved that it should be before his father noticed its absence. "What did you pay to redeem it? I'll give you a draft."

"Not me, made that bawd do the pretty." Freddie looked exceedingly pleased with himself.

They entered Travellers' exclusive portals and Granville paused in the cloakroom to draw out his pocketbook. He scribbled a note and folded several large bills inside it. "Do you have a wafer, Hansard?" he asked the porter.

"Certainly, Sir." The servant produced the requested bit of wax.

Granville affixed it and dashed an address on the outside. "Can you have this taken around?"

The servant produced a silver tray to receive the note. "Certainly, Sir. Very good." He received his tip. "Thank you."

Granville and Freddie went on into the coffee room. "What you about, Gran?"

"A note and subscription to one of my mother's charities, The Forlorn Female's Fund of Mercy."

Freddie laughed, "You're bamming me. You sending a fistful of flimsies to Fifi?"

"To the Society. For her care—and Clarissa's too, if they can find her."

Freddie was speechless for a moment, then said, "Better to call out Bow Street than some Friday-faced almsworker. Not to say that Fifi ain't plenty forlorn, of course."

Granville smiled at his friend's sentiments, but spoke seriously. "I'll admit my first impulse was to call out the runners, but a recent experience of mine made me think mercy was more appropriate than judgment."

Freddie's eyes got large. "You been messing around with that lightskirt Grace again?"

Granville was too thunderstruck at Freddie's misapprehension even to laugh. "Yes, Freddie, 'grace' is the word, but you've got it

174

all wrong—I'll explain sometime."

A waiter arrived to take their orders and the quickly served refreshment brought a new topic to Freddie's mind. "Merry's coming to Town Wednesday. Want to make up a party to the theatre?"

Granville started to agree, then stopped. "Sorry, I shall be required at a family assemblage that night—in honor of my uncle. He's finally been translated."

Freddie stared. "Translated? What's that? Don't mean to say he's become French, do you?"

Granville threw back his head in an open, carefree laugh which he had employed all too seldom in his recent months of struggle.

Freddie regarded him thoughtfully. "I say, Gran, thought religion would ruin you. I was wrong. Like you better this way."

Granville wiped his eyes with his napkin. "I like me better too. That's the whole thing."

The next evening, the crush of elegant carriages outside Lady York's house in Berkeley Square was only a prelude to the multitude thronging her Georgian mansion.

Granville presented his card and was announced by the powdered and liveried butler, then began strolling through the flower-banked reception rooms filled with people and music. It seemed that he saw everyone of his acquaintance in London—except the one person he sought. And when he did encounter the Duke of Beaufort's daughter in the long gallery, it was the elder Miss Somerset who came to him smiling with outstretched hand to be bowed over.

Charlotte was radiant in an evening dress of figured ivory silk with gauze insets, and the jewels entwined in her hair sparkled under the chandeliere as she danced the Boulanger with Granville. When the music ended, Granville offered to secure a glass of ratafia for her; but instead of answering his question, she looked across the room and cried, "My, doesn't George look splendid tonight!"

But it wasn't the flamboyant Mr. Agar-Ellis in his high-cut waistcoat of French silk enriched with silver thread and embroidered in silver purl and spangles that captured Granville's attention, but the young man's partner—Georgiana in a pink satin dance dress, cut low on her white shoulders, its bell-shaped skirt adorned with appliqued trimming and padded rosettes, a fillet of pink French roses in her hair.

"Shall we join them?" Charlotte asked.

Granville was about to suggest an alternate activity when the couple spotted them and moved forward. Before Georgiana and George could cross the room to them, however, their hostess hurried in.

"Granville, I'm so glad I've found you. I wanted to be the first to give you the news. You haven't heard, have you?"

Granville's reply to her confused question was lost when a lady nearby gave a muffled scream. Servants hurried in to fold the shutters across the windows. All dancing stopped as a buzz of gossip flew around the room.

Lady York grasped Granville's arm. "I don't know how accurate the report is, but we've just received word that there has been an attempt to assassinate the Cabinet. Is it true that they were dining at your father's house tonight?"

Granville stiffened to attention, as if his captain had just brought word of an enemy attack. "Tell me what you have heard, Madam."

"There has been an attack on our uncle's house—a plot to kill the cabinet!" Charlotte siezed Georgiana's hand and pulled her into the circle to hear Lady York.

"Indeed, I am not sure what I have heard, the reports are so garbled—twenty to thirty conspirators, the foot guards ordered out to support the police, shots fired—oh, my Dear, I hardly know what to tell you. Indeed, it could be nothing, but it does sound very bad.

"Very bad, indeed. I know you will excuse me, my Lady." Granville bowed and turned toward the door, his mind filled with gory visions of his parents' blood staining the pale blue walls of their dining room.

· 17 ·

"GRAN, I'M GOING WITH YOU." Georgiana grabbed his arm.

"Certainly not. I have no idea what the situation is, but if one-tenth of the report is to be believed, it is not a circumstance I wish to take you into." He hurried on toward the entrance hall, barely ahead of numerous other guests preparing a hurried exit. But Georgiana matched her step to his.

Granville was obliged to wait for his carriage to be pulled forward. "Georgiana, we have no idea if the conspirators have been apprehended. They may be lurking about anywhere, lying in wait outside our house. Or the scene may be—" he spoke the word through clenched teeth "—grisly."

"Precisely why I am going. You may need me."

Further argument was stopped by the simultaneous arrival of Granville's phaeton and a breathless servant, running from the house with Georgiana's evening cloak. Granville sprang into the carriage, leaving the servant to hand Georgiana in.

The short drive down Carlos Place from Berkeley Square to Grosvenor Square provided evidence of the incredible alarm that had spread through London—troops from the Hyde Park Barracks were struggling to keep order in streets choked with traffic, as dinner parties, assemblies, and balls quickly dispersed. Passersby called to one another for news, and each report grew more alarming.

"How many killed?"

"Nine, I heard."

"Yes, and Liverpool."

"Liverpool? They've killed the Prime Minister?"

177

"The King? An attempt on the King?"

Granville set his features and looked straight ahead, driving his most skillfully in impossible circumstances. Beside him, Georgiana sat very still, her hand tucked gently under his arm.

"It will be all right, Gran. I know it will."

One of the officers stationed outside Harrowby House recognized Granville and sprang forward to hold his horses as Granville leapt from the carriage. Another officer handed Georgiana down. At the doorway they were joined by Sandon who threw the door open and rushed ahead, calling over his shoulder, "Glad you're here, Gran. I heard the news at Almacks; got here as soon as I could." He threw the door to the dining room open and stood frozen, blocking Granville's view.

Sure that he was to be faced with the reality of his blood-spattered visions, Granville attempted to shield Georgiana when Sandon exclaimed, "What the deuce!" He moved on into the room. "It's all over London that the whole Square has been blown sky high and the government with it—a real Guy Fawkes—officers filling the streets—couldn't make my way through the cordon outside—and here you sit sipping coffee!"

The enormous flood of relief that washed over the viewers of a placid domestic scene—the Earl and Countess dining quietly alone—brought with it near hysterical laughter. It was considerably later before Granville demanded to know what had taken place.

"I told you of the warning I'd received," the Earl spoke calmly. "Most of the ministers were disposed to treat the matter as unworthy of serious notice; but Wellington and Bathurst had heard previous rumors, and so insisted we formulate a plan.

"The Duke brought forth a noble scheme worthy of the hero of Waterloo, with two hundred men from Portman Street on alert until the moment they saw the gang assemble for action, when they were to approach double-quick and the Life Guards were to gallop across the park and occupy the surrounding streets.

"But since that scheme entailed the Cabinet members actually dining here, it was decided that the member's carriages pull up at their doors and drive here as if all was going forward. But the carriages actually arrived empty, while Bow street constables and a piquet of foot guards went to Cato Street to apprehend the conspirators on their home territory."

Granville, still unable to rid his mind of the horrors it had conjured up, shook his head. "And absolutely nothing happened here?"

The Earl shrugged. "I observed men watching the house, front and rear all day, but I ordered dinner as usual."

The Countess gave a small gurgle of laughter. "Well, there was one casualty: Jean-Luc threw his hat on the floor and trampled it in a rage when he heard his dinner was to be canceled."

Sandon laughed. "There'll be delicacies in the schoolroom for weeks. I envy my infant brothers and sisters."

Granville, however, was not taken with the humor of the situation. "But, Father, didn't it occur to you to remove to another place? It's all very well for the other ministers to stay at home, but here you sit at the center of the bulls-eye. If the conspirators had escaped arrest, they might well have come on here and blown you to eternity. After all, the arrival of all those empty carriages gave the impression that they could accomplish their ends. And what of Mother's safety?"

"He did think of that, Dear. I don't think he took a single thought for himself, but he did urge me to order dinner served in the upper sitting room. I thought that quite nonsensical—which, as you can see, it would have been. Would you care for some coffee?"

Granville shook his head. "Pluck to the backbone, both of you."

"Anyone?" Lady Harrowby touched the coffee urn. "It may yet be a long night."

Before she had finished pouring a cup for Georgiana, the butler opened the double doors of the room and stood aside. "Sir Richard Birnie," he announced as the police magistrate entered. "And, er— Mr. Lavender." It was clear that although service in a house which was the focal point of the most audacious assassination plot in British history had not ruffled this worthy servant, the necessity of announcing the most felonious-appearing of the Bow Street Runners had very nearly overset him.

"Thought you'd want to know as soon as possible, my Lord, so I came around with the news myself," Sir Birnie said. "We got the ruffians in the Cato Street stable, just like your informant said. My first man in was shot in the head, but it's only a wound. The one who followed, though, was stabbed and killed. Smithers, his name is . . . er, was. The conspirators put out the light and attempted to escape, but by that time the soldiers had arrived. We took nine prisoners. Thistlewood and the rest escaped, but we'll soon get

179

'em, no worry. Have 'em strung up for treason quicker 'n you can say 'Jack Spratt.' "

"But what was their object? What can they possibly have hoped to obtain by such an act?" The Earl's overriding reaction to the whole event seemed to be perplexity.

"Near as we can make out, yer Lordship"—Lavender twirled the hat he had refused to surrender to the footman—"the ideer was to fire a rocket from the 'ouse soon's they'd completed their work of destruction. That was to be the signal for the risin' of their friends. There was some notion of settin' an oil shop on fire to increase the confusion, then throw open the Bank and Newgate.

"The 'eads of the ministers, beggin' your pardon, me Lord, was to 'ave been cut off and put in a sack which they'd prepared for the purpose—but we got the sack all right and tight." He finished with considerable satisfaction, as if securing the sack had been the coup de grace to the conspiracy.

"Those poor, misguided creatures." The Earl shook his head. "Did they actually believe they could pull off such a thing?"

"The plan does seem to have been attended with a remarkable degree of disorganization," Birnie said. "And the mob, even if they had espoused such a cause, though possibly very dangerous in creating confusion and making havoc, would be quite inefficient for a regular operation. It would never have done."

"All that for some vague notions of revenge, liberty, and instant prosperity by a band of desperate destitutes." Lady Harrowby leaned her forehead against her hand. "And now I suppose they will be executed. Do they have families?"

"Don't be wastin' no sympathy on them, Ma'am. Their notion was to stick the 'ead of your murdered 'usband and 'is compatriots on staves and carry 'em through the streets of London to rouse the mob. Beggin' your pardon, Ladies," Lavender nodded to the Countess and Georgiana. "But you'd best know the truth."

"And to think that was all prevented by the pure chance of a member of the conspiracy knowing and liking you, Father—our milkman, no less."

"No, Granville. I don't believe it was chance," the Earl replied.

"The Honorable Mr. Frederick Calthorpe and Lady Charlotte Somerset." The butler might have been announcing late arrivals at a formal ball.

"Where is my brother? They said he'd been murdered!" Fred

looked quite distracted.

"Georgie!" Charlotte flew to her sister. "Are you all right? You can't imagine the stories that are flying everywhere. The whole Town is in an uproar. Lady York's guests were barricading her house with arms when we left."

The essence of the matter was reported to the newcomers and a much calmer Mr. Calthorpe and the men from Bow Street departed to escort the Somerset sisters to their father's house. Lord Sandon suddenly remembered his wife whom he had left in the care of their party at Almacks.

"I know you'll do better for our parents' comfort than I, at any rate." Sandon clapped a hand on Granville's shoulder, then hurried off to put Lady Sandon in possession of the facts.

"The Town will be abuzz till long past daybreak, but there is no need for me to be. If you will excuse me, my Dears." Granville and his father stood and saw the Countess out of the room.

While all London surged outside, father and son faced each other across the tranquil room. "Father, I—" Granville could find no words to express his relief at finding his father unharmed, and his sudden increased realization of how much this man meant to him.

"Sit down and have a drink, Granville." The Earl handed his son a glass and resumed his seat at the table. "We have needed to talk for some time. I apologize for allowing my Parliamentary duties to get in the way of my duties as a father."

"No, Sir, it is I who must apologize. But I won't embarrass you by speaking of what should never have risen between us."

"I appreciate that, Granville. Allow me to say only that I now realize that I was far too impatient in pressing you to develop the abilities with which I knew you had been endowed . I had a very fine letter from Charles Simeon—he had some superior things to say to your character."

Granville grinned, "Doesn't know me well, huh?"

"On the contrary, I should say he knows you far better than your own father. But I think we might remedy that in the future." The Earl extended his hand and Granville clasped it warmly.

"The prodigal has returned, Father." Granville exchanged the handshake for an embrace.

"Shall we kill the fatted calf?"

Granville chuckled, "I fancy that won't be necessary with all Jean-Luc has prepared."

The Earl gave him a final slap on the back. "Now to bed with you, you young scapegrace. Have you no compassion for a tired old man with an abominable headache?"

But in his room, the image that filled Granville's mind was not his newly sympathetic vision of his father. He now saw pictures of Georgiana which his mind had been capturing all through the harrowing evening, but had found no time to focus on. Georgiana, insisting on going with him to face possible murderers or rioters because, "You might need me." Georgiana, all delicate pink, white, and gold as the streetlamps lighted her, enveloped in a long rose cloak with a shoulder cape, the whole garment edged with the softest fur. Georgiana, sitting beside him with her calm support, while panic ruled in the streets.

He picked up his pen. The letter he wrote, however, was not addressed to Georgiana, but to God:

> O Lord God, the great and merciful God,
> Thou hast caused, in Thy good providence,
> that I be companion with one
> whom Thou hast richly endowed with charm of person,
> mind, and disposition, and above all,
> with a heart desirous of loving and serving Thee.
>   O Lord, it seems to me that she is particularly suited
> to me as a helpmeet, above all others.
> That her character, by its strength and decision,
> by its gentleness, purity, truth, and conscientiousness,
> is one calculated to be most useful to mine.
>   Therefore, O my Lord, I pray Thee, that I may love her
> more faithfully and truly, and above all—unselfishly,
> so as to desire her happiness in preference to my own. . . .

He held his pen poised above the paper. His next thought brought an agony he could hardly bear, but it must be faced. What if his great desire for her was not compatible with her happiness—with God's best plan? He dipped his pen in the inkwell and resolutely continued:

> . . . . even if that be inseparable from that
> which be most painful to me.
>   But, O Lord God Almighty, if it be possible,

consistent with her best interests here and hereafter,
turn her heart to me, to love me above all others.
That we, loving each other above all things else on earth
—but loving Thee above all—may, by Thy great mercy
in Thine own dear time, have a way made for us,
that we may marry and enter upon that holy estate
with a deep sense of our responsibility to Thee
and to one another, and with the firm determination
of being helpmeets to each other, of uplifting one another,
and being to one another the cause
of as much earthly happiness as Thou knowest
to be compatible with our heavenly welfare.

He was suddenly struck with the audacity of what he was asking,
what an incredibly precious prize he sought—next to the gift of
salvation, the greatest life could offer. In an attitude of deep
supplication he wrote slowly:

All this I dare only pray in the humble hopes that Thou,
having caused me to be so long with her,
thereby learning to know thoroughly her character,
to appreciate its excellence,
to believe her to be peculiarly suited to myself,
and to love her very tenderly, would in Thy great goodness,
grant me this rich gift, utterly unworthy of it though I am.
But, my Father, Thou canst make me worthy
of more, even of heavenly gifts, through Christ Jesus.
Oh, I pray Thee above all to do so;
and then I shall be worthy of this earthly gift,
great though it be!
But, O Heavenly Father, I pray Thee especially,
that I may more than all desire Heavenly kinship.
And shouldst Thou decide to deny me this greatest
earthly blessing,
O enable me, in this and all trials,
to submit humbly and cheerfully to Thy divine will,
saying from the bottom of my heart,
"Not my will, but Thine be done."
Amen.

· *18* ·

But many weeks later, at Troy House in the lush green Welsh mountains, it was not Granville's letter that Georgiana was reading, with her white brow knit in thoughtful furrows, but one from George Agar-Ellis:

My Dear Georgiana,
My very, very dear Georgiana, my heart's desire—but more of that anon. I am torn with regret over my misfortune which prevented me from speaking with you and unveiling that which is in my heart before you left London. But for that dreadful Cato Street affair—but enough of that.
What I wish to communicate to you most particularly is that affairs require that I should journey into Yorkshire and stay a few days with Lord Carlisle at Castle Howard. From there I propose to journey to your side where I shall have something most particular to say to you which—I take great leave to flatter myself—I do not believe you shall find unpleasant.
Yr most humble and devoted servant,
G. A-E.

"Well, that is rather pot-sure of him." Georgiana smiled and laid the letter on her writing desk. And yet, as she so often reminded herself, George was not an unpleasant companion. In spite of his propensity for puffery, he was never vicious or profligate and he was entirely free from anything like severity or austerity. But if she were to accept his offer—and she had no doubt that was his allusion—

there would never be a less romantic, or more businesslike attachment; for in spite of his protestations, she did not flatter herself that his heart was seriously engaged, but she felt assured that she might contrive to rub along quite well with a man so active and ambitious in his pursuits and magnificent in his tastes. *He is devoted to literature, politics, society* . . . she coached herself, *and since the one other of whom you think tenderly, considers you only as a cousin* . . . Yes, George Agar-Ellis might do . . . If only her heart were not already engaged elsewhere. She sat long thinking of Granville, of their last, dramatic night together in London and of the other times they had spent together in Town. All through the dismal months of January and February, she had hoped that when she saw Granville again he might give her some indication that he reciprocated the tender feelings she held for him. But no such declaration had come when she had seen him in Town.

She sighed as she tossed George Agar-Ellis' missive onto her desk and thought how far different her reaction would be if the letter bore a different signature.

She had also hoped that Granville would join them at Troy House for Easter, but that day was long past and still there was no word. Had all she thought Granville felt for her been only wishful thinking? Had her judgments been colored by the strength of her desire? What should she do if Granville had no more to communicate to her and George sincerely sought her hand?

In London, Granville was wondering if he would ever be able to leave Town and seek his cousin's companionship. The demands upon his time following the upheaval of the uncovering of the conspiracy left him no leisure for even writing to Georgiana. He had barely managed to scribble a hasty note to Peacock in Cambridge and inform his crammie that events in London would delay his return to Trinity for Lent term. With the Earl and Sandon busy in the House from morning till night, family responsibility for assisting the officers and responding to the public fell on Granville.

Although nine of the conspirators were immediately apprehended in the Cato Street stable, several others, including Thistlewood and Edwards, the ringleaders, were still at large. Two days after the alarm, Lavender called at Grovesnor Square and inquired if the Honorable Mr. Ryder would be so kind as to accompany him to view the evidence Bow Street was collecting for the trial.

The sight was an alarming one, as Granville contemplated what might have been the result had this arsenal been put into use in the hands of an unruly mob. There were piles of muskets, carbines, broad swords, pistols, blunderbusses, ball-cartridges, and gunpowder; then in another room, a bundle of singularly constructed stilettos, pikes, pike handles, and hand grenades. . . .

Granville turned to Lavender. "It makes one excessively thankful to Providence."

Lavender wiped his forehead with an ample handkerchief. "That it does, Sir. And now, if you would be so good as to accompany me to the 'orse and Groom. Beggin' your pardon, but it seems only fittin' . . ."

"Yes, of course." Granville went out the door Lavender was holding for him. "I should be glad to pay my respects to the officer killed while saving our country from this terrible affair."

Pending the inquest, the body of Officer Smithers was laid in a first floor room of the public house across the street from the stable. The slain man was still in the clothes in which he was killed, his chest and neck covered with blood. Granville took a brief look and, as so often in the last two days, breathed a prayer of thanks that it was not his father's body he was viewing.

"What of this man's family?" he asked Lavender. "Has anything been done to see to their needs?"

The runner wasn't aware that any action had been taken, so Granville set about to initiate a public subscription for the support of Smither's widow and children, and also a fund to reward the officers engaged in the apprehension of the conspirators. He also endorsed Sir Birnie's plan to offer a thousand-pound reward for the information leading to the arrest of Thistlewood.

Meanwhile, each day's post brought another stack of letters to Harrowby House. Anonymous letters came full of threats; others brought unwelcome offers of help. Granville sat at the desk in Lord Harrowby's study shaking his head as he read yet another public-spirited proposal:

My Lord:
   If you will enclose in a Letter the sum of two or three pounds to enable me to act with certainty, I will write you by Friday next information of the utmost importance. If you do not comply with my mode of information, no other will be

noticed and I shall seal my lips forever.

Your Lordship's Humble Servant,
John West

Granville tossed the note aside and turned as the butler opened the door and announced Sir Birnie. "I don't know what to expect next, Sir." Birnie sat on the edge of a wing chair. "We've had the good fortune to uncover another plot—"

"What! More conspirators?" Granville jerked to attention.

"In a manner of speaking, that is. A couple of 'public-spirited' radicals have formed a committee for conducting the prisoners' defense."

"Surely that isn't out of order? They are entitled to a fair trial."

"Right you are. But it seems they aren't willing to take their chances with justice. They meet every other evening at the Crown and Anchor in Shoe Lane—where we are careful to see that two spies meet along with them," he said the last with a note of conspicuous pride.

"Well, what have you learned?" The strain of the last days showed in the edge of impatience in Granville's voice.

"We have secured a paper from one of our spies containing a list of the men eligible for jury duty who have been canvassed in the interest of the prisoners. The names of those found to be favorable to them are marked with an X, very favorable XX. Those they are afraid of are indicated with an O, very fearful OO. They feel if they can secure jury seats for only two of their men, they can prevent a verdict of guilty."

"But surely you can prevent such tampering with justice now that you are alerted?"

"Indeed we shall. You may rely on it, Sir."

The next day brought even more dramatic events as Edwards, the chief conspirator, gave information on the whereabouts of his friend Arthur Thistlewood for the promised thousand pounds. Edwards collected the reward, then disappeared. But Thistlewood was captured and, after a visit to Bow Street for the usual formalities, was taken off to be examined by the Privy Council.

Especially since Thistlewood was the son of one of Lord Harrowby's Lincolnshire tenants, Granville desired to accompany his father to the Home Office for the hearing. The room was filled with those from the highest rank of society and government as public interest in the conspiracy continued to grow.

Thistlewood, led in by strong guards, was dressed in shabby clothes he hadn't been out of for days. His features were emaciated and he sat with his eyes looking only at the floor.

A Bow Street Runner named Westcott identified Thistlewood as a conspirator. "Yes, my Lord, that's the man. He turned round and presented a pistol to my head; I put my hand in this kind of way to defend myself." And the witness folded his arms over his face. "He fired at me. There were three holes made in my hat. I went to make a rush and received a blow on the right side of my head. I fell with it. He was out of sight before I could get at him."

"I won't miss next time, Guv'nor," the prisoner muttered. Under questioning from the council, Thistlewood admitted to being influenced by the ideals of the French Revolution, and then he told how the plan took form. " 'Bout 'leven or twelve of us was gathered to talk over what we could do to stir up the people when Edwards bursts in with the newspaper. 'There's to be a cabinet dinner tomorrow at the Earl of 'arrowby's!' 'e said. Then I declared, 'Now I'll be damned if I don't believe there is a God. I've often prayed that those thieves be collected all together in order to give us a good opportunity to destroy 'em. God has answered my prayer!' President of the Provisional Government I was to be."

The questions continued, but Granville had heard enough. "Send the chaplain to them," he ordered Birnie, and then walked back to Grosvenor Square.

Sandon met him in the entrance hall. "What's the news of the interrogation?"

Granville tossed his hat and gloves to the butler and led the way into the sitting room. "Poor devils. Such ignorance, such discontent, such desperate idealism. They have no notion of what they've done. Or, by the grace of God, were prevented from doing." He paced the floor. "And I can't get away from the feeling that in some horrible way they're a symbol of what any of us might be capable of, if we were bereft of money, friends, education, family, God. . . . "

"It sounds as if you've been listening to revolutionaries yourself."

Granville gave a tight laugh. "Maybe I have. No, don't worry, I'm not about to lead a revolution; but when I get into Parliament, I do mean to work for reform. There has to be a way of alleviating the desperation of such poor creatures as these. What Wilberforce has done for the blacks in the colonies is all very well, but there are those on our own doorstep whose situations are equally desperate."

While the brothers were still talking, the Earl entered, rubbing his forehead. With the slightest hint of amusement in his eyes, he said, "Well, it seems that at least one person has profited from this sorry business. Some fellow quite unauthorized has taken possession of the stable and demands a shilling from each person who desires admission. They tell me thousands surge through Cato Street to see the site of the drama."

A few days later the trial began and the Earl of Harrowby was one of the first called to give evidence regarding the Council's prior knowledge of the conspiracy and the warning delivered to him by Hinden, the milkman.

Hinden, the cow-keeper, was called next and told of meeting one Wilson at a shoemaker's club. "Wilson asked me if I would be one of a party to come forward to destroy 'is Majesty's ministers. 'E said they 'ad some such things as I never saw, which 'e called by the name of 'and-grenades. 'E said they were to be lighted with fuses and put under the table, and all that escaped the explosion was to die by the edge of the sword, or some other weapon."

"On Wednesday the twenty-third, did you see Wilson again?" the Attorney-General asked.

"I did."

"You were going with some milk?"

"No," Hinden corrected. "I was going 'ome with one of my little girls in my 'and."

"And what did Wilson say?"

" 'E called me by name and said I was the very man 'e wanted to see. 'E said there was going to be a Cabinet dinner at Lord 'arrowby's and that I was to go up to Cato Street and meet the others by the stable."

"But instead you took word to Lord Harrowby?"

Hinden agreed to the accuracy of that, and then Arthur Thistlewood took the stand.

Thistlewood was definitely proud of his plan, as he told it in detail to the court: "I proposed going to the door with a note to present to 'is Lordship. When the door was open we would rush in directly, seize the servants what were in the way, present a pistol directly and threaten them with death if they offered resistance.

"This done, a party would rush forward to take command of the stairs. The man 'aving firearms would be protected by 'olding the 'and grenade. When the 'ouse was secure, those to do the assassination were to rush in directly after.''

His tale was continued by Ings, another conspirator, in a likewise defiant and excited tone: "I was to enter the room first with a brace of pistols, a cutlass and a knife in my pocket, and after the swordsmen 'ad despatched those 'igh and mighty rascals, I would cut every 'ead off that was in the room and bring it away in a bag.''

A shiver of horror went through the courtroom as the plan continued to unfold: one conspirator to throw a fireball into the straw at the King Street Barracks to stifle man and beast; others to capture the cannon. The Royal Exchange to be set on fire. Next the Bank of England to be attacked and plundered of all they could get, but the books not to be destroyed, so that they would provide evidence against others to be assassinated throughout the country.

Day after day the tale unfolded. As more and more bloody details emerged, Granville's gratitude for God's protection increased, as did his desire to have the apalling affair ended. It was clear that the conspirators would be hung, but Granville determined to be out of London when it happened.

As far from London as she was, Georgiana heard little of the stirring events gripping the city, and the verdant beauty of the Welsh countryside offered meager distraction to aid her determination not to think of one who had so obviously forgotten her. She was in her room studiously not thinking about Granville when suddenly Charlotte flew into the room in a welter of sprig muslin skirts and beribboned curls. "Georgie! Hold my hand. I'm in such a flutter I can't contain myself.''

"Char! Whatever is wrong, my Dear?" She flew to her sister's side and grasped her trembling hands.

"Wrong? Whatever made you think anything is wrong? Nothing could be more right! Frederick Calthorpe has just made me an offer—and, and I have accepted. He has gone now into the Oak Room to find Papa. O Georgie, Papa won't refuse, will he? He's normally the most amiable of men, but the gout sometimes makes him crotchety and—" She squeezed her sister's hands. "O Georgie, I can't bear it, my whole happiness depends on it.''

"Charlotte! I had no notion you had a tendre for Frederick— indeed, I had thought—"

"Oh, yes! For some time I have considered him the most amiable of men and the handsomest, of such superior manners and breeding—and then that dreadful night when those ruffians tried to blow up London and Fred was so distracted, not knowing what had befallen his brother—Georgie, he turned to me for support—to me! Then I knew that there was no other way I could spend my life but in supporting him in everything."

Georgiana's smile was wistful. "Yes, I know exactly what you mean, I had a similar experience. . . . " Then a more practical consideration struck her. "But Char, you say you have been with him just now? When did he arrive? I thought him in London with Worcester and Lord Lauderdale."

"Yes, yes, he was. He has driven directly from London to bring Papa a letter from our brother. O Georgie, you don't suppose it's bad news, do you? If it is, Papa will be all out of sorts and not at all ready to hear Fred's suit." She clasped a hand to her mouth, "Oh, I didn't think of it! What could be so particular that Frederick should be obliged to bring a letter from Worcester? Why couldn't he have sent it by post? O Georgie, I'm worried to distraction—hold me!"

And so it was that Agatha found the sisters locked in one another's arms when she entered the room a few minutes later. "His Grace is asking for you, Miss—"

"For me?" Charlotte cried. "Oh, how did he look? Was he smiling? Oh, say he was. He must have been smiling."

"For both of you, Miss Somerset and Miss Georgiana."

"Both of us? How very singular. O Georgie, I am glad you are to come with me—I'm all in a quake." Charlotte practically pulled her sister down the stairs, barely pausing to catch her breath and smooth her hair before entering the Oak Room.

The room, named for the black oak Jacobean paneling which had been brought to Troy House for safekeeping from Raglan Castle when the castle was threatened by a Roundhead seige, was already occupied. The Duke sat with his left foot on an elevated stool, while the hurriedly summoned Duchess sat in a chair near his, and Mr. Calthorpe stood before them. Charlotte squeezed her sister's hand until Georgiana winced.

The Duke cleared his throat and waved a piece of paper with a broken red wax seal before them. "Mr. Calthorpe has been so good as to bring us word from Lord Worcester. He was married three days ago at a private service in St. George's Church, Hanover

Square."

"Married!" Georgiana cried. "To Emily? Did they find a way around the degrees of affinity?"

"Your brother was advised that since the connection was within the proscribed bounds, the match *would* be voidable, but not void. Therefore, he thought it best to make the object of his heart's desire a *fait accompli*, and trust that no action should be taken by an ecclesiastical court to set it aside. Since the lady's stepmother is very much in support of the match, it seems that Culling-Smith will not take steps to overset it." He turned to Frederick. "Sir, will you ring for some port that we may felicitate them in absentia?"

The Duchess wiped her eyes. "Oh, I am so happy for them. I knew at Christmas that she was the right one for him. It was clear he was head over ears in love with her.

"And it was certainly time he should be married, m order to put a stop to the reports and stories that have been circulated about him. My Sister Granville informs me that the Town have married him to three different people since Christmas." She held her glass before her and said, "Joy to them."

"And progeny," the Duke added bluntly. "That young Corinthian had best remember his duty to the family and produce an heir."

The family laughed and sipped the deep red liquid; but Charlotte, who had not let go of Georgiana's hand through the entire proceeding whispered, "Is that *all?* Hasn't he anything to say to my happiness? *My* fagot band was the first to break."

"Hush," her sister whispered. "It's unlikely Fred has had opportunity to speak to him on the matter."

"Oh, I shall die if I'm obliged to wait longer."

But such dreary prospects were not to occur, because the Honorable Frederick had indeed spoken on his own behalf as well. "Fill 'em again, Burton," the Duke ordered. "We have another matter to toast as well." He looked at the Duchess. "Seems our Charlotte has given her heart to this young scalawag here. I told him we might abide him in the family, if you think you can bear it, my Dear."

The Duchess rose and enfolded her eldest daughter, who at last dropped Georgiana's numb hand. "O my Dear. I am so happy for you!" Then she dabbed at her eyes again. "Oh, my cup runneth over, *two* in one day! I don't know that I can bear it." She released Charlotte who flew to her betrothed's side.

Georgiana, observing the scene, smiled to herself. It wouldn't do to speak of it now, but she too just might have an announcement for them as soon as Mr. Agar-Ellis arrived. If only she could be as thoroughly enveloped in the joy of it as her sister was.

Three days later Lord and Lady Harrowby arrived at Troy House to be present for the stonelaying ceremony at the Duchess' chapel. Georgiana greeted her aunt and uncle and assured herself that she wasn't in the least disappointed that their second son was not of their party. "And where is Charlotte?" the Countess asked. "I understand that we may wish her happy."

"She must not be aware that you have arrived, Aunt Susan. I'll go find her." Georgiana kissed her aunt and fled, glad of an excuse to escape before she betrayed her dejection over Granville's absence. She had held out just the tiniest shred of hope. . . .

She found her sister in the upstairs front drawing room, looking out the window. "Lord and Lady Harrowby have arrived and our aunt is asking for you."

Charlotte gave the dreamy smile that was characteristic of her these days. "Yes, I know. I'll go down soon. But I want to see who that is approaching. Can you make out the carriage crossing the bridge?" She pointed to the high curving lane that spanned the river on the main road to Troy House from Monmouth. "Fred said he would return as soon as he had informed his family. I suppose it's too soon to expect him, still . . . "

Georgiana could see nothing but the thick, verdant foliage lining the road. "You'll know soon enough. Come greet—" At that moment a pair of perfectly matched greys turned into the private lane that led up the hill. There was no mistaking that pair of high-steppers. "Oh, I do see them. Yes, those are the horses George calls his sweet-goers."

"What, pray tell, is he coming here for?"

Georgiana gave her sister a mischievious grin. "Do you think you're the only sly one in the family? He's coming to offer for me."

"No! Oh, dear, how awkward. Shall I tell Mama to send him away?"

"Indeed you shall not! I intend to accept him."

"Accept *George?* but Georgie, I thought you and Gran—"

"George always said we were eminently well suited—destined even, because our names were the same. I find that I am of quite the same mind."

"But Granville—"

"Granville Dudley Ryder is quite the handsomest man I've ever seen, with charm of manners, person, and address, but I fear we have no tendre for each other."

"No tendre? What a whisker! I've seen you look at each other—it's been all midsummer moon with you two for ages past."

"You quite mistake the matter, Sister." Turning away from the window so that Charlotte couldn't see what her admirable control cost her, Georgiana continued, "George is a remarkably agreeable man. He is hospitable, courteous, and cordial. He collects about him the most distinguished persons in every rank and condition of life; he has a constant flow of high spirits, much miscellaneous information, and excellent memory, a great enjoyment of fun and humor, a refined taste, goodness of heart. . . . "

Charlotte exploded with laughter and choked out, "In short, he would make an excellent host for a weekend house party! O Georgie, don't be so idiotish—go send him packing."

Georgiana's spirits were dampened by her sister's unvarnished words, but she was determined on her course of action.

"I want to be useful, to be needed, to make someone happy. It is true, I had hoped—" she choked, then tossed her head bravely. "But never mind. As our cousin doesn't have need of my affection to complete his happiness, I must find another who does. Mr. Agar-Ellis has made it quite plain that I stand able to make him the happiest of men. It would be selfish in me to refuse when the happiness of another is in my power."

"Georgie, that's so like you! So sweet and giving, and so wrongheaded."

Afraid her own resolve would weaken under the onslaught, Georgiana pushed her sister out the door with the reminder that Lady Harrowby wanted her. Then she went down the stone steps, across a small stretch of green lawn, and stood beside the gravel circle drive just as the carriage rounded the last curve and swung into full view.

When the horses came to full stop and the driver dismounted, she couldn't credit her eyes. She blinked to be certain they weren't cutting a sham with her. But it was true. "Gran!" she cried and only with the greatest restraint resisted throwing open her arms to greet him.

194

And he seemed in danger of the same unseemly conduct as he tossed his reins to a groom and jumped down. "Georgie! I would have been here sooner, but one of my pair threw up lame outside Bristol and I had to talk like the Dutch to make the hostler at The King's Head allow me to hire the pair Agar-Ellis keeps there. I assured him we were friends, and had to quote my pedigree, but in the end it was the color of my coin that carried the day."

Then Georgiana's young sisters spilled down the stairway to meet their cousin, followed by the Duchess and Countess, so that it was considerably later that Granville said to Georgiana, "Would you care to go for a drive—to Raglan, perhaps?"

Georgiana didn't even bother saying yes, just, "I'll get my bonnet."

As they drove through the sweet, green countryside, Georgiana thought of the generations of her ancestors who had made similar journeys when Raglan was their home, of the lords and ladies of Worcester who had lived there in a Castle that provided manorial elegance and comfort inside medieval defense requirements. And then of the Cromwellian troops marching in determination to conquer the Earl's defenses in what proved to be the final battle of the civil war and earn Raglan the title of The Last Castle. And soon after, the same ground was covered by Lord Worcester's garrison in retreat which, in spite of defeat, marched out with horses and arms, colors flying, drums beating, trumpets sounding, and bullets held in their teeth. It must have been spectacular, even if soon after the terms of capitulation were shamefully broken and the aged Worcester taken prisoner and kept in confinement until the end of his life. And still Raglan stood, broken but unbowed, a symbol of devotion to duty, loyalty to friend and king, and determination to do right— no matter what the personal cost.

"So quiet, my Dear."

She caught her breath at Granville's use of the familiar term of address. "Oh, I was thinking of the men and women here before us—as real as we are today, with their own thoughts, their own feelings, but now all gone—one generation vanishing into another."

He nodded, "I was thinking of similar things, and how someday we shall be gone, and our ch—er—others will take our place. I only hope our family motto may be true, that 'As they increase, so shall they shine.' "

Then the ivy-mantled towers rose into view before them on their terraced green hill. Up a gentle drive to the gatehouse, Granville hitched the horses and helped Georgiana from the carriage. They crossed the drawbridge high above the moat and went through the entrance protected by a double row of portcullises.

Granville looked around him, as he asked, "Isn't this where some forebear of yours is supposed to have invented the steam engine?"

Georgiana had hoped to talk of things nearer her heart, but answered in good grace, "Oh, yes, it's a rather unsubstantiated claim, I fear, but Lord Herbert, the second Marquess of Worcester, was fanatically interested in scientific research. He set up a laboratory and workshops here for his experiments in the time of Charles the First. His pride and joy was his 'Water Commanding Engine'."

"Does the machine still exist?"

"No, but his hydraulic machine, which he claimed solved the problem of perpetual motion, is said to have been buried with him in Raglan parish church."

"What a pity. It would be most instructive to see it operate."

"I fancy that wasn't quite the reaction some recipients of the honor of observing his inventions had." She laughed and pointed toward the Great Tower. "He contrived some waterworks in there by which water poured from the top through artificial channels, causing reverberations all over the Castle.

"One of his favorite jokes was to send a servant ahead to set the machine in motion, while Herbert approached the drawbridge with visitors. Suddenly the deafening roar of the waterworks would come from the castle and a servant would rush up shouting, 'Look to yourselves, my masters! The lions have got loose!'"

They laughed together, then walked on in silence. As the silence deepened, Georgiana sensed that Granville was holding something back. But as he had not yet spoken, she could only hope she was not being deceived by the desires of her own heart.

Without conversation, but with hearts in tune to the history and beauty around them, they climbed to the top of the hexagonal tower and looked across the countryside—a patchwork of spring-green wheat fields bordered by darker hedgerows and wooden clumps of trees, and over all, a gentle blue sky with mounds of soft white clouds. They looked down on the broken arches of the buff stone, covered with gold and green moss, patches of grass and purple wild flowers blooming in the windows, and everywhere a riotous growth of ivy.

196

Granville took her hand to lead her down a corkscrew of stone steps to the walk along the moat filled with bright green moss and gold and black fish. Shafts of sunlight pierced the water as precisely as Cromwell's arrows must have in an earlier time. But now there were no stirring battle cries, no clash of arms, no snorting, stamping war steeds—just the pounding of Georgiana's heart and the singing in her ears that closeness to Granville was wont to produce.

Then they entered the Great Hall and sat on a bench, provided as part of the Duke's restoration. From their seat in the bay of an oriel window, they could see the hints of former splendor remaining in the Castle's finest apartment: Mullioned and cross-beamed windows, molded roof, corbels projecting from the walls, and a huge fireplace. Georgiana hoped she could think of something to say before the silence became awkward.

But Granville spoke first. "I believe the usual opening is, 'I have something of a particular nature to say to you.'"

And then he was silent. "I guess the reason I can't find any words is that I've already used them." And he drew two folded sheets of paper from his breast pocket and handed her the love prayer he had written long weeks ago.

By the time she finished reading, tears were streaming down her radiant face. "Granville," her voice choked, "if I hadn't loved you before, I would now." She handed the papers back to him. "You must put these away very carefully. I am afraid any woman who read them would tumble into love with you and that could prove most awkward, because I intend to make a very absolute piece of work of our marriage."

But in the logic of things, it was necessary that first Granville should make a very absolute piece of work of kissing his beloved in the hall where her ancestors had lived and loved since the fifteenth century. And she knew that in at least one way, the Harrowby motto was already fulfilled—her love for Granville was increasing to a brilliant shining.

They drove through the soft spring evening back to Troy House, Georgiana bursting to share their secret, and at the same time, savoring it and hugging it to her heart. But her heart sank when they pulled up to the house and found another carriage arrived just ahead of them—*Oh, no, not George. This could prove very awkward.*

But the slash-up-to the-mark Mr. Agar-Ellis would have been highly insulted had he known the lady had accused him of owning such an old-fashioned equipage as that driven by Lord and Lady Granville Levenson-Gower.

Before Georgiana could remove her bonnet or give her Aunt Harriet a proper greeting, Lady Granville began regaling her with the latest on-dit which had London by the ears. "And my Dear, the tittle-tattles are saying that Mr. Agar-Ellis intended to end his tour here and offer for *you*, but of course, we know that's quite absurd. But at any rate, after a short time at Castle Howard, he found that Lord Carlisle's second daughter suited his purpose very well and would confer upon him a very agreeable family connection without the trouble of going any further. So after three or four days, he proposed to Lady Georgiana Howard.

"It seems that the lady was not less surprised than pleased and proud at the conquest she had so unconsciously made, and she immediately accepted him."

"O Aunt, I do believe that's the most famous story I ever heard! Do you suppose they'll suit?"

"The reports are that the lady is mild, gentle, and amiable, full of devotion to and admiration for her betrothed—qualities which should blend very well with his vivacity. The results produced should be quite felicitous."

"Yes, Aunt, but you omitted the lady's most outstanding mark of eligibility."

"What is that, my dear?"

"Her name is Georgiana—proof that they were destined for each other by a kind Providence." Laughing delightedly, Georgiana took the arm of the waiting Granville, and leaving her baffled aunt, led him into the garden. "And what do you say to so famous a romance?"

"I wish them joy, but I believe we have a much surer basis for building a happy marriage."

And as Granville very scandalously kissed her for the second time that day, Georgiana thought so too.

Author's Afterword

The major events of the book are all recorded history, and the characters (including most of the servants and animals) actually lived. To the extent that they have been recorded, I have used the characters' own words.

With one exception the events all occurred between 1820 and 1825, although not necessarily in the order presented here. The rainy afternoon that gave the world the game of Badminton was in 1863.

In 1835, on the death of his father from the "family enemy," gout, Lord Worcester became the seventh Duke of Beaufort and was succeeded in time by the son born of his marriage to Emily Culling-Smith. Frederick Gough Calthorpe succeeded his brother as the fourth Baron Calthorpe. He and Lady Charlotte had four sons, three of whom succeeded to the title, and six daughters. George Agar-Ellis, later first Baron Dover, and Lady Georgiana had four sons and three daughters.

The Slavery Abolition Act to which William Wilberforce dedicated his life was passed in 1833, one month after his death, although he lived to see the successful second reading of the bill.

True to his pledge, Granville Ryder was elected Member of Parliament for Tiverton in 1831 and for Hertfordshire in 1841. He and Georgiana made ther home at Westbrook Hay, Hemel Hempstead, in West Hertfordshire, where they had three sons and five daughters.

Badminton is still the seat of the Dukes of Beaufort and the Beaufort Hunt continues. The present Earl of Harrowby lives at

Sandon Hall, Staffordshire. He is the author of *England at Worship*.

Holy Trinity Church, Cambridge, carries on Charles Simeon's heritage of an alive, Spirit-filled ministry to students and community, and maintains an active vision for world missions.

Donna Fletcher Crow
Boise, Idaho
1986

TIME LINE FOR
THE CAMBRIDGE COLLECTION

UNITED STATES		ENGLAND
George Whitefield begins preaching	1738	John Wesley's Aldersgate Experience
	1740	
French and Indian War	1756	
	1759	George III crowned
	1760	Lady Huntingdon opens chapel in Bath
	1766	Stamp Act passed
Boston Tea Party	1773	Rowland Hill ordained
The Revolutionary War	1776	The American War
	1787	Wilberforce begins antislavery campaign
Constitution ratified	1788	
George Washington elected president	1789	
	1799	Church Missionary Society founded
	1805	Lord Nelson wins Battle of Trafalgar
	1807	Parliament bans slave trade
War of 1812	1812	Charles Simeon begins Conversation Parties
	1815	Waterloo
Missouri Compromise	1820	George IV crowned
John Quincy Adams elected president	1825	
	1830	William IV crowned
Temperance Union founded	1833	William Wilberforce dies
Texas Independence	1836	Charles Simeon dies
	1837	Queen Victoria crowned
Susan B. Anthony Campaigns	1848	
California Gold Rush	1849	
	1851	Crystal Palace opens
Uncle Tom's Cabin published	1852	
	1854	Florence Nightingale goes to Crimean War
Abraham Lincoln elected president	1860	
Emancipation Proclamation	1863	
	1865	Hudson Taylor founds China Inland Mission
Transcontinental Railroad completed	1869	
	1877	D.L. Moody and Ira Sankey London Revivals
Thomas Edison invents lightbulb	1879	
	1885	Cambridge Seven joins China Inland Mission

WORD LIST

Ashen fagot—a bundle of ash sticks, burned in the west of England instead of a Yule log

Bosky—tipsy or drunk

Bow Street Runners—London police before Scotland Yard

Boxing Day—first weekday after Christmas, celebrated by giving Christmas boxes to servants and poor

Bumblebroth—situation that has been bungled

Buttery Book—signed by students before eating in Hall

Corinthian—fashionable man-about-town, sportsman

Dipped—short of money

Double First—first class honors in two different subjects

Drop-fences—the ground is lower on one side of the fence

Fistful of flimsies—handful of paper money

Fives—fist

Haricot—lamb and vegetable stew

Hilary term—second academic term, from mid-January to Easter

Kern Baby—a doll fashioned from kerneled wheat stalks

Knee smalls—tight-fitting breeches worn above riding boots

Mill—prizefight, or free-for-all fistfight

Neats—cows

Oak—heavy outer door on university rooms, for extra privacy

Pamphylians—prostitutes

Perch phaeton—a light, four-wheeled carriage with the seat perched over the wheels

Pietradura—a sytle of cabinetry developed in Florence by the Medicis, ebony inlaid with polished semiprecious stones.

Pockets to let—pockets empty of money

Punting—gambling or betting, a play against the bank in faro

Ratafia—a fruit juice liqueur

Reverberator—Charles Simeon's name for his hearing aid

Roundaboutation—beating about the bush

Sarcenet—soft, thin silk

Sizar—a student who acts as servant to other students in return for an allowance for his college expenses

Smalls—short for examinations, required for matriculation

Sprig Muslin—a plain-woven cotton fabric patterned all over with sprigs of flowers

Tilbury—a light, two-wheeled carriage with an elaborate spring suspension system

Ton—(pronounced tone) style, the fashionable world, smart set

Treat—to negotiate a settlement

Waits—rustic serenaders who sing for small gratuities

Whippers-in—hunter's assistants who whip the hounds

MAJOR REFERENCES

*With my deep appreciation to those
who have walked this ground before*

The Right Reverend William Meade, D.D., *A Faithful Servant, The Life and Labors of the Reverend Charles Simeon,* selected from the larger work of the Reverend William Carus, New York: Depository of Protestant Episcopal Society for Promotion of Evangelical Knowledge, 1853.

William Wilberforce, *An Appeal to the Religion, Justice, and Humanity of the Inhabitants of the British Empire in Behalf of the Negro Slaves in the West Indies,* 1823.

Hugh Evan Hopkins, *Charles Simeon of Cambridge,* Grand Rapids: William B. Eerdmans Publishing Co., 1977.

Hugh Evan Hopkins, *Charles Simeon, Preacher Extraordinary,* Brancote Notts: Grove Books, 1979.

Christiana Hole, *English Traditional Customs,* London: B.T. Batsford Ltd., 1975.

Ford K. Brown, *Fathers of the Victorians: The Age of William Wilberforce,* Cambridge University Press, 1961.

Horatia Durant, *Henry First Duke of Beaufort and His Duchess, Mary,* Pontypool: Hughs & Son, 1973.

Letters Between the Hon. Elizabeth Ryder and Her Brothers, Privately printed, 1891 (in the British Library).

R.I. and S. Wilberforce, *Life of William Wilberforce,* vol. 3, London: 1838.

Parliamentary Debates, New Series, vol. 10, 3 Feb—29 May, 1824.

Horatia Durant, *Raglan Castle,* second edition, Great Britain: The Starling Press Ltd., 1980.

Abner William Brown, M.A., *Recollections of the Conversation Parties of the Rev. Charles Simeon, M.A.,* London: Hamilton, Adams & Co., 1863.

Jonathan Edwards, "Sinners in the Hands of an Angry God," preached at Enfield, Conn., 1741.

T.F. Dale, M.A., *The Eighth Duke of Beaufort and the Badminton Hunt,* Westminster: Archibald Constable and Co., Ltd, 1901.

The Greville Memoirs, 1814-1860, in 8 vols., Edited by Lytton Strachey and Roger Fulford, London: Macmilliam & Co., 1938.

George James Welbore Agar-Ellis, Baron Dover, *The Letters of Horace Walpole Earl of Orford:* In 6 volumes, vol. 1, London: 1840.

Michael Lewis, *The Navy of Britain, A Historical Portrait*, London: 1948.

Horatia Durant, *The Somerset Sequence*, London: Newman Neame, 1951.

The Victoria History of The Counties of England, Edited by R.B. Pugh, University of London Institute of Historical Research, 1970.

G.M. Trevelyan, *Trinity College, An Historical Sketch*, Cambridge University Press, 1983.

D.A. Winstanley, *Unreformed Cambridge*, Cambridge University Press, 1935.

John Charles Pollock, *Wilberforce*, New York: St. Martin's Press, 1977.

Lt. Commander C.F. Walker, R.N. (ret), *Young Gentlemen, The Story of Midshipmen*, London: 1938.

From the HARROWBY MSS TRUST (The Ryder Papers) Used by permission:

Precis of the Cato Street Conspiracy, unpublished.

Prof. G.C.B. Dacies, *The First Evangelical Bishop, Some Aspects of the Life of Henry Ryder*, London: Tyndale Press, 1958.

Thomas Dudley Ryder, M.A., *A Memoir of The Hon. & Rt. Rev. Henry Ryder, D.D., Bishop of Lichfield & Coventry*, by His Son, London: Harrison & Sons 1886.

Granville Ryder Papers 1822-1880, Harrowby Mss. Trust, Vol. 1037.

Lt. Gen. Lord de Ros, *Memorials of The Tower of London*, 1876.

V.S. Anand and F.A. Ridley, *The Cato Street Conspiracy*, London: Medusa Press, 1977.

From King's College Archives; used with permission:

Charles Simeon, *University Sermons on The Law And Gospel in King's College Chapel*, London: 1828.

Acquaintance with God, Printed & sold by J. Downing in Bartholomew Close, 1726.

King's Old Court 1822-1825, by a Scholar of the Period [i.e. by William Hill Tucker, 1803-1901]; typed transcript, formerly owned by M.R. James.